Water under the bridge

by

Simon Murch

Grosvenor House
Publishing Limited

Published by Grosvenor House Press 2009

First published in Great Britain in 2009 by
Grosvenor House Publishing
Crossweys
28-30, High Street
Guildford
Surrey GU1 3HY

www.grosvenorhousepublishing.co.uk

ISBN 978-1-907211-53-9

For Dolly, George, Rosy and William

and in memory of Eulie Peto, John Elias-Jones
and Roy (Danny) Kay

Water under the bridge

A sporting novel

Simon Murch

Faintly as tolls the evening chime
Our voices keep tune and our oars keep time

Thomas Moore (1779-1852)

Prologue

The road from Wimbledon to Valhalla cannot reasonably be described as straightforward or easy. But Heidar was not a straightforward or easy man, even for an Icelander.

His saga was inspired by the written word. Not ancient runic script on faded yellow parchment. Not hard words hewn by rough hands in dark huts, to the keening refrain of the bleak northern winds. Something more modern entirely.

Well, perhaps not entirely. If you're into Blame Culture you can pin this one on the Sunday Telegraph. Scout's honour.

CHAPTER 1

The Sunday Telegraph does not try to change lives. That is the business of lesser papers. Its columnists deliver thunderous judgements on issues great and small and invariably conclude that things aren't what they used to be. Its loyal readers take deep satisfaction from this editorial constancy. They need to. Many have yet to recover from the traumas of 1991, when within six short months Margaret Thatcher was forced from office and Dunn's Gentleman's Outfitters ceased trading.

This Sunday the Observer was sidelined by industrial dispute. Most of its gentle readers received the Sunday Times instead, experiencing just mild annoyance until reaching Clarkson's column. Morley's newsagent was made of sterner stuff. He achieved quiet satisfaction by unsettling his customers with provocatively off-message newspapers whenever opportunity arose. A Barbour or Range Rover would earn a Socialist Worker, while a Save the Whales badge or Prius scored a Telegraph or Spectator. Helen Morley's Venezuelan hand-knit and Friends of the Earth bag made this almost too easy. The paperboy squashed the Sunday Telegraph through the Morleys' letterbox, ignorant of his role in events.

Peter Morley was driven reluctantly from his Sunday bed by a combination of calls from his bladder wall stretch receptors and complaints from his methane engulfed wife. He trudged downstairs in that state of peculiar contentment induced in men of middle years by emphatic bowel evacuation. His benign world view, augmented by the bright May sunshine and the success of Stockport County in yesterday's Division 2 playoffs, was dimmed by the sight of the alien newspaper on

1

the doormat, emerging from under the capacious rump of Farquhar, the family's labrador.

"Bugger" was thus Peter Morley's first word of the morning. This was not rare – indeed, since the kids had reached their teens, it was his usual opening salvo on coming downstairs to make tea. Today the lights were off, the television silent, the freezer door closed, the living room tidy without tomato-sauced plates or liquidly half-full tubs of Ben and Jerry's on the table, his wine rack intact with no obvious signs of pillage. Either they were inexplicably losing their touch, or more likely sleeping over at some other poor sod's place.

Farquhar's name had been chosen by the boys, inspired by Morley's bellow when he found the puppy devouring his new running shoes. He was understandably popular amongst local schoolboys, who liked to call him loudly on the common. Seeing his master retreat with the paper, he heaved his bulk off the mat with the most appealing expression he could muster. Since his annual booster his quality of life had taken a turn for the worse. The vet, only able to get him up onto his treatment table at risk of a hernia, had issued a dictat limiting him to just one meal daily. Farquhar was by any standards a good eater, his legendarily prodigious appetite and resourceful food-seeking techniques having been offset for years only by runs with his master. Sadly, he had developed arthritis in the last year and thus now had an almost Iowan energy balance. As quick on the uptake and as expert in psychology as any labrador, Farquhar had rapidly identified the weak link in the united front so far presented by the family. He recognised his mistress to be entirely resistant to appealing facial expressions or supplicant body posturing and nuzzling, as his master had rediscovered last night. By contrast, Morley, despite his constitutive foul temper and even worse language, was what is known in the psychological literature as a soft touch.

Morley sat at the kitchen table, nursing a mug of Earl Grey and staring balefully at the unwelcome paper. Farquhar was reacquainting himself as quietly as a labrador can with the delights of Baker's organic. Morley roamed the contents guide on the first page with mounting disdain. *"My wilderness years by David Cameron, page 10"* – I bloody well hope they're to come mate. *"George Osborne's favourite garden furniture, in Telegraph Style"* – oh, come on! What the hell's next in this bloody rag? New Tory response to global warming - Ann Widdecombe's hot tips for bikini waxing? What does that bloody half-wit newsagent think he's doing? Helen's going to be fit to sodding well tie. At least it wasn't the bloody Mail on Sunday – be thankful for small flipping mercies.

The grunting settled as he reached the sports pages. Morley had to accept that Stockport County would not have had so much coverage in the Observer. He appreciated the profile of their new manager, described by their football correspondent as a charismatic Belgian, words that looked unusual in juxta-position. He turned the page idly then sat up straight.

"Fuck!!" was his immediate response, loud and sudden enough to cause Farquhar to make a startled and energetically improbable jump. Although Confucious said that a a journey of even a thousand miles must begin with a single step, Morley's commenced with a single word.

CHAPTER 2

What is it about men and sport? Can it be blamed, along with so much else, on the lack of that civilising second X chromosome? Does there lurk a sports susceptibility locus next to the nostalgia gene on the Y chromosome? Forced to choose between giving up Athenian ideals of democracy and good citizenship or the Corinthian spirit of honourable sporting contest, most men would need to agonise at length over their decision. Apart of course from Millwall supporters, who are frankly unimpressed with both schools of thought.

Some sports have understandable universal appeal. Football, the "beautiful game", provides moments of drama and skill that might satisfy any aesthete. The fearsome confrontations of top-class rugby and the head to head challenges of track athletics touch some ancient nerve, reprising atavistic human instinct for direct challenge.

For other sports the attractions are less obvious, the passions difficult to understand. Not least rowing. Dull and seemingly pointless to the outsider, as I suspect you might agree, it exerts a vice-like grip on the soul of all who fall under its spell. Say what you like about the Sunday Telegraph, they know this. They are second to none in their coverage, reaching a febrile peak on Henley finals day each July. This is the day when old oarsmen squeeze themselves into their prized old blazers with the ease and aesthetic effect of a condom slipped over a fire hydrant before reacquainting themselves at length with the Henley one way system.

These days Henley Royal Regatta is viewed as a bastion of unearned privilege and conspicuous consumption - a pointless relic of Edwardian England where dimwitted blazered oafs show off in front of their wives and girlfriends. It may well provide useful benefit only to the growers of strawberries, the blenders of Pimm's, the bottlers of Bollinger and the shareholders of Laura Ashley. However for any serious oarsman it is also a place of myth and legend, of dreams, aspiration and deep nostalgia. To win there is a prize for the very few, often the very highest peak of a sporting life. The competition is intense, the training so severe that there is no room for ironic detachment.

To have engaged like this but to have just missed out, losing closely in semi-final or final, is the worst fate that can befall a rower. The winners and no-hopers can always return to Henley untroubled in their enjoyment. The nearly men, the close losers, have a more troubled relationship with the regatta. They may need a decade or more after retirement before they can face returning, and even then pass the time assailed by thoughts of what-if. For many this pain is remediable only by devout pilgrimage to the Pimm's tent.

Peter Morley was one such emotional casualty. Not one of nature's more spangly rays of sunshine, his outlook had not been improved by the experience of narrowly losing one Henley final and two semi-finals while at university. A quarter of a century later, this still rankled. He had returned just twice since, and had struggled to share the enjoyment of his non-rowing friends. Against his better judgement, he had been persuaded in the New Year to attend this year's regatta Saturday, for the twenty-five year reunion of what had been called the Famous Four. He had not seen his crewmates Dave, Heidar and Gareth since the emotionally overwhelming day of their only Henley final. They had been without doubt the closest and most trusted friends he had ever had, engaged on a venture of passionate intensity that entirely dominated their lives. What unfolded in those desperate eighteen hours had left all scarred and scattered, with no contact sought or wanted for over two decades.

Morley stared, a man lost, at the paper. The small headline, *"Stewards announce new Henley event"* had initially aroused

no more than general interest. The text beneath, which dyna-
mited the calm pond of his Sunday morning, might appear
innocuous to the uninitiated. However this was probably the
single greatest moment of marital subversion inflicted on readers of the Sunday Telegraph since an unwary and rapidly
sacked sub-editor had let through an article suggesting the existence of the female orgasm.

*"The Stewards have announced the inauguration next year
of the Princess Alice Vase for men's coxless fours, each member
of which will have reached his forty-fourth birthday by the first
day of the Regatta."*

CHAPTER 3

Long distance running becomes lonelier when you lose your running companion. Morley's Sunday runs around Wandsworth Common now seemed longer and less rewarding. He had become one-paced, lacking the sudden turns of speed required when he saw Farquhar crouch to evacuate his bowels by picnicking families or police cars. As much as he had cursed at the time, he now missed the company. He had become unsettled by the thought of the reunion, and troubled by returning daydreams about racing. He had fought against this nostalgia for years, and had steadfastly refused to go back to any of the local rowing clubs. The time demands were inconsistent with family commitments, and he viewed the sort of guys who carried on with competitive sports through their middle years as sad acts, not far removed from the losers he saw pestering the assistants when he used to take the twins to the Warhammer shop. The announcement from Henley had hit him more strongly than was comfortable.

He arrived home, sweating yet dissatisfied. He had achieved some satisfaction this morning from burning off assorted joggers, before being brought back to earth by two young athletes in club tracksuits who cruised past him at high speed. Helen was now up and was preparing to go out to pick up the twins, who indeed turned out to be staying over at a friend's house.

"When did they go out? Nobody tells me anything. Not unless they need a lift or some money," he grumped.

"Darling, you're a middle-aged male. That's the human condition, get used to it," she replied breezily. Morley simply grunted.

He worried about all three boys. David and Alastair had graduated with the onset of puberty from a taste for pranks that had worried their mother and teachers but secretly delighted him. Now they had entered a more subversive and edgy testosterone-fuelled zone. He was still reeling from their confession a few weeks back, which even now he could remember word for excruciating word:

"Dad, sit down, we've got something to tell you," had said a contrite David, with Alastair in tow, both looking unusually serious.

"Bloody hell, not again. Sounds like this is going to be bad. What's it this time? More porn through the headmaster's letterbox? Fireworked next door's cat again?"

"Dad, don't joke. It's worse than that."

"Shit. Been caught by the police with dope? I have told you the bloody consequences of that. Don't you be coming to tell me that ..."

"Don't be stupid, Dad. That's normal. Everyone at school does dope. What's the problem? Anyway, it's not that – it's much worse."

"Normal! Normal!! I'll come back to that one later. What the hell is it you've done then?"

"Dad. Um – don't know how to tell you this.... um ... Phoebe's pregnant."

Phoebe was a girl from the year below who travelled on the same school bus. Alastair had ungallantly, but to Morley's eye not entirely unfairly, christened her The Warthog, stupidly repeating this in front of one of her friends. Girls of that age don't do discretion, and Phoebe had not spoken a word to Alastair since.

"You are bloody joking! Come on, that girl's a bloody visual contraceptive." Morley's initial smile quickly faded. "Oh God. No! You're not joking are you? Oh bloody hell, no ..... This was your doing then David?"

"Not just me Dad," said David. "Both of us."

"Both!!" Morley held his head in his hands. "What the hell are we going to do?....... Both of you! ......When?"

"I only went out with her a couple of times, Dad," David explained. "I got bored, so I got Alastair to walk her home. You know what it's like, Dad. She was so keen. We just didn't want to hurt her feelings. It seemed the kindest thing to do."

"Oh, bloody brilliant. Perfect bloody gentlemen. Well done you. For God's sake, you're just fifteen. She can only be fourteen." He shook his head in disbelief. "What the hell can we do? Her dad will kill you, if I don't do it first. You pair of bloody irresponsible idiots."

Morley eventually calmed down enough to promise to discuss it with Helen when she got back. Temperamentally unable to control himself until then, he decided to take the bull by the horns and call Phoebe's family. He spent one of the most miserable ten minutes of his life on the phone to her increasingly irate father, intermittently screaming at a wailing Phoebe in the background, who finally slammed the receiver down after a parting volley of abuse.

He explained the whole miserable situation to Helen when she returned. Although shocked, she was calm and practical by comparison, and quietly called the perpetrators in to account for themselves. They looked remarkably untroubled until Morley recounted his conversation with Phoebe's father, when both suddenly exchanged looks of alarm. Alastair's response was unexpected in the circumstances.

"Dad, you are such a dickhead!"

"Don't you call your father a dickhead," said Helen, either out of loyalty or because she viewed that as her perk these days.

"Well he is Mum."

"Why the hell are *you* calling *me* names when you've just bloody well ruined several lives?" Morley shouted, control fast evaporating.

"God, Dad, you are such a nob-jockey phoning her dad like that. Think about it, what day is it?"

"Saturday, what the hell's that got to do with it" said Morley, suddenly aware of the pitying looks from all around him.

9

"Oh my God!" said Helen, suddenly aghast. "What the hell have you done, Peter?"

"What the hell have I done? Me??"

Alastair gave him a look of patient resignation. "Dad, it's April Fools' day. It was a joke. At least it was until you called Phoebe's dad."

Grossly unfairly in his view, the blame for this entire episode was laid at Morley's door, and the twins seemed to have had only very peripheral responsibility as far as Helen was concerned. He had found the follow-up phone call even more cringe-making, and had begun to reflect that the privileges of the modern family man in his middle years appeared to be limited to becoming a chimera composed of part mobile cash-point, part all-hours chauffeur and part all-purpose family scapegoat.

Although he worried about David and Alastair from the viewpoint of likely imprisonment, he had a feeling that they'd be all right in the end, although no idea where this end was and how they'd reach it. He actually worried more about their older brother Thomas. Always shy, he had retreated in puberty behind a wall of dark lank hair, wearing nothing but black. When Thomas announced that he had become a Goth, the twins immediately christened him Vizzy Goth. The name Vizzy had somehow stuck, even after he decided he had now become an Emo. Morley had not found Wikipedia reassuring on this, and kept watch on Vizzy for signs of self mutilation, de rigeur for any self-respecting Emo.

Helen, by contrast, appeared blithely unconcerned. The strong alternative streak that had first attracted him twenty-five years ago ran deep in her. She did not share his shock upon finding the first bag of dope in Vizzy's bedroom three years ago. The only household members to benefit from Morley's volatile and graphic outburst over this, of the kind known in family lore as one of Dad's Wall of Death moments, were the twins, inspired into conducting a covert operation on Vizzy's bedroom while he was downstairs under parental cross-examination. Quiet as Kraftwerk Unplugged, they employed a stealthy precision that would have brought joy to the heart of a US Marines special ops supervisor. Vizzy's anguished howls of outrage at finding his whole precious stash filleted from his room had fallen on, if not exactly deaf, certainly very stoned twelve-year-old ears.

A deep bass line made itself felt. Vizzy had clearly re-entered the land of the half-living. A vision emerged in grubby and pungent black T-shirt and boxers, the latter recognisable to Morley as his own. He was trailing an aroma of cigarette and what smelled suspiciously like the tail end of Morley's Christmas bottle of Jack Daniel's. In such circumstances, there are more thoughtful morning greetings to your troubled firstborn than "Up at the crack of noon, Mr Doherty?" Vizzy's first words of the morning, spookily echoing in spirit his father's own hail to the dawn, were thus "Fuck off."

Genetics works in strange ways, its effects sadly invisible to those who perhaps need to see them most. Morley, for whom wisdom and insight were rarely close travelling companions, elected to follow up immediately with a blast about Vizzy smoking in his bedroom. Vizzy, clearly temperamentally suited to a career in politics, denied vigorously what for any normal non-teenager would be patently undeniable.

With the return of the twins, the Morley household promised to settle into its comfortable Sunday routine of clandestine mischief, botched DIY, Rugby Special and roast beef. All would have remained fixed in its orbit had Morley not decided, against all better judgement and the evidence of his recent track record, to make another unsolicited phone call to a surprised recipient.

CHAPTER 4

In his youth, Morley had serenaded his neighbours with Deep Purple's Machine Head at high volumes, as had many of his generation. He had always liked the neanderthal chords of Smoke on the Water, launchpad for a million air guitarists. He loved its references to Frank Zappa and the Mothers, one of his particular favourites before age and responsibility tunnelled his emotional vision. The twins, currently murdering these chords at indecent volume, had probably never heard of Zappa, although the great old man himself would undoubtedly have appreciated their inadvertent forays into syncopated atonality.

Smoke on the Water's *dum dum duuuuh, dum-dum-di-dum, dum dum duuuuuuh, duum du-uuuuum* probably vies with *daaaah dah-dah-dah-dah-dah-dah, dum-dum-dum-dum-dum daaah dah-dah* from Beethoven's Ode to Joy as the most recognisable musical motif in the world. While the latter is beamed into the furthest reaches of the universe by NASA, in a so far unsuccessful attempt to signal our existence to alien lifeforms, Morley felt that the former had more chance of getting interesting replies. You get an invitation through your letterbox to a coffee evening in the church hall on Tuesday and you're on the phone to the babysitter in a trice? Are you bollocks. The Brian May lookalike up the road, with the wine cellar to die for and the wife who flirted with you last New Year's Eve, is having a Rock & Roll party on Saturday week and you're half way to Camden Market by lunchtime via the cashpoint. Don't even begin to deny it. Until NASA comes up with a half way decent musical policy, we're alone in the universe.

Taking the phone into the least sonically challenged room he could find, Morley took out his address book and dialled. A male voice answered, smoothly covering any surprise he might have felt at hearing Morley's voice for the first time in a quarter of a century. If one word could be used to describe Dave Hewitson, that word would be smooth. Society expects no less of its gynaecologists.

Morley cut straight to the chase. "Dave, have you seen the Sunday Telegraph?"

"Blimey Peter," came the swift reply, "you've changed your tune – you were a Socialist Worker man weren't you?"

Morley demurred, saying perhaps the Guardian, but no not the Socialist Worker. Dave would have none of it.

"Peter – that's utter bollocks. You Manchester Grammar boys were all the same. Good thing too, considering. Do you remember those bloody amazons from the Young Conservatives – a vice like grip on your wrist when you got within ten inches of anything with elastic in it and a piercing squawk of *get your hands off my knee you beast*!"

Morley agreed that this must have seemed desperately unfair.

"I have to thank you Peter. Your Young Socialist friends saved my sanity. God, were they gagging for it, even if they did spout a load of crap."

Not for nothing had Dave been known throughout the Boat Club as Shagger. He set off happily down an unusually salacious Memory Lane. Morley knew better than to interrupt the flow, leaving him on full reminisce for a further few minutes before trying again.

"About the Sunday Telegraph ..." said Morley hopefully.

Dave was having none of it.

"Come on, Peter. You're the one with the good memory. Who was that tubby girl with the spiky hair who doled out the Socialist Worker in the Union building? Didn't look like she was into men, if you know what I mean, but you'd never have guessed it."

Morley groaned. "Go on then, Dave, surprise me."

Dave continued unabashed. "Amazing really, once you got to know her. Pardon the sordid detail, but it's all flooding back now. Happy memories. I promise you, Peter, without a doubt, the best blow job in forty miles, no contest. Nice kid actually. Could have gone for her in a big way if she wasn't so hardline feminist about body hair. Those legs were bad enough, but I tell you, not even David Attenborough would have dared go down without a machete and a native guide. Come on Peter, you must remember the name? Punky hair, bit fat, dungarees, nose piercing, Socialist Worker."

"Julianne Robertson?" said Morley uncertainly, by now glazed over with Shagger's lubricious reminisces. He wondered how many more half-remembered conquests Shagger would dredge from the memory bank before he could jolt him back towards reality, and hoped that the poor sod who'd been his best man had possessed some pretty exceptional diplomatic skills.

"No, hang on. It's on the tip of my tongue. I've got it – Helen … Helen Dutroy. Bloody brilliant name – God, she must have loved her parents for that. You must remember her – come on, you know. We called her The Face that Munched a Thousand Chips. Where do you think mad socialist buggers like her went when Maggie swept away the loony left councils? Anyway, enough dirty old man talk. What's all this about the Sunday Telegraph then, Peter?"

CHAPTER 5

Morley's marriage, while subject to bickering from time to time, was essentially strong. Both appreciated the other's passion and commitment to their work and family, however strangely the latter had evolved in the last few years. He was proud of his wife's work, more vocation in fact, and the efforts she put in for the less privileged in her job at the local Housing Association. She had even won two awards for innovations she had made in the field, proudly but discreetly displayed by the drinks cabinet. All of us do like some recognition, and it tends to come all too rarely these days. Morley wondered how prominently Helen would care to place a plaque confirming her as the best purveyor of blow jobs in a forty mile radius. Particularly, he couldn't help thinking sourly, as she hadn't seemed to demonstrate any aptitude or real inclination for that particular pastime for the best part of two decades, at least in his direction.

He had reeled when Dave recalled her name, having had no idea that he had been referring to Helen. His revelation had placed Morley in a quandary. He now wanted to question Helen in some depth, particularly about the timing of her relationship with the man he could now only think of as Shagger. He was now pretty certain their connections must have been in parallel rather than series. However he realised that the sensitisation likely to be induced by such emotional archaeology would place their reunion at risk.

Morley's uncharacteristic forbearance with Dave had been rewarded. When he finally got to mention the new event, Dave gave a low whistle. Both speculated on the potential impact on lives and families across the world. He rang off to look up details on the Henley website, phoning back twenty minutes later with more information. The races would be over the full course of 1 mile 550 yards, over double the normal veteran racing distance. Morley suggested they should call it the Coronary Cup. It turned out that Dave had himself returned to rowing three years ago and was now racing in a veteran four at Thames Rowing Club. He then made a few of the thoughtful *Hmm* sounds that Morley remembered usually preceded some expedient but morally dubious proposition.

"Hmm. Bad luck on young Bateman. He's our two man. Not a bad oarsman at all. Sad thing is, the poor sod's only forty-one. Well, that's him buggered for a couple of years. So, Peter, what are you doing on Wednesday evening?"

CHAPTER 6

Morley put away his multiply-revised sketches with a groan. The lot of the modern architect was not a happy one, particularly when designing kitchen extensions for city bankers' wives. He had developed, with long experience, a theory that the only way that a banker's wife would be remotely reasonable in her architectural requirements was if she was being royally serviced by her personal trainer or other appropriately qualified therapist. Following his conversation with Shagger on Sunday, he was beginning to wonder whether he'd save himself a great deal of grief if he were to invite him into the firm as a novel type of sleeping partner.

He retrieved his bike from the basement and set off for Putney, glad of the diversion. He took his life in his hands at Clapham South by attempting the right turn down Nightingale Lane, deaf ear turned to the hooting motorists he delayed for whole milliseconds in their daily odyssey towards the zen experience of rush-hour Balham High Road. Apart from the speedbumps, he generally tended to feel safer when he got to this part of his journey, at least until he reached the boutiques and smart restaurants of Wandsworth Common, where the 4x4's leap from their parking places like predators after a limping ungulate.

His next moments of increased alertness usually came when he turned right into Trinity Road, which has a dual nature of part-time parking lot and part-time unlicensed race track, both potentially tricky for cyclists. For once he didn't take the next left towards home but headed on towards the sphincter-challenging demands of West Hill and the Wandsworth one way system. Many a cyclist has sadly met his ultimate destiny in this traffic-clogged half mile, shuffling off his mortal coil to the sound of Kiss FM, emerging at industrial volume from the open window of his tattooed van-driving nemesis. Again it was the right turn that he was relieved to negotiate. On a bike, it's always your right turn or the van-driving bastard's left turn that gets you. Apart from Richard Hammond at the wheel of a Bendy-Bus, Morley could imagine no greater hazard for a cyclist than *homo alboplaustrum*, white van man. He was relieved to head down the lower Richmond Road towards Putney, feeling that sense of hopeful anticipation mingled with vague apprehension familiar to all those starting a new school or stopping to buy condoms on the way to a blind date.

As he finally turned down the old familiar sliproad to the towpath he saw that the river was low but the tide incoming. He got off his bike before passing the navy blue flag on the London Rowing Club boathouse, spotting the emerging bows of an eight and letting it pass in front of him down the slipway towards the water. He saw the red and black of Thames Rowing Club a little further on. He wasn't familiar with the club, and stood pondering where to go when he was loudly informed by a man emerging from the clubhouse with a sour expression and a sculling boat that he should get out of the fucking way unless he fancied a fucking bow-ball up his fucking arse. This did not strike him as the mark of a particularly welcoming club.

He spotted Dave by the boat house door and wheeled his bike over. "Natives not particularly friendly," he said, gesturing towards the sculler, who was now trudging his boat down the slipway with a body language that simply demanded exclamation marks.

"Ah, that's Bateman," said Dave. "Bit bad really, should have phoned him first. He was expecting us to be practising our starts for Thames Ditton this evening. Not best pleased to hear about the Princess Alice and his red card." He did not look desperately saddened by Bateman's fate, and Morley recalled just how hard-nosed rowing could be.

Morley followed Dave into the boathouse, surprised how moved he was to see the rows of racing shells on their racks. He saw the cleaver shaped blades, which had also come in since he had last raced, and wondered whether they would feel different.

Dave pulled him to one side. "Now Peter. No pressure, but you need to put up a reasonable show today. I know you keep fit with cycling and running so it should be pretty basic. The guys weren't so happy about giving Bateman the bum's rush like that. But, you know, that's Henley fever. Anyway, I've told them that you're ex-national squad but that you've been out for a couple of years. I've said that we'll be faster than ever in two or three weeks."

"For God's sake Dave. It's not a couple of years. It's nearly a quarter of a flipping century," said a thoroughly alarmed Morley.

"Peter, look at me. You know that. I know that. They don't. Class is permanent, OK? You were ten times the oarsman they were. Just don't bloody well say that the blades look different to the ones in your day – I did when I first came back and they didn't take me seriously for a year. You've just got to get through the next few weeks without cocking up too much, and we're warp factor 5 towards the Princess Alice. As I said, no pressure."

CHAPTER 7

Morley followed his old friend to the changing rooms, which had the old familiar smell and untidy appearance, discarded socks and other oddments littering the floor. Seeing various wellingtons, lone and abandoned like widows in a Victorian novel, he remembered with annoyance that he'd forgotten this virtual necessity for Tideway rowing. On this part of the Thames the rise and fall of the tide rules out landing stages or pontoons. Feeling slightly awkward, Morley was led down to the boat racks to meet his crew members. He hadn't quite known what kit to bring, and had gone for the nondescript cycle pants and sweat shirt option. Dave had managed to unite two wellies of approximately similar size in a hopeful second-time around fling. Morley realised that he probably didn't look too professional, and was aware of the appraising eyes of John and Chris, his soon to be crewmates. They were guarded but friendly enough, asking him where he'd rowed with Dave before.

Chris, stroke of the crew and plainly its leader, began the pre-outing discussions. "Well, welcome Peter. We've heard a lot about you. We're expecting great things. Dave says its three or four years since you were last on the water. That about right?"

Aware of Dave's gimlet stare, Morley made non-commital grunts and a shrug. "Can't remember exactly. Been a while, I guess."

Morley did not want to create a bad impression, but did worry that his lack of recent practice might betray him. As they finally embarked, pushing the boat away from the bank with their oars, he felt a sense of unreality. After so many years, he was back on the water.

The first few minutes were spent doing warm-up exercises before turning to follow the incoming tide towards Hammersmith. The feel of the rowing was unexpectedly familiar, although the catch of the water at the start of the stroke was sharper with the new cleaver-shaped blades. He was managing to row fairly cleanly despite his long break from the sport. Even allowing for his rustiness, he recognised that Chris was probably not the smoothest of strokemen.

With no more than occasional wobbles and no really catastrophic lurches the four made steady progress at light paddle or half-pressure past the Fulham football ground. Despite it going reasonably level and in time, Morley did not feel entirely comfortable. He was grateful to hear Dave's call of "easy all" just before Hammersmith Bridge. His comfort was short-lived. The strokeman Chris turned and gave the orders for their first piece at racing pace. "OK. Time for a quick sharpener. Three minute piece, off at 38 then settle to 34. OK?" Morley turned to Dave behind him, who simply shrugged his shoulders. Three minutes it was, then.

Chris clearly came from the crash-bash-bash school of racing strokes, attempting rather jerky application of brute force rather than sweeping smoothly past. It was a difficult rhythm to follow and the boat felt hurried. The first thirty seconds nevertheless went fairly well. By around a minute, Morley was beginning to be out of breath, and by one and a half minutes he was beginning to regret having gone off as hard as he had. The oxygen debt in rowing feels somehow more global and profound than in just about any other sport. While undeniably uncomfortable, the debt when running or cycling feels like it might be owed to an impersonal financial institution, pressing for payment by letters couched in polite but firm terms, and only getting really shirty after a few reminders have been overlooked. In rowing, the debt appears to have been passed on to a particularly unprincipled underworld enforcer, who has just sent round his least house-trained henchman to do nasty things to your body until you cough up.

Morley had always wondered whether Einstein used to row. No one who has experienced the last two minutes of a balls-out racing piece could ever think of time as progressing in a linear fashion. Twenty seconds can take a subjective equivalent of several minutes. With thirty seconds to go, he was hanging on for dear life. All nostalgic feelings for rowing were long extinguished and his form was going, his blade dropping in a good six inches short and starting to wash out at the end of the stroke. About two strokes after Dave had shouted "last ten", a by now terminally knackered Morley got caught in at the finish, slewing the boat sharply sideways and down onto stroke side. This brought the piece to an inglorious premature finish, embellished by a cascade of water that soaked John and Chris in the stern. He could hear the grunts of "fuck" from all the others, including Dave behind him. Morley's misery was compounded by seeing a sculling boat about twenty yards away towards the Surrey bank, containing a widely grinning Bateman, looking directly towards him while rhythmically moving his opposed right thumb and middle finger in the internationally recognised, though yet to be EU sanctioned, symbol for "wanker".

"Shit hot, lads. Bet the oppo will be crapping themselves," shouted the utterly delighted former incumbent of Morley's seat, before setting off with an impressive burst of speed back towards Putney. There was a profound silence within the boat, save for the rasping of breath.

CHAPTER 8

One means of torture inexplicably overlooked by the Geneva Convention is the Concept 2 rowing ergometer, conceived initially with cruelly ingenious misuse of bicycle parts. Its cycling origins are now hidden by vaguely designer looking panelling, as if its natural home should be in some quiet corner of Tate Modern or a Docklands warehouse conversion, rather than its usual aromatic subterranean haunts. However its ability to inflict pain remains fearsomely intact.

Morley was suffering as only a man on a Concept 2 can, shouted on by Dave behind him. "Come on, Pete, push! .... push!! ...... push!!! – Now go! ... Last 10!! ... Go!!! Come on!!!"

When Morley began to get some breath back he fixed Dave with an unamused grimace. "That push, push, push business, Dave. Do me a favour and save it for bloody work, OK?"

"Bollocks, Pete. You can do it. OK now, thirty seconds to the next interval. Then just two more. Deep breaths now."

"What the bloody hell do you think I'm doing – hysterical hyperventilation?"

"OK, ten .... five seconds .... go. Come on .. push ... push ...."

Since the mortifying end to their first racing piece, the four had shown some improvement. Morley was on a steep path of improvement, limited by the pain from the blisters on his hands and his aching back. The work on the water was improving, and he could last better through racing intervals. The technique was also coming together, although he still felt that Chris rushed the catch in a way that made it feel hurried. Dave's bow steering was also less erratic than he remembered.

Bow steering is one of the great skills of rowing, requiring rapid glances over the shoulder every few strokes while continuing to row or even race at speed, performed sufficiently sensitively to avoid unbalancing the boat or falling out of time with the rhythm coming down from stroke. Heavy tweaks of the rudder both slow the boat and reduce the efficiency of the steersman's leg drive as his right foot pivots to right or left to move the rudder cable. Thus a skilful bow steersman will minimise use of the rudder by adjusting his catch, easier said than done as oxygen debt takes its toll in a close race.

When two such tenuously controlled beasts race side by side in narrow lanes between hard wooden piling, as at Henley, this allows all sorts of possibilities. Many races are won by the weaker four with the smarter bow steersman. It is one of the more enjoyable black arts of the sport, and a good bow steersman will learn just how much he can possibly get away with before the umpire waves the red flag of disqualification. He will hover as near to the exit line in a tight race as a yellow-carded Italian defender 1-0 up in the last minutes of a Champions League semi-final. This puts his opposite number under extreme pressure to maintain his line and the dreaded booms seem ever nearer. There is no more anxiety-making sensation at Henley than seeing your puddles stretch back into the distance within inches of the booms. Once hit, the booms usually ensure it's game over. For the perpetrator, a return towards his own station on what he recognises to be the umpire's final warning often pulls the other crew with him. They then tend to veer off their station in turn, provoking the wrath of the potentially gin-soaked Henley umpire. You can almost see the anxiety begin to bite and the suckered crew shorten up into an inefficient staccato rhythm. The spectators at the finish are usually unaware just how much skullduggery has been required to engineer this happy outcome against the odds.

Helen had not been dismayed to see Morley develop another mid-life obsession. At least it was better than a mistress. If she had given a bit more thought to this, she might have decided differently. Sunday football in the park is undeniably less of a problem for a mid-years marriage than a pouting stocking-clad nymphette up for the cup in whatever position Sir would care to try tonight. Granted. Rugby presents few additional problems, the aftermath of all the beers and curries being balanced by the likelihood of injuries leaving him free for child care three weekends out of four. Golf potentially impacts more on the caring-sharing business, but any woman who has knowingly married a golfer has really only herself to blame. Rowing, despite the advantages of regaining the lean and toned husband of twenty years ago, is worse for a marriage than any dimwitted trollop with piercings and an eye on his pension fund. It is the ultimate mistress. If he has once shaken the habit, for God's sake don't let him go back. Let him choose the good-looking au-pair next time. Let him take his clients to Spearmint Rhino or get Customer of the Year on Friends Reunited. Anything but let him start rowing again.

Any man who has ever rowed for any length of time comes out with spookily similar stories of lost self-will, his spirit now in terrible thrall to this most seductive and infuriating of pastimes. "It's like a virus" is probably the most common expression, but there are many variations on this basic theme. However awful the outings, however bad the beatings at regattas, there still may come this moment of ineffable beauty that all rowers experience from time to time, tweaking irrecoverably all the relevant neural receptors, as the boat runs like a dream across glassy smooth water in an idyllic sylvan setting, the blades locking in and flicking out together. It becomes transiently just the simplest, easiest, happiest, most exhilarating sport. Like a night of wonderful lovemaking in a struggling marriage, such moments can sustain for years.

CHAPTER 9

"I am not wearing my fucking school uniform, and that's final!"

"Vizzy, darling. Be reasonable. There'll be lots of school-boys there, and most of them will be wearing their school uniforms. For goodness sake, do you want Dad to have yet another of his Wall of Death moments?"

"I don't care if he does. He looks less boring when he goes purple."

"Darling, it's not much to ask. They simply won't let you in without a jacket and tie. You just don't get Goths in the Stewards' Enclosure at Henley."

"Mum! I'm not a fucking..."

Helen cut in quickly. "Sorry darling. Emo's – even fewer of them, believe me. You can't go in there looking like you're on day-release from the crypt. It's got to be a jacket and tie with smart trousers or a suit. Honestly, dear. School uniform is best."

A semi-articulate bellow came up the stairs, following about a minute after its predecessor. Linguistic analysis would suggest its nearest equivalent in intelligible English would go along the lines of "Get a bloody move on up there. What the bloody hell's going on? We're ten bloody minutes late already."

"Nearly ready, darling," shouted back Helen, in the strained tones of a woman deciding whether to strangle her firstborn or husband first. As a consequence of the attraction of opposites, presumably an evolutionary tactic to reduce the chances of inbreeding, many couples such as the Morleys contain one partner who likes to arrive three hours early for flights or major social events, just in case an asteroid impact closes the motor-way, and another who views arrival more than five minutes before the gate closes as a waste of time that could have been spent more usefully fiddling around. This all adds to the gaiety of life.

Ten minutes later, Morley having settled on the tactic of sitting in the Volvo with the twins in the back and the engine running, hooting the horn vigorously at two-minute intervals, Helen emerged with an unusually scrubbed-looking Vizzy. Morley was not as pleased as he might have been.

"Bloody hell, Helen. That's my best bloody suit."

"Darling. Did you want him to come or didn't you?"

"And my new Ermenegildo bloody Zegna tie."

"Darling, he's here. Just be grateful."

"It's all way too big for him. He looks like David Byrne in that Talking Heads film. What the hell were you playing at?"

Helen fixed him with a look he knew all too well, a look recognised by all husbands when they have gone just too far for just too long. Her clipped tones brooked no argument whatsoever. "Darling! Just drive. And if you could do us all a favour by taking a vow of silence until we leave the M4, you might just have a chance of surviving until lunchtime."

Morley drove in the required silence, too cowed to check whether Helen had packed the Stewards' Enclosure tickets, or even to protest when Vizzy won the rear-seat battle for in-car entertainment and Helen had to slide the new Lost Prophets CD into the dashboard.

Some time later, Lost Prophets a distant and unpleasant memory as they sat in the traffic inching down Remenham Hill, Morley was filling in the boys about his friends they'd be meeting for the first time. He skimmed over the circumstances when the four had broken up so painfully in the aftermath of their defeat in their only Henley final. He remembered the black eye and broken nose that Dave had sustained on the evening before their final, and the fact that none had wanted to contact the others for two decades afterwards, until Gareth initiated the flurry of emails this Christmas. Apart from Dave, who he knew had finally got married to a younger physiotherapist and had two young children, he did not know what the others had done since.

"So, if you were all such good mates, Dad," asked Alastair, with his unsettling knack of getting straight to the uncomfortable point, "how come we've never heard of them before?"

"I guess people just drift apart," said Morley, attempting to downplay the issue.

"More of an explosion than a drift, dear," chipped in Helen, such disloyalty explicable on the basis that she was still smarting from his behaviour two hours earlier. Once they've passed their elastic limit, women don't do the quick forgiveness thing, unless they have a sufficiently good ulterior motive. She was still at least a couple of Pimm's short of any genuine reconciliation.

Mention of explosions galvanised the rear seat occupants from their state of torpid acceptance of what was shaping up to be a seriously boring day. In the twenty minutes before they finally got to their allotted parking space, Morley had to give the boys a brief history of the four, on as much of a need-to-know basis as he could sustain after Helen's intervention and in the face of Alastair's formidable interrogation skills.

"So why did Heidar hit Dave? Didn't that mess up your race? Is that why he stopped, Dad?"

"It's complex, Alastair. Not so easy to explain."

The motivations may not have been but the facts were straightforward enough. On the evening before their final against the Isis four, all coming from that year's victorious Oxford blue boat and future Olympians, they had sat down for Heidar's special big-race ritual. This was only employed before apparently impossible challenges. Heidar Kjartansson had a large horn drinking mug, a precious inheritance from his father who had died five years before, into which he would pour mead for them to share in turn. Recognising the depths of his Icelandic feeling and sensitive to his act of homage to his much-missed father, the others always indulged him, and in fact felt touched and bonded by the ritual. He always stood tall, and looked each in the eye in turn. "My crewmates," he would begin ponderously, his accent more prominent than in usual speech, "join me in this drink of the Gods. For tomorrow we must be heroes, and not all may return." And they would toast, and feel feelings complex and ancient. And on the morrow they often were heroes, and won more than any formbook would have suggested.

On that fated evening, Gareth Jenkinson, their bowman, managed to misjudge the mood. Thinking the moment for seriousness had passed he turned to Dave and said, "Hey Shagger, it's not mead you should be drinking, is it? I've heard on the grapevine that this bird you're knocking off calls you Merlot, 'cos you're so smooth ..... Shit, what have I said now? .... What's up, Heidar? ....Will someone tell me what the hell's going on? .....For God's sake, Heidar, sit down...... Oh, shit."

Heidar had rearranged Dave's face within ten seconds, and the two had to be separated by the others. After a period of imposed calm, Dave was helped away by Morley for an evening in casualty, pausing only to say a nasal "Thanks, Gareth. You're a mate" and "Sorry, Heidar. Really sorry", before climbing into the car with a towel clamped to his face.

Morley had been shocked by the revelation as much as the fighting, and realised that Gareth had completely misunderstood the implications of what he was saying. Heidar, intense in love as in all things, had been smitten to his core by a French drama student named Margaux, whose vibrancy and often surreal humour provided striking Gallic counterpoint to his dark northern seriousness. Somewhat scared of his intensity, Margaux had maintained a semi-detached relationship with him for the two previous years. Heidar had to accept this, however much it hurt, recognising that attempts to pull her closer would simply push her away.

Named with deep vinous reverence with her twin sister Lalande by her father, the love of wine ran through Margaux's family genes and veins. The Delacasse family had made their generous reds in their rambling family home in the Haut-Médoc for four generations before they were devastated to be omitted from the lists of the Grands Crus Classés in the great classification of 1855. Even now, any Delacasse will tell you, with some justification, that a bottle of Chateau Belle Pensée is better than most 3rd Growths. Margaux had left the family business somewhat against her father's wishes, deciding not to follow her brother Estephe down the well-trodden family route to the degree in oenology at Bordeaux. Her love of Hollywood movies, also anathema to her deeply patriotic father, led her to wish to study drama where she could learn English. Heidar saw her first, and lost his heart, in a not entirely convincing adaptation of Ibsen. Even he had to admit later that her forte was comedy, and the revues that she had put on with her group of otherwise intense and politically active performers, including Helen Dutroy and at least two of Dave's old girlfriends, were sensational by student standards. One was good enough to take to the Edinburgh Festival, the experience apparently the stuff of hushed legend.

Heidar was a deep, complex and proud member of a deep, complex and proud race. He had been devastated by the drowning of his father Kjartan, who he adored and whose love of nature he had inherited. He was almost as badly destabilised when he was uprooted from the lakes he loved to the tamer charms of Bushey, when his mother was remarried to a British Airways pilot. Hating everything about England and teased at school about his accent and his naïve and sometimes otherworldly attitudes, Heidar had found his only moments of peace on the river. Having got into the Hampton first eight in his lower sixth year, his independence reasserted itself. He chose instead to row alone in a single scull against the wishes of his rowing master. Heidar ended up winning the National Schools and the junior national championships. Not content with annoying his rowing master with his stubbornness, he next stuck two fingers up to the Great Britain selectors by electing to represent Iceland in the Junior World Championships, taking his country's first ever medal.

Reading Scandinavian Studies at Queen Elizabeth College, his obvious next move would have been to gravitate to the University of London Boat Club, then probably the outstanding university boat club in the country. A combination of a face to face argument with the UL chief coach, a respect for the efforts of Morley and Gareth Jenkinson in the gym, and the arrival of a charismatic coach at QEC had led him to choose to row for his college and not the university. The arrival from Cambridge for clinical studies of Dave, a former Radley first eight and Cambridge second eight oarsman, completed a potentially very good quartet.

As is the way with young males where emotional honesty is concerned, it took two years of rowing together before Heidar admitted to Morley the depths of his feelings for Margaux. He recognised that her period of wildness was probably a necessary reaction to the tight-knit upbringing that she'd had, but still felt hurt that she did not seem to recognise how deeply he felt. She was quite open about playing the field, grading her lovers in a backhanded compliment to her father's obsessional style of upbringing. She teased Heidar by calling him her sensitive Pinot Noir, saying he was so much finer but so much more delicate and difficult than those simple earthy Grenaches, Syrahs and Mourvèdres in the student union and drama club. Something then seemed to change in her third year, as she returned from Bordeaux for the autumn term despite her mother's illness, now recognising that family gravity was likely to prevail and she would have to return before long to help her father with the business. She began to let Heidar closer to her soul, her wildness tempered now by something deeper. By about Christmas they had become inseparable, and he began to think and hope that they would be together forever. When Gareth, ignorant of all this, mentioned that July evening that Dave's secret lover was calling him Merlot, there was only one devastating conclusion that Heidar could draw.

Morley's rather limited diplomatic skills were never needed as much as that night. By midnight, neither Heidar nor Dave was prepared to row with the other ever again. Heidar, still tearful after a long and very painful phone call with Margaux, was sitting with his head in his hands. Dave, not long returned from casualty, where he'd had his nose painfully straightened and a rather comic plaster applied, was by this stage looking for a return match with Heidar. Having been without a coach for three months, also down to Dave but for rather different reasons, Morley felt the burdens of leadership fall on his shoulders. Gareth, crew joker and usual maintainer of morale, was shocked by his inadvertent complicity in this disaster and could do little more than go from one to the other saying how sorry he was. The best that Morley could broker by 2am was that they should go and sleep on it, as the only people gaining from this were the Isis crew.

Heidar came down for their rather tense breakfast with a look of determination of an intensity they had not seen before. After a few mouthfuls he put his fork down and looked round the table. "We do it?"

A slow series of nods was returned.

"Yeah. OK. We fucking well do it and we do it fucking well....... Oh, sorry, Mrs Holland."

Mrs Holland, whose Henley house the crew were renting, was not too taken aback by the language. She had heard a fair bit of last night's events and clearly disapproved of Dave's behaviour, judging by the looks he was getting. She clearly had a softer spot for Heidar.

"Don't worry, Heidar. The kids aren't around. You just go and beat those Oxford boys. We've never had any winners stay here before. Semi-final was our best, Princeton in '73. The amount those Americans ate, it was a wonder that boat floated. Now eat up lads. You won't beat Isis without a proper breakfast."

It had been a long and quiet walk, past Henley railway station, along past the shops on the high street, then across the bridge towards Leander. Gareth tried to lift the mood with the odd call of "Sorry Mrs Holland" in an execrable Icelandic accent or "It was a wonder that boat floated" in his best Life of Brian impersonation. No one had the heart to engage in the banter, and he finally gave in to the silence. All were acutely aware of the privilege and challenge of getting through to Henley final Sunday. Just two crews survived out of the twenty to fifty entrants in each event. Never was the disparity of the Henley experience more obvious, the dense streams of day trippers, many neatly turned out with Stewards' Enclosure badges prominent, filtering past the more scruffily attired surviving oarsmen, most grey with nerves. Still with three hours to go before the 14.50 start, they filtered into the vast boat tents and began to change in silence.

The silence was maintained on the paddle up to the start. They saw Isis boating just before them, then followed them towards the start in the batch of crews allowed briefly onto the course between races. The booms attendant slid open the gap, allowing them to leave the course and progress up towards the start between booms and bank. They stopped to watch the final of the Diamond Sculls as it passed, waiting until the wash from the Umpire's launch settled. Some wag from the bank pointed out Dave in the three seat to his mates, calling him Rocky 3 to their huge amusement. When they got beyond the start they practiced a series of starts with quiet intensity. As they backed onto the stakeboat, it was an almost overwhelming moment. The honour of their first Henley final, as clear underdogs against a crew who should properly have been racing in the open Stewards' Cup. There was an intensity in the air he had never felt before.

Isis taughtened their already screaming nerves by attempting a false start, unwise given the Cambridge blue blazer in the bows of the Umpire's launch. The QEC four replied with their best ever first twenty in the restart, leading by a third of a length at the top of Temple Island. Morley could feel the power, greater than he had ever felt before, coming down from Heidar in the two seat. Against all the odds, against the form book, and despite going two to five seconds slower to each mark in the semi-final, QEC were leading the Isis blues. Because of Heidar's dramatic efforts, Gareth at bow was having some difficulty holding the boat straight along their station on the Berkshire bank, and they were encroaching slightly towards the Isis crew on the Buckinghamshire station. This was actually just about perfect tactics, putting Isis under pressure, and they had pulled out to three quarters of a length lead by the Barrier, the first timing mark.

An intuitive stroke, Morley had seen the Isis stroke side oarsmen struggling with the puddles coming down from the QEC bow side and recognised the danger of disqualification if they were to sprint enough to clash, while QEC were illegally in their water. Even a Cambridge umpire would have to give Isis that one. He shouted for an unplanned spurt for twenty strokes, pushing the rating up to an unsustainable 42, and was relieved to see them pull out to a length and a half lead, which they maintained to the second timing mark at Fawley Lock, just before the three quarter mile point. It was a surreal experience, as they raced on, to be able to hear the race announcer inform-ing the crowds that their time to the Barrier had equalled the Visitors' Cup course record and their Fawley time was a new record. He knew they were racing out of their skins, and was aware that Isis were now inching back. Another warning for steering, just before Remenham Club near the mile mark, thwarted Gareth's attempts to carry on washing out Isis with their puddles. The volume of support from the banks was getting louder – the only time oarsmen get an acoustic insight into what it must be like to be a professional footballer is during the closing stages of a close race at Henley, and by that time their auditory nerve functions are being stepped down through oxygen starvation.

Isis were overlapping, rating in excess of 40, by the Regatta Enclosure and had closed further to just under three quarters of a length at the start of the Stewards' Enclosure, with at most 300 yards remaining. By the mile and a quarter post, QEC were just hanging on by just under half a length, when things started to unravel. Heidar's astonishing early efforts had taken their toll, his pace judgement skewed by emotion and tiredness. He had gone, and Gareth was now fighting to stop the four piling into the booms lining the Berkshire bank, amidst a volume of noise from the Stewards' he would have thought unimaginable. With fewer than ten strokes left, Isis were through and the 6 or 8 feet they'd opened up was now an unbridgeable chasm. In the last two strokes Heidar had utterly nothing left. Despite rudder full on, his right foot desperately turned beyond 10 to 4, and softening his catch as much as feasible in a tight race, Gareth suffered the ignominy of the stroke side blades hitting the booms by the judges' box on the last stroke, causing the boat to slew across the finish at an angle of thirty degrees, with water cascading over the stroke side riggers. The recorded verdict of three quarters of a length was a horribly unfair reflection on the most desperately tight of races, and the fact that the winning time of 6 minutes 49 was a new record was of little consolation.

Heidar was inconsolable in the boat tents afterwards. Morley, gutted to his very marrow, shook hands with the Isis crew. Dave, tears welling from his blackened eye, unaware now of his ridiculous mask, was cut to the core with guilt when a red eyed Margaux came up to the beleagured crew with a friend. From the depths of his dark northern being, with the force of all the spirits and water sprites that can impassion an Icelander, Heidar turned towards Margaux and said with chilling venom, "Just fuck off. And stay fucked off."

Margaux had departed with dignity, tears coursing down her cheek. From what Morley had heard, she had left the next day for Bordeaux and they had never seen each other again.

Chapter 10

Henley Royal Regatta is professional in its arrangements and careful over small details. It is highly selective in its choice of attendants who blockade the gates of the Stewards' Enclosure against those without the correct badges or dressed inappropriately. They perform this task with the zealous assiduity of the Guardians of the Gates of Heaven faced with a crowd of adulterers and estate agents, taking it as a personal slight if they have to let in five consecutive emigrants from the long and patient rows outside, who show the stoic acceptance of a particularly well-dressed Moscow meat queue. It is easier for a lady to blag her way into the VIP area at Live Aid by saying she's Noel Gallagher's masseuse than to get into the Stewards' Enclosure wearing culottes. The attendants can spot the surreptitious use of a mobile phone at forty paces and be at the miscreant's shoulder before he's finished saying "I can hardly hear you, this brass band's so loud."

There are usually two or three of a more menacing disposition, large and Hackney-bald, clearly sunlighting from their night-jobs as bouncers at the rougher East End clubs. Their job is to deal firmly with the more persistent bloggers and escort out those who have become, as quaintly described in the Stewards' guidelines, confused by the alcohol. There are many possibilities for confusion. Bottles of Bollinger are common but viewed as such, Pimm's more classic and classless, although class becomes difficult to project after drinking three or four. Gins and tonic and glasses of white wine abound. There are even members, usually looking defiantly around like Elizabethans with a papal missal, who nurse pints of bitter.

Having finally got to their allotted parking space in Butler's Field, which looked for all the world like the legendary mating grounds of the Range Rover, Morley tried to brush the three boys into some vague semblance of neatness and pinned on their Steward's badges. Helen did last minute checks on the picnic in the back, and reassured herself that her husband had put the ice in the large wine cooler. Rather impetuously, she had volunteered to bring the reunion picnic, although Dave's wife was apparently going to bring some puddings. She hoped that she hadn't forgotten anything.

Rather less mortified than he had expected by the boys' behaviour in the entrance queue, apart from the twins sniggering at the sight of a fat elderly gentleman in a deckchair-striped blazer and boater and Vizzy moaning on that this was all just so fake, Morley stood patiently and awaited their turn. When they got to the front, he was relieved to see that all got let in, although the scrutiny that Vizzy received from one of the more thug-like attendants was a little more prolonged than good manners would have dictated.

The reaction of the kids when they got inside was much as Morley had expected. The twins were highly amused by the inhabitants, probably feeling that they had been taken to some strange and exotic theme park, where doddery old boys in scarlet blazers and matching cap tottered alongside ladies demonstrating impressive acreage of floral print. The bright red high heel, previously the perquisite only of the lady of easy virtue and designed for walking up and down the naked spine of the more louche Edwardian gentleman, had clearly crossed over to the mainstream since Morley last visited Henley. Whereas it was theoretically possible that a good percentage of the ladies of the Stewards' Enclosure were now of easy virtue, Morley felt that there were precious few who Health and Safety might allow anywhere near an unprotected vertebra even if wearing sneakers.

Vizzy was less impressed than the twins and less ready to appreciate the gentle English absurdity. "This place is bloody weird.... OK, sorry Mum ... weird. Look at all these pathetic people trying to pretend to be upper class nobs."

"Darling, that's because they are," said Helen, herself not entirely reconciled to the place on only her second visit.

"Come on, it's not that strange," said Morley ill-advisedly, and frankly on rather thin ice.

"Then why's the band playing Monty Python?" asked Vizzy. "Are they taking the piss?"

"Vizzy, I don't think the Band of the Household Cavalry would know how to take the piss if they wanted to. It's Souza's Liberty Bell March."

Vizzy did have a fair point. Viewed from any dispassionate perspective, the Stewards' Enclosure does have a frankly surreal air. For a sensitive teenager, being subjected to Henley is probably a cruelty on a par with being kissed by his mother at the school gates or having had his first name chosen by Bob Geldof.

Morley guided them towards Poplar Point, a large tree close to the finish supporting a notice board where the results of races are faithfully inscribed in copperplate handwriting. No LED screens at Henley, all visual aids have remained unchanged since Lloyd George commenced puberty in hopeful anticipation. There are wooden boxes by the wooden booms on the Bucks station in which white coated men, looking like aquatic cricket umpires, push boards inscribed with the crews' names to demonstrate the current state of play in races further down the course. The only electricity consumption comes from the champagne chillers and the PA system, seemingly manned by former 1940's BBC continuity announcers.

Helen was quietly nervous, wondering if this was the same Dave Hewitson she half-remembered. She had only visited Henley once previously, and was not particularly impressed, quietly sympathising with Vizzy's viewpoint. Morley, by contrast, was enjoying the experience more than he would have envisaged and was looking forward to catching up with his former crewmates. He had enjoyed spending time with Dave, and they had reminded themselves of some of the funnier moments. They had laughed to remember some of Gareth's one-liners, usually delivered in his strong Welsh accent with impeccable timing. Even the initially dour Heidar had succumbed to his sense of humour, laughing longer and more fiercely than anyone.

He looked at the crowd mingling by the results board, some competitors and coaches scribbling into their programmes, others also simply using this as a meeting place. There was no sign of Dave, and Morley did not initially see any of his former friends. There were more tall males than would be expected in an unselected group, a few younger and probably still competing, others of more mature years. Then he saw the unmistakeable shock of fair hair, now greying, the same upright stance, little changed in a quarter of a century. "Hey, Heidar," he called, and was pleased to get a big bear hug and a slap on the back.

"Ah, it's young Peter. Still just about keeping out of the bathchair," came the reply, the accent still as before. "It's great to see you again. And to meet your family. Hi guys," he nodded towards the boys. "You look like your father, in different ways. I hope you're not so grumpy."

The boys exchanged amused glances. Their body language suggested they had taken to Heidar.

"And, of course. Please excuse my rudeness. Mrs Morley. I don't believe we have met."

"I'm sorry to correct you Heidar," said Helen, "but we have. Helen – Dutroy as was. You even came to see me perform."

"My goodness, Helen. Please forgive my rudeness. It is so good to see you again. I had no idea – Peter, always the dark horse, as you say. Despite the undoubted strains of living with Peter, you look absolutely wonderful."

"You mean you wouldn't have recognised me," said Helen, these days able to raise a smile about her former self.

"Reunions, always a time for nice surprises," rescued Heidar, winning by the genuine warmth of his smile as much as his words.

Helen made the introductions. "Well Heidar, this is our oldest, Thomas - better known as Vizzy for reasons too complicated to discuss. And the twins, David and Alastair. They look innocent enough. However, do not, on any account, leave your drink unguarded for a second."

"Boys, we have clearly much to discuss. And it sounds as if there is no better venue for such discussions than the Pimm's tent. Remind me later – there is much you need to know about your father."

Morley groaned audibly. The boys were visibly perking up. Heidar looked over their shoulders. "Look, here's a man who needs a long overdue kiss and make up."

Dave was striding towards them, with a broad grin. Heidar stepped forward, arms wide, and embraced him. It was a moment that even touched the boys. "You've come alone, guys?", asked Morley.

"No way, Peter," said Dave. "Jane's in the Regatta Enclosure with Lucy and Ben – they don't allow under-10's in here."

"No, she's nobly parking the car," said Heidar. "I'd forgotten what this damn traffic's like, and we decided the only way we'd make it on time was if I walked ahead down the hill."

There was a sudden increase in the background noise, the mark of a close race. Dave looked in his programme. "Come on, guys. It's the Grand. National Squad's taking on the Canadians. It sounds close."

All three rushed the twenty yards to the bank, craning over the spectators to see. Helen stayed put with the somewhat bemused boys, shrugging her shoulders and raising her eyes. They returned, conversing volubly about the chances of the GB eight at the forthcoming World Championships.

Dave looked concerned. "Please excuse my bad manners. I didn't say hello. You must be Peter's sons. I've heard a lot about you."

It was the boys' turn to look concerned.

"And of course Mrs Morley. Very pleased to meet you."

"It's Helen. I think you'll find we've already met," she said, with just a hint of asperity, having recognised him immediately.

Morley's warning look went unheeded. Dave's smooth gene kicked in. "I'm sure I couldn't forget such a pleasure. I insist – give me a clue."

"At QEC – surely you remember now?"

"No – it can't be. You're far too young," soldiered on Dave.

"David Hewitson, you always were the silver tongued charmer," said Helen, quietly pleased despite herself. "Helen – Helen Dutroy. Surely you remember?"

It was like a Roger Moore convention. Dave's eyebrows shot up in surprise. He looked at Morley, whose eyebrows followed suit in more quizzical vein. Helen saw the looks pass between Dave and her husband. Her eyebrows followed the emerging trend and she shrugged, colouring slightly.

Morley broke the silence. "Don't worry. I keep a strimmer behind the bed for emergencies."

Further discussion was put on hold as they stood back to let a waiting group through to the results board. Morley felt a momentary annoyance as the bald overweight man seemed to be taking an age to pass through with his family. "Sorry, we're in the way. There's quite a few of us," he said, attempting to avoid any impression of rudeness.

The man did not appear to be mollified. He folded his arms theatrically. "Peter Morley, you daft bugger," he said, with a very familiar Welsh voice. "A chap just has to lose a bit of hair and put on a few pounds and all his friends go off with the other boys."

"Gareth!" shouted Heidar, favouring him too a bearhug. "Oh, and Mrs Gareth?" he said, smiling at the rather anxious looking woman with him.

"I'm sorry. Didn't get round to introductions. Heidar, Dave and Peter – this is Lynette. And of course vice versa. And these two," he said, indicating a boy and girl in their early teens, "are Gwen – short for Gwenhwyfar, for which I am apparently never to be forgiven – and Thomas. We've torn them away from their music for the day."

"Oh, we've got a Thomas too," said Helen brightly, "only he prefers to be called Vizzy. And these are David and Alastair. They love their music too. How lovely."

In less than a minute of parental interchange, all five teenagers were thus scowling. The Morley boys' interest in the proceedings was reignited by Gareth's surprise at discovering their mother's identity, and by another exchange before they set off to find Dave's family outside.

"Hang on, Heidar, we can't go until your wife gets here," said Morley.

"Don't worry," said Heidar, "I can see her now. As our powers of recognition don't seem so great today, I'd better make the introductions. Peter, Helen, Dave, Gareth, Lynette, Vizzy, David, Alastair, Gwen, Thomas – some of you may have met my wife Margaux."

CHAPTER 11

In around 1907, a Bostonian called Lawrence Luellen invented the Dixie Cup, the first disposable cup made from paper. Its potential contribution to the health of nations was cemented by an article published the following year by an eminent Lafayette microbiologist called Davison, entitled "Death in School Drinking Cups". Honestly, it's been downhill all the way for health scares since. This article was widely redistributed by the Massachusetts State Board of Health in 1909, and the paper cup was thus launched on its trajectory to world domination. Distant successors of Luellen's creation emerge from fast food outlets across the globe. While the taste of many of their contents might have given Luellen pause for thought, there is no holding back a good invention. Except, that is, at Henley Royal Regatta, where most are of course held back very effectively. Particularly in the Henley car parks, where the grandest picnics outside a Merchant Ivory production may be seen. Mr Luellen's invention is not welcome here.

A Henley car park picnic is no ordinary picnic. Indeed, for the poor person organising one, it's no picnic at all. Few social challenges are quite so daunting, and little guidance is available for the novice. Producing Tesco scotch eggs, tara and Australian shiraz from the back of an Astra is not the behaviour expected in Butlers's Field on Regatta Saturday. Sausage rolls and a Ginster's pasty would probably get you ejected, and a Mitsubishi Evo would already have been turned away at the gate. Presenting your guests with plastic cutlery is utterly beyond the pale, equivalent to donning a knotted handkerchief at a Royal Garden Party. The ideal, and be assured it does happen, is to have your butler serve a full silver service luncheon from the boot of the Rolls, with a selection of Corney and Barrow's finest. By the time Helen had navigated the first fifty yards across the field, with Margaux, Jane and Lynette in tow, her heart sank at the sight of so many pristine white cloths, crystal glasses, bottles of champagne and whole salmons or haunches of beef.

She had been utterly delighted to meet Margaux again, but there was still the reserve engendered by too long separation and maybe too little wine so far. She was, for the moment, reserving judgement on Jane and Lynette. It went against the grain to have a girlie party getting the picnic sorted out, but she reckoned that life would be smoother if they let the boys and assorted kids meander over a few minutes later. Margaux was sensitive to her unease in the presence of so much opulent consumption around them, and teased her gently. "So which is your Bentley, then?"

"Oh, the Bentley, sad story that," she replied, glad to get just a taste of former banter.

"Have you got a Bentley?" asked a wide-eyed Jane.

"No, sorry," said Helen, "Margaux was just teasing me. We used to be in revues together – she always tries to wind me up. I was beginning to get worried that she'd stopped. No, Margaux, we've got a very elderly Volvo. And I," she gestured with her eyes towards the picnic by a Range Rover on the left, "simply forgot the wild boar."

They all laughed. Jane looked relieved and owned up to feeling nervous about the puddings she'd brought. They reached the old estate, looking much shabbier now than it seemed to be in Wandsworth. Helen opened the boot. She rummaged inside a large cold box. "Here we are. Just what the occasion demands. How about some Chablis before the boys get back?"

There was general assent. Helen poured four glasses while they unpacked lunch. She looked apologetic. "If we'd have known you'd be here Margaux, we'd have given a bit more thought to the wine."

Margaux smiled. "Don't worry. I'd never meet up with old friends without at least a few bottles of Belle Pensée. Heidar will fetch it."

Seeing the blank faces of the others, Helen felt explanations were called for. She was keen to get Margaux on her own, to begin to find out how she and Heidar had managed to reunite after such a parting of the ways and her return to France. Launching into a very superficial explanation of the past events for the benefit of Jane and Lynette, she was then interrupted by Margaux, who held court with all her old humour and verve. There was no stopping her.

"So, the old Viking bastard gave me the, how do you say it, heave-ho. And I guess I deserved it. OK, I definitely did. How you say – a fair cop. I learned more that day than I had since I came to London. There is always responsibility, even when you choose not to see it. Well, I went back to Bordeaux – I had to hitch as I was broke by then. Always so, the end of term. Unless you live like a hermit, and that is something I could not. It took three days. I thought I was going to die. The kind people who picked me up must have thought I was a madwoman – sobbing every few minutes. I realised then how much I loved him, what I had robbed myself of. I had got stuck in bad ways – I think Dave was too at that time. Silly things. Silly children we were."

Jane looked perturbed.

"Don't worry, my dear Jane. It is, how you English say, all water under the bridge. I hadn't realised how serious Heidar was. Lots of boys said they loved me – and of course a few girls. It was the 1980's my darlings, and a girl's only young once. Isn't that so, Helen?"

Now Helen looked perturbed.

"Well I got home. What a disaster. My mother, so much worse than I had thought. Thin, tired, in bed and in pain. My father, my strong father who used to hold me and Lalande up in the air at the same time. He was like a broken thing. I could have cried. And I did, oh God I did. Estephe, like me, escaped and hiding in University. Lalande, so ground down by this, just walking round in a daze. Where before I just knew what she thought and she me – all gone. I think she had just shut down all emotions to protect herself. And everything the Delacasse family stands for – our glorious Belle-Pensée, just nothing."

She paused, lifting her glass towards the others and shaking her head. "Did you know that the last year, 1982, had been the best for fifty years in the Médoc? The very best – better than 1945, even. Shit. Belle-Pensée 1982, born in sadness and neglect that great year, well it is not worth tasting. Awful, thin, a disgrace to the name. And that shame saved me, and saved my father, and my sister and brother, though I am sorry that nothing could save my mother. Because I am a Delacasse, and sometimes a family needs someone to stand up. And I stood up and I took charge. And I bullied the workers who needed to be bullied. And I praised those who needed to be praised. And I, stupid and silly little girl I was, I had the sense to delay the grape harvest when everyone – my father included – said it should be brought in."

Margaux paused, took another large sip of wine, then tapped her arm. "I felt it in my bones – and let me tell you, darlings, if you feel something in your bones, never ever ignore it. Every day of that marvellous sunny week in September, I smiled. I had been right. And I, almost one by one, chose the grapes, and bought new casks of American oak. My father said that the cost would ruin us. I said that another wine like the '82 would do that anyway. My dear mother, in her last week of this life, said that I was right. Anyway, she said that she wanted the oak from our old casks, which had lived with her for all those years, to make her coffin. The choice of a special woman, who had become a true Delacasse. And Belle-Pensée '83, my special intense year, my '83 is the best Belle-Pensée of all time. The very best. On the day I am to die, I hope to drink Belle-Pensée 1983."

Helen hugged her. The others, wide-eyed, were silent in the face of such emotional outpouring on a day of expected superficiality.

"So, before the boys arrive with all their talk of rowing – my, how they talk. If any woman could inspire like that, she would be the muse of the ages. So, I settled down, and tried to forget Heidar. How do you forget? A boy can join the Foreign Legion. But a girl? Well, I do what we all do. I buried myself in the work. And my father began to grow strong again, although he was never the same. And Estephe came back with his degree and his big ideas from Bordeaux University. And Lalande and I became more close – never the same as before, but close enough. Until Paolo arrived. My big Italian hunk. OK, hands up, I'm with friends. Lalande's big Italian hunk. He was gorgeous, but such a baby. Always missing his *mamma*. And Italian. What do they know about wine?"

Helen took this as a cue to pass round the Chablis. Jane and Lynette, now fully engaged, gladly topped up. She was beginning to revise her opinion positively about the younger two.

"Well, my darlings, maybe you are getting the impression that I could not be trusted around men. And you would have been right then. But not now. But then – oh my God. Paolo, my Tuscan stallion, rich, vain, from one of the best known families in Montalcino. His family made a Brunello, not bad for Italian wine, even I would admit. They sent him to Bordeaux for a summer the next year. His Papa, sorry - his *Babbo*, was a clever man, wanted to see what French secrets he could bring back. To see Paolo in the fields, no shirt, what can I say?" She raised her eyebrows archly, pausing for another sip of wine.

"Well I never loved him, not really, and Lalande did. But I wanted him so I stole him. Stole him with my tales of London, and of cinema, and the stage, and the crazy nights at Edinburgh. How could Lalande compete? She looked like me. But she had not lived. What stories could she tell to compete with the Scheherezade that London had made me? And I, vain and selfish girl, I married him even though I did not love him and I broke my sister's heart. And then there came the times when I broke his heart, and I think my father's. Shit, Helen, where's the wine when a girl needs some? The boys are coming. Chablis is far too good for them after all that Pimm's they'll have been drinking."

Crossing the field towards them came a loosely aggregated throng, the four oarsmen in animated conversation, Dave carrying little Ben as he chatted, followed by Vizzy, alone and palely sauntering with a look of ineffable boredom. There followed a group clearly ring-led by David and Alastair, with Gwen and Thomas sniggering at their latest remark, and little Jane tagging hopefully along on their coat-tails.

The next quarter of an hour was spent sorting out the lunches for the assembled group, the mothers as usual putting their own needs after those of the children. Morley had to caution the twins, who were returning for second helpings before many of the adults had been served once. He then followed it up with a sterner warning after spotting their rather suspicious withdrawal and finding a bottle of Belle Pensée tucked under Alastair's jacket. It was decided that the older kids could be allowed a glass or two with their meal but no more. Morley was not entirely pleased to see the wink that Heidar had given the twins during their dressing down.

Conversation picked up. There was a lot of catching up to do. Gareth, who had started this particular ball rolling, did most of the filling in of background. He was able to supply details about other members of the QEC boat club, with whom it seemed he alone had kept in contact. After a while of such reminiscing, clearly boring the children and at least some of their wives, Heidar looked suddenly concerned. "What about George? Didn't you ask him ?"

"Of course. I tracked down his email and sent him the same one."

"Perhaps he didn't get it. Maybe he's changed email address," said Heidar hopefully.

"I don't think so," said Gareth. "It's not usual to reply saying Piss Off in those circumstances."

Junior interest was immediately rekindled. "Who's George," asked Alastair, as always quickest to home in to interesting gossip.

"He was our coach," explained Heidar. "Probably the main reason I ended up rowing with these wonderful people. A truly great man. If he had stayed with us for those last three months, who knows …"

"So was he ill?" persisted Alastair, ignoring signs of discomfort from his father and Dave.

"No, not exactly ill," said Heidar. "Although he thought he was. Didn't he, Dave?"

Dave looked extremely discomfited. He mumbled a few syllables and then sat quietly, looking sheepish. Jane was intrigued, and clearly not about to let him off the hook. "Do tell us, darling. It sounds very traumatic."

"It was indeed," replied Dave, with clear reluctance, "traumatic, and the stupidest bloody thing I've done in my life."

"Go on, what happened, Dave?" asked Alastair, merciless.

"Oh God," said Dave. "I'd forgotten about it. Blanked it from my memory. This is mortifying." He paused, gathering himself, shuddered and started. "George. Great guy. Also a medic in my year. He'd stroked the Blue Boat and rowed in the GB eight while at Cambridge, then did his back in weight-lifting during winter training. Took up coaching for us. No qualifications, but totally brilliant. Anyway, he fell for this nurse, Angela, and it got serious really quickly. Then they found she was pregnant, and brought forward the wedding to Easter. Well, to cut a long story short, it was the stag night."

He now had the full attention of the teenagers, and would have been concerned if he had noticed the more appraising looks he was beginning to get from Jane, who was clearly getting hints of another side to her smooth and urbane gynaecologist.

"I was the only one of the crew there that week. The others weren't medics and had been able to get a few days at home. As always, it got a bit silly. George was bladdered and fell over.

He'd hurt his leg and one of the lads suggested the old dodge. We carted him off to Casualty, holding him one either side. A couple of the guys ran ahead to get it set up. We knew all the housemen and nurses on shift – different days then. They all played ball – a bit of fun like this made a change from the aggressive midnight punters. Well, we did the old trick. After his X-ray, someone dug out the old films from a motorcyclist who'd broken his leg. The Orthopaedic Reg shows him the film, tells him he's got a fractured femur, needs eight to ten weeks in plaster. The houseman then put him into a full hip spica plaster, groin to the toes of his right foot. It covered most of his pelvis with just a small gap to pee through. My God, it was a monster. We pissed ourselves laughing in the coffee room."

He shook his head, clearly struggling to counterbalance the horror and humour. "Of course he should have guessed there was something up by the way people were smiling. Silly sod, what do they always tell you to do for Finals? If they give you an X-ray in the viva, read the name first and look at the date. Well the silly bugger didn't, too pissed or too shocked when he thought about the wedding. He just sat there moaning about what he could say to Angela."

"Darling, that is dreadful," said shocked Jane. "How could you?"

"Well, it wasn't actually so bad. It's a fairly standard Med School stag night joke. Any medical student should know that one, and you'd expect them to go and check the films the next morning when they see everyone's more amused than sympathetic. If the penny still hadn't dropped, the etiquette was that you turned up the night before the wedding with a plaster cutter – everyone then has a good laugh, you buy the groom a pint once you've cut him free and the Best Man has got a flying start for his speech."

Jane looked somewhat mollified. The twins still looked expectant.

"Well, it went belly up. I woke up the next morning feeling like there was a road drill inside my head and several hyenas had crapped in my mouth. Then I got called to the phone. My dad had had a heart attack and was in a bad way, so I shot home. They didn't think he'd pull through, but thankfully he did. The next time I even thought about George it was the following Tuesday, when I'd obviously missed the wedding. Even then, I thought that one of his other mates would have sorted things out. When I got back, Heidar told me that he'd had to cut one leg off his morning suit and had got married on crutches. No one knew where they'd gone on honeymoon. Oh, shit. What a fuck-up. Those days, no way of tracking them down."

"Oh shit, indeed," said Jane. "Were they OK?"

"No they weren't," said Dave miserably. "Tourist class on a charter to Sri Lanka, as it turned out. No chance of an upgrade. Just an aisle seat and him having to stand up every time the trolley came round. Both out and back. He had to sit in the shade – couldn't go into the pool - apparently the itching inside it drove him mad in the heat. He said that they'd consummated the marriage just the once – God knows how they could with that plaster, must have been desperate – apparently Angela couldn't sit down for days afterwards. I didn't know what to say. Of course I put my hand up and told him, and Angela."

"What happened?" asked a wide-eyed Vizzy.

"George gave me the biggest mouthful I've ever had. Angela slapped me, burst into tears and ran off. I was crying too, to think of the pain I'd caused them. He never spoke to any of us again."

"You know what?" said Vizzy. "That's shit. But it wasn't your fault. Your Dad was sick. If he's still behaving like that he's got a lot of growing up to do." He coloured, then stuttered, "OK, OK. I know I have to as well."

Heidar nodded appreciatively. "Vizzy Morley, you are absolutely right. Spot on. I like straight talking and honesty. You and I will be friends, I can tell. Dave, Vizzy is right – George needs to grow up and maybe I will have to tell him so one day. It is his loss, and Angela's, that they're not here today. Now, some of Margaux's family lifeblood – Belle Pensée. From the millennium."

Morley had heard that 2000 clarets were good. Indeed it was. He noticed that the boys, who he'd thought would have difficulty telling Petrus 1970 from industrial meths, were showing signs of genuine appreciation. Remarkably, Vizzy appeared relaxed and even expansive. Morley was quietly proud to see him taking little Jane and Ben under his wing, chatting with them and gently making sure that they were included. He nudged Helen, who had already spotted it for herself. They shared a rare moment of hopeful happiness about Vizzy.

There are some people who have the great gift of being able to lift the spirits of those around them. Sometimes couples display the same ability, usually because of their ability and willingness to give. This may not relate to goodness in the conventional sense – often such people may have foibles, habits and flaws entirely sufficient to ward off any such label. But they are good to be around. Heidar and Margaux were one such couple, and even the tough hard-bitten Morley boys were captivated. Heidar was regaling them about his passion for Norse mythology – it turned out that he was an academic in the Department of Scandinavian Studies at QEC. His tales of Thor and Odin were engrossing and entertaining.

"Odin's wife Frigg is best known for sleeping with another man to try to get her husband's gold. Very modern attitude, if you think about it. She must have been pretty good at it, because she gave her name to the practice. You've heard the word frigging, boys ? Oh, of course you have, sorry. Well, I don't think it's a way that I'd want my wife remembered."

"I don't know, darling," cut in Margaux, who had clearly been hitting the Belle Pensée for a while. "Better than being remembered for bog cleaning. Poor old Ajax."

Lynette cut in, sensing that Margaux was in expansive and uninhibited mood. "Now Margaux, you've kept us waiting for too long. I'm dying to hear how you got back with Heidar."

Heidar rolled his eyes and shrugged his shoulders. He called his old crewmates together in a bid, as he put it, to escape the girltalk. Vizzy was clearly torn in two, wanting to listen to both. Margaux was oblivious to the subtleties and ready to fly on a heady mix of company, memories and Belle Pensée.

"Darlings, it was so romantic. But I insist on some more of this wine first. Oh, and a cigarette. Blast. None of these damn rowers smoke. Not even Gareth?" she asked hopefully. "Damn it. This ridiculous fitness business. Oh Vizzy. You sweet kind boy. And you're rolling it yourself. What a darling."

Helen faced a number of conflicting emotions with this interchange. On balance, the look of happiness on Vizzy's face won out. She relaxed and smiled.

"Now, Paolo. Make no mistake. Very handsome boy. And like all handsome Italian boys, he knew this very well. We knew he was coming. Lalande was excited – she'd heard about him from Papa. We heard his car from half a kilometre away, before we could see it. Bright red Alfa Duetto, with the hood down. He looked so romantic – really casual, but maybe not really deep-down. You know the type, girls?" she asked conspiratorially.

Receiving nods all round she continued. "Anyway, he had not shaved. Looked a mess, but somehow a tidy and – how do you say – studied mess. His shirt crumpled but, you know, something expensive about it. Later I found they were made by the family tailor in Siena. A grey silk neck scarf – dove grey, looked like a film star. His trousers – you don't see them now, but so 60's retro, even then, I think velvet cord with flares. And his boots, his precious desert boots, his precious Clark's desert boots, his design icon. He would have died in those Clark's desert boots if he could. And the cigarette – of course he trod it out before he shook Papa's hand. Vizzy, if you find one half of

Paolo's style, OK, maybe cheap and empty style, but you will have more girls than you can fight off. Unless, and who can tell with you English, you prefer boys?"

She gave him an amused and quizzical glance. Vizzy, reddening rapidly, goggle-eyed, stayed mute, lost as a Yorkshireman in Yo Sushi.

"Dear Vizzy. I am so sorry. And you have been so nice. You choose your own style and you will be fine. Maybe a smaller suit next time? I guess this is not your normal style. Henley style, not normal for anywhere. Did you see all those fat men in their pink ties?"

She laughed, inhaled deeply from Vizzy's roll-up, drained another half glass and continued. "Well, it is a long story for another day. Lots to say. But the reason I am here today? Well, anyway, one day the next May, water falling from the sky but not as much as from Lalande's eyes, we married in the village church. Now I'm Mrs Montecchini. His *Babbo* and my Papa, oh the competition. Which? Castello Montecchini or Belle-Pensée for the toast? Nearly a fight. In the end, two toasts. His mother, from the very start, she looked at me like a rival lover. I knew there would be trouble. And there was. And I knew I should never move to Montalcino, but I had to. His family called him back for the harvest and he was like iron filings to a magnet. Also Lalande would not stay in the same room as me. My father was being torn in two. So I went. And we fought, my vain Paolo and me."

She paused, dragged on her cigarette, snorted contemptuously. "Look at me. Vizzy, I said look at me. You can tell I could be the match of any Italian boy, especially one who dresses like a Bohemian but is really a sly conservative. Shit, I bet he votes for Berlusconi on the quiet. Of course I am a match, more than a match. But with a boy, plus his *Mamma*, that bloody mother, the bitch, plus his *Babbo*, who knew everything about everything and always had to be right, plus his brothers and sisters, all five. Shit, I just shut up, switched off and planned inventive ways to kill them all. So, that dark night with the thunder, that wild night, when my wild thing arrived, it was my fate. My fate. Heidar, my Heidar, at the door with his motorbike. He had water dripping from his nose. He said he had come to take me back – he'd thought I was still in Bordeaux and had ridden on from there through the rain and the dark. I looked at him, asked him what had taken him so long, called him an idle bastard. I got on his bike, in the rain. That bitch of a mother cursed us. Paolo – he was not there – off drinking with his awful hunting friends. I did not see him again, even when he married Lalande. So, I see the lightning strike the vines in the next field as we head off in the rain. I am soaked in five seconds, but happy, so happy. Heidar's bike, so loud, so fast. And so, yet again, as at all big moments in my life, I just left and went. And here I am, at Henley, with my Belle Pensée 2000 and Vizzy's cigarette, and here you are. Here we all are. Here's to us."

Vizzy appeared transfixed. Helen, Jane and Lynette were deep in thought, all recognising that they had been living in the emotional slow lane. Conversation was stalled by the return of some of the other children, who had presumably been rubbernecking the men's conversation. There had been loud guffaws of laughter from their group for the last few minutes, and Gareth was clearly holding court.

David, sidling up to Helen with a look of some bemusement, tried to whisper a question, managing to make it perfectly audible to all.

"Mum, why did Gareth think you used to be a dyke? Were you?"

Helen sat, mouth open, paralysed. Margaux rescued her.

"Darling, we were all artistes. It was all so long ago. And what if she was then? Does it matter now?"

Helen had recovered her poise.

"Darling, I guess, umm, I guess I may have thought about it. Lots of people do at that age. But when I actually had the chance, well ..."

"Well ... what?" cut in Vizzy with some determination. Margaux looked appraisingly at her, maybe the hint of a smile. Helen glanced back and hesitated before replying.

"Oh, darling. Um, what can I say? Oh dear... how can I put this?" She shrugged. "Well, darling, I had my chance - and I guess I muffed it."

The silence after this, profound in its way, was broken by the return of little Ben. In his loudest five-year-old voice, tugging at Jane's skirt, he bellowed loudly enough to turn heads in the adjacent picnics.

"Mummy, why are they calling Daddy Shagger?"

CHAPTER 12

Morley had not been red-carded in the last two decades. A six month relationship with a fellow trainee architect, following his split with Helen after finals, had been terminated abruptly when she took up with a young banker from the city. He had last seen her roaring off in the passenger seat of a new Porsche, and felt insult was added to injury when her brother turned up the next weekend to take back her records. He still had complex feelings about the departed Lexicon of Love, the one relic of their past that he truly missed when she'd gone. Even now he had fought shy of buying a replacement. The pain from his ejection from the national rowing squad later that year actually ran deeper but had long been blunted by denial mechanisms. These had been stripped away tonight, and he was emotionally raw and vulnerable.

He cycled home from the club, feeling angry and humiliated, not least by the cruel banter from a delighted Bateman. Dave had looked mortified as Chris told him that he wasn't going to be up to it, and Bob Dawson from the rival London Rowing Club four was going to have his place. With a shrug and a nonchalant "Sorry, mate," his tenure of the two seat was terminated. Dave looked desperately upset, and said that he'd call him later. Chris, showing as much subtlety in his personal interactions as his stroking, called the crew to action. "Right lads. Here comes Bob. Snap to it. See you some time, mate. Good luck."

Morley maintained his dignity as an evidently happy Bob Dawson came in. Seeing Morley, he had at least the grace to say "Sorry, mate," which was evidently the greeting of the day and was at least refreshingly free of sentimentality. Morley returned to his bike, unpadlocking it and starting to head for home. His fervent wish to avoid Bateman was thwarted by a deliberate effort to humiliate him.

It felt undeserved, particularly as his crew had beaten the London four at last weekend's Veterans' regatta, their margin the greatest between the crews in five meetings. After little more than a month back, he had thought it a triumphant return. He had encountered the second of Kipling's imposters in the semi-final, as a Nottingham crew took them apart by nearly two lengths. They in turn were beaten by the same distance in the final by the new Leander four, all medal-winners from the Moscow or Los Angeles Olympics. It was an open secret that their strokeman, Adrian Heyward, a Henley Steward for the last two years, was the driving force behind the new Princess Alice Vase, and clearly had intentions on securing it for himself.

Morley thought dark thoughts on his cycle home. He felt that Chris, who he suspected would think Kipling's two imposters were a type of teacake, had not given him a fair chance. He had not enjoyed the racing rhythm sent down by Chris, and just knew that he could make the boat go faster if he were at stroke. Well, no chance now.

He arrived home to find the twins had plugged their Xbox into the family television and were blatting aliens at high volume. They were competing with each other on different halves of the screen, down which lurid green bodily fluids trickled after each successful lunge of their digital daggers, each accompanied by the kind of piercing shriek that only a more histrionic Alpha Centauran might make if his day were spoilt in that way. They bore the initial brunt of his hurt. "Will you turn that bloody thing down. For God's sake, haven't you got any homework?"

"Ohh, Dad! That's not fair. I'm winning," said an unabashed David, paying him only partial attention. Even that momentary lapse in concentration was enough to allow Alastair, who had not been deviated in the slightest by his father's interruption, to snatch an apparently insuperable lead in the quantitated alien carnage, eliciting more unearthly shrieks in rapid succession than a Mariah Carey CD on fast-forward. David was outraged. "You bastard. That's not fair. You always cheat."

He aimed a punch, receiving one in return. Morley had had quite enough. He felt a Wall of Death moment coming on, as always rather amazing the twins by the force of his outraged passion. For once, they had some justification in feeling unfairly treated.

Helen stormed in. "What the hell's going on? Peter! What on earth have the boys done? I don't like it when you shout like that in the house. Why are you here anyway ? It's your rowing night, isn't it?"

She glared at him angrily, then paused, body language softening. Sometimes long-established couples get sudden insights that cannot be explained logically. And sometimes, when partners are behaving least lovably they actually need most love. Helen saw something in her husband's eyes, a moistness just one step away from tears, that she had not seen combined with burning anger since one night over twenty years ago. He had turned up on her doorstep, unexpected and emotionally lost, the night he had lost his place in the national squad. She had not then heard that he'd already broken up with his enviably slim architect girlfriend, and had previously thought that she was over him. The bonds they had reforged and then forged anew that night had lasted ever since.

She looked him straight in the eye. "Darling, you need a hug. And a drink. Which do you want first? OK, the hug then. Boys, switch off that damn machine."

The paucity of alien shrieks suggested that even Alastair had been paying attention. The sudden loud squelching from the television, followed by an even louder "Oh, shit !" from Alastair suggested that he had paid the price of his lost concentration with virtual demise at the tentacles of one of the aliens.

The drink followed, the twins and Vizzy being treated to their share of one of Morley's better bottles, with hopeful designs on the second. Helen decided that she could do without cooking that evening, and Morley telephoned an order to the local curry house. He decided that a full-on sensory experience was warranted in the circumstances and went for the Vindaloo. All three boys followed suit, leaving Helen as the only one going for a softer option. She took the gentle ribbing from the boys and calls of "wuss" in good part.

Morley was regaling them with the tales of his evening, and was touched by their loyalty.

"That's really unfair, Dad. They were much better with you there. And you'd only just joined them."

Morley was beginning to mellow, and had taken a more reasoned view. "Thanks Vizzy. That's kind. Trouble is, we were two lengths down on a crew who were then two lengths down in the final. Simply no chance for Henley next year. Any decent oarsman would kill his grandmother for a Henley medal. Bob Dawson is way the best oarsman in the London boat. Shame for me he's stroke side. Otherwise it might have been Dave on his way home."

Alastair was unimpressed. "Well, I think Dave was a bastard. Should have stood up for you."

Morley demurred. "No Alastair. I'd only just joined. He's desperate for his chance of a medal. Rowing is a hard-nosed sport."

Alastair looked dubious. "OK, Dad. Say it was the other way round. Would you have stayed on and let him walk?"

Morley thought about this. "Point taken, Alastair. You're right. I wouldn't. He's my friend, plus I don't really like the others. Plus, that Chris is a crap stroke and it wouldn't be any fun. Plus we'd never win at Henley anyway."

"See, I told you so, Dad. He's a bastard."

The doorbell went, prompting a search of Morley's pockets and Helen's handbag for the curry money. Vizzy headed off to the front door and Helen to the kitchen to get the plates. "Bring the bag in here darling. David, get out the trays. Come on, look lively."

Vizzy re-emerged, empty-handed. "Dad, it's not the curry man. It's Dave."

There was an air of tension in the sitting room as Dave followed Vizzy through the door. Hair still wet from his post-outing shower, he looked flustered. "Peter, I'm really sorry, that was shit. I had no idea."

Morley was at a loss, simultaneously embarrassed by having to face his friend so soon after a public humiliation, jealous of his place in the crew and grateful for the thoughtfulness. He just shrugged in reply.

"Well," continued Dave, "I guess we're both in the same boat. Or not, when you think about it."

"What do you mean?" asked Morley, slow on the uptake. Realisation dawned. "You mean you've been kicked out as well?"

"No way, mate," said a cheerful Dave. "I told them to sling it and find someone else. Just didn't enjoy it. You're right about Chris. That bloody rhythm – hate it. And I hadn't realised just how much I enjoyed rowing with you. Soppy, isn't it?"

Morley was at a loss for words. Vizzy wasn't. "Dave, that's brilliant. Really brilliant."

Alastair didn't miss his opportunity. "Dave – why *are* you called Shagger?"

Dave was saved, temporarily at least, by the bell. Invited to stay for dinner, he appeared relaxed and happy until his first mouthful of Vindaloo.

"Oh God, I'm going to pay tomorrow. The Morley chicken vindaloo therapy for irritable bowel syndrome. With my bowels this is the dumbest thing I've done in a long time. The price you pay for rowing with your mates. Well Peter, lucky you're rowing in front of me tomorrow."

Morley looked puzzled. "Rowing tomorrow? What do you mean?"

Dave smiled. "Just because we're not rowing with those two doesn't mean we're giving up. No way. Coxless pair tomorrow. Then we'll see."

CHAPTER 13

A moment of truth. Fully aware of the baleful eyes from the balcony and having endured the barbed comments from former crewmates, Morley and Dave carried out the pair to the water's edge. The tide high, combining with the wind to make a typical Tideway "sinker", this was not the day for new experiments. Few other crews were boating, most doing ergometer sessions in the gym. Both however were keen to get going, just to see what if anything remained of the old synergy.

Feeling a sense of significance, Morley kicked off from the shore with his right foot, his left balanced in the middle of the boat. They set off slowly, keeping close to the bank against the outgoing stream. Almost from the start it felt comfortable, something right about the rhythm that had been missing in the four. Discretion the better part of valour, they cut short the outing before Hammersmith Bridge, where the water became less and less rowable. Returning cautiously, still keeping close to the bank while keeping a sharp lookout for crews coming the other way, they got back to Putney in good spirits.

Inhibited from further discussions while in the clubhouse, they considered their options over a pint of Young's Special in the Duke's Head just up the towpath.

"Peter. It's still there. We can make a go of this. We just need to find another pair. I'll ask around. Leave it with me."

Morley shook his head. "No Dave. We don't need A.N Other and his mate. If we're going to do this, we do it as we did before. We've all got unfinished business with Henley."

"Come on, Peter. That's crazy. Heidar perhaps. But Gareth? Did you see the shape he's in?"

"Did you talk to him, Dave? OK, he's put on some weight. But a year ago he was three stone heavier, and smoking. He decided to pull it together – down the gym three days a week. Bet he could beat both of us on the erg with a little training. Come on. It feels right. It's the right thing to do."

Dave remained unconvinced. "Bloody hell, Peter. Even if they could, do you think they would want to take on that sort of commitment? Would they even get permission? Margaux might be OK, but did you see that Lynette? I bet Gareth is on a short leash. No way he'll be allowed."

"Dave, there's only one way to find out. We're long overdue a lunch party at Morley Mansions. Keep Sunday week clear. I'll let you know if the date's OK for the others."

CHAPTER 14

There were mixed feelings. Both Vizzy and the twins were delighted at the prospect of seeing Heidar and Margaux again, and quite happy to see Dave and Gareth. However that was where it ended.

"Bloody hell!" said Alastair. "Not bloody Thomas and Gwen. Pair of bloody wusses. *We play our music at church, you know*," he simpered, in ruthless imitation of Gwen. "*And I can play keyboards, not just sing.*" That bloody Gwen. Stuck up cow. How did someone like Gareth end up with kids like that? Bet it's that bloody Lynette."

David looked equally sulky, asking whether they had to stay for the lunch or could go over to friends. It was only the prospect of Gareth's jokes that seemed to reconcile him to the event. Vizzy by contrast was quietly thrilled to be seeing both Heidar and Margaux again. Compared to the Vizzy of a month ago, there was a definite change in his outlook that had quietly pleased both of his parents. Helen was looking forward to seeing more of Margaux. Although quietly sceptical that the rowing would last for longer than some of Peter's other crazes, she was happy to see him engaged and optimistic again.

The day, thankfully, was turning out beautifully. After a week of rain and low clouds, it had dawned bright and clear. Morley, in prime alpha male mode, had elected to take on a barbecue and was intently employing the full range of his architectural skills on a large mound of charcoal and a few fire-lighters. The birds, celebrating their deliverance from persistent soaking, were singing lustily in competition with the decidedly less natural noises emerging from the twins' open bedroom window. Helen was putting the finishing touches to her three bean salad and a large summer pudding. Morley paused in annoyance as a motorbike revved noisily in the street, its engine noise a throbbingly powerful bass baritone growl punctuated by loud backfires at frequent intervals. There was something familiar to him about this combination, suggestive to the musically minded of Bryn Terfel attempting to pass a cantaloupe melon while lighting firecrackers.

The penny dropped. "Heidar and that bloody Harley," he muttered. "Should have scrapped it years ago."

The boys emerged quickly when it was clear that Heidar and Margaux had arrived.

"Aren't you the rock-chick?" asked Helen, as Margaux peeled the leather biking jacket from over her short summer dress. She accepted the two bottles of Belle-Pensée that Heidar had produced from the panniers of his ancient Electra-Glide.

"I thought we should try the '97," said Margaux. "Much better than you'd think, and it's still drinking really well."

"I'll take your word for it," said Helen. "You'll be pleased. I've got some lovely ginger beer to mix with it .... joke, darling."

It was a relaxed start to the lunch, and all were in good spirits as the others arrived. The twins did not show any apparent antipathy towards Gwen and Thomas, and good humouredly tolerated the attentions of Lucy and Ben. Vizzy was intermittently quizzing Heidar about Norse mythology. Helen was delighted to hear Margaux in full flow, presenting her offbeat view of life in her inimitable French accent, perhaps touched these days with a little South London.

"So darlings, I tell you there really are aliens. From outer space. Truly. Trust me. You can always tell. Their civilizations are so advanced, they cannot cope with our primitive notions of money. That's how you can always spot them. They get to the front of the queue at Sainsbury's, pack their bags with shopping, then what? Nothing. They try to transfer payment mentally like they do on their planets. Pouf – nothing happens. Twenty, thirty seconds, they look puzzled, then they remember. Then, at long last, they hunt in their bag for money or a credit card. You see that all the time. That's not a stupid human, that's a clever alien, just too clever. All the time they think what a backward hole of a planet they've landed on. Same at cash-points. They queue for five, ten minutes, get to the front of the queue. Go to the machine – try to converse with it in digital, maybe. Then the same. They think *shit, what a bunch of prim-itives*, they hunt through all their pockets. Of course it takes them ages, because they can't remember which galaxy they're in and whether they need a cashcard or a silicon-based octuped, and they're stored in different pockets. Then they can't remem-ber the number because it's too simple and needs no four dimensional calculation. Aliens, always aliens. You look closely, next time you see someone doing that. There's always something a little different about them. Not quite right. Aliens. Perhaps they take over the planet."

Gareth cut in, in cheerful Welsh counterpoint.

"Margaux. You don't half talk some crap sometimes. They're not aliens. They're just Scottish. They don't look quite right either. It's just the thought of having to pay out money that does their head in and paralyses them like that."

Dave was not to be outdone.

"Scots. Well, you know what doctors say about Scots. Those you find in England are like piles. They're never much fun at the best of times, but it's the ones that come down and stay that become the real pain in the arse."

"Piles, Dave ? I guess you'd know all about that. Especially after that vindaloo," laughed Morley.

Dave looked pained.

"I don't need to be reminded about that, thank you Peter. It's a wonder that I made it to the pair next day."

Heidar was suddenly intrigued, pausing in his conversation with Vizzy. "A pair. I thought you guys had started rowing in a four. Veterans' regatta or something."

Morley grabbed his chance. "Heidar, I'm glad you mentioned that. Part of the reason you're here today, apart from the pleasure of your company."

"Part of the reason? Part??"

"Thank you Vizzy," clipped Morley, with a stern look. "Yes, part. It was wonderful to see you all at Henley. Far too much wasted time. You three were the closest friends I ever had, apart from Helen, obviously. It was just far too long and I'm not letting you lot go again. But, and it's a big but – sorry Gareth, no offence – there is the small matter of the Princess Alice Challenge Vase."

"What the bloody hell's the Princess Alice Challenge Vase when it's at home?" asked a puzzled Gareth. "I'll deal with the butt issue later."

"The Princess Alice Challenge Vase is unfinished business, Gareth. For all of us, I hope. No, I expect."

Explanation followed after Morley and Dave dealt with barbecue issues, and returned with a large plate loaded with steaks. Helen had correctly forecast that the younger children would go for the chicken option, and would turn up their noses at the baked potatoes in favour of oven chips. Morley saluted her perspicacity with a grateful nod, graciously acknowledged.

The twins had leapt on their steaks at speed. While the rest of the table went at more sedate pace, they quizzed Gwen and Thomas in what was clearly a continuation of earlier cross-examination. "So what sort of music do you play in church? Tell us more about the Youth Club on Sunday evenings."

The replies were lost as adult conversation picked up. Distractedly, Morley allowed the children to leave the table for a while as the adults chatted on, leaving a pause before puddings. Vizzy stayed, interested and engaged. About two minutes later, loud music emerged from the twins' bedroom window, with powerful rhythmic drumming and a coruscating guitar solo.

"Peter. Your boys are really good," said Heidar.

"No they're not," cut in Vizzy. "They're total shit. If that's Alastair and David, then I'm an alien."

He looked round, realising that, dressed as he was, perhaps he hadn't made the best of points. He rallied. "And I'm not. I'm not even Scottish."

Lynette smiled. "No, that's Thomas. He's very good on the guitar. I just don't like it when he plays that loud stuff. Especially on a Sunday."

Gareth looked pained, making a subliminal shrug towards Morley, who replied with an understanding smile.

Helen broke the silence. "So, girls. Are we going to let this bunch of old has-beens go on their crazy Don Quixote quest? Have our kitchens invaded by disgusting smelly rowing kit? Our evenings ruined by moaning about blisters? Our weekends blighted by taking on all the child care? In short, are we completely mad?"

"Are there any upsides?" asked Lynette uncertainly.

"The muscle tone," said Jane.

"And the libido," said Helen. Vizzy blushed.

"Doesn't seem much compensation to me," said Lynette doubtfully.

"Count me in," said Margaux forcefully. "When can he start?"

A decision was reached. A provisional decision, a tenuous decision, a decision to be reviewed in a month. But a decision. Like a rather overweight phoenix arising from some very old ashes, the QEC four had been reborn.

As he and Helen saw off the guests on that emotional day, Alastair and David managed to startle Morley more than at any time since the Phoebe episode. Thinking about it, at least that had been in character.

"Dad. Next Sunday, can you do us a favour ? Will you take us to Church?"

CHAPTER 15

The movement of a boat through water is subject to a variety of physical constraints, familiar to applied mathematicians and marine engineers if not its occupants. Accelerated by motive force and retarded by viscous drag, its resultant motion is a consequence of the dynamic balance between these opposing forces. It is possible, and indeed achievable by those with an unhappy dynamic balance between their own opposing forces of mathematical interests and social life, to derive a series of equations that might explain the respective motions of Michael Phelps, the GB coxless four and the fat bloke who dive bombs into the deep end in the beer ad. What they cannot begin to do is to quantify feel.

The feel of a boat, intangible, difficult to pin down and yet hugely important to its resultant speed, is apparent to most occupants, albeit to varying degrees. There are some who can perceive subtle changes early, responding with appropriate minute alterations in their stroke rhythm and timing to restore harmonic integrity and boat speed. If also possessed of bravery and a little ruthlessness, they would make an ideal stroke. There are others, less sensitive to these changes, who can end up as initiators of, or unknowing participants in, an almost viral spread of clipped movements and panicked rush that both strips all aesthetic enjoyment and retards boat speed. Whatever their current level of physical conditioning, whatever the scales might say, however long the break had been, all four of the former QEC crew fell into the former category.

The outing having been sanctioned by the club captain, they had congregated late the next Saturday afternoon, when there were likely to be fewer witnesses. There had been some nerves, understandable in view of the potential significance. Remembering the UL coach from the 1970's who had left his labradors by the boathouse, Morley had relented and allowed Farquhar into the back of the car. The dog was almost pathetically grateful to escape the twins, as would be any human who enjoyed the original Sweet Child of Mine and the integrity of his eardrums. Farquhar roamed up and down the towpath, finding enough new smells and interesting puddles to keep his tail wagging continuously. His attempts to aid in the boating process were less appreciated, and he had to be dissuaded from swimming after the departing crew, ending up sitting a trifle forlornly on the bank.

It felt different to Morley, almost from the start. Not consistently, and certainly not a joyous return to their former fluency. But different enough, enjoyable and encouraging. He made sure that they took things gently, making frequent stops to prevent fatigue and its consequent effects on posture and rhythm. He remembered his own returning outing well enough to know how Heidar and Gareth might be feeling. He had promised Gareth that they wouldn't do any hard racing pieces, provided that Gareth promised in turn not to wear Lycra until he'd lost a further twenty pounds.

They decided eventually to turn just after Barnes Bridge, turning into the middle of the stream which was now outgoing towards Putney and eventually the North Sea. Dave spotted a dark figure, unmistakeable even from this distance, on the Surrey towpath. "Peter! Bloody hell. It's Farquhar! How the hell did he get here?"

Morley was amazed. Farquhar had not voluntarily travelled this far in at least two years. Gareth and Heidar shouted and clapped their hands. Farquhar, recognising that he was the centre of attention, barked happily back. As they set off back towards Putney, their canine shadow padded off in pursuit. Morley thought that their pace must suit him better than his running, or that he had just got bored of Wandsworth Common. Well, fitness for all in the Morley household.

They decided to try a few short pieces at three quarters pressure, and even a minute at higher rate and full pressure. Definitely promising, but a long way to go. It was a happy crew that disembarked at Putney, hindered by a now aquatic Farqhuar who swam to join them as they stopped to adjust their approach to the bank. Morley had never had his calves licked as he lifted out a boat before, and was in sufficiently good mood to enjoy the experience.

Boat and blades racked, they congregated on the towpath as they looked at the famous stretch of river while Farqhuar explored the water's edge. Morley, leader in most aspects of the crew's daily life, knew that Heidar had the biggest say in their big decisions. He deferred to him, waiting until the Icelander was ready to speak.

"Peter, Dave. You present us, in our middle years, with a heroic and possibly futile task. We have had one outing – a good outing, OK. But I now have five blisters, a sore back and a problem. Do I change my life, the calm structure that I have built up around me, at a time when I have achieved some contentment? Do I do this crazy thing when I have the even crazier problem of the Research Assessment Exercise to deal with at QEC? It would be mad. Completely mad. What do you think, Gareth?"

Gareth, still sweating heavily, looked at his friends. "Heidar's right. It's completely mad."

He paused, looking at the disappointed expression on Morley's face. "But on Monday I go back to the Traffic Planning department at Twickenham Council. If I had known where my Maths degree would take me, I'd have done Sociology. At least the girls were better looking. Oh, why didn't I go into financial forecasting when I had the chance? And if I go back to that life tomorrow, missing this opportunity for madness and futility? Now that would really be mad. Two years ago I was a mess – fat, smoking, bored at work and, I'm sorry to say it but you're my best friends, bored at home. It was only Gwen nagging me that made me pull it together. Now, I don't know where this train is going, but I'm along for the ride."

Heidar looked round him, fixing each in turn. He spoke with emphasis.

"OK. I guess I'm repeating myself. But I'll say it again. *We fucking well do it and we do it fucking well.*"

"Sorry Mrs Holland," chorused the other three, in their best Icelandic accents.

"The amount that Gareth ate, it's a wonder that boat floated," added Dave, in his best Monty Python falsetto.

CHAPTER 16

The acquisition of race fitness is a long and unavoidably painful process. For rowing, the mantra that mileage makes champions has been proven time and again. For the full-time professional athlete, the winter is thus a time of dark misery and untold horrors of endurance training, underpinned by the sapping uncertainties of squad life and ruthless selection rites. For Morley's crew there was at least the certainty that, injuries allowing, they were in it together. That did not make the physical side easier, and they had decided that their only chance of beating opponents of such calibre was to row and train more intensively than them. They trained side by side on the ergometers, clocking up 10,000 metre intervals at gratifyingly improving speed. Morley sensed that they had moved in the eyes of his old four from quaint joke to serious rivals.

It was playing an increasing role in family lives. The Morley boys were beginning to see their father in another light, and engaging in new social interactions. The twins did indeed go to church, but demanded the Catholic church in Twickenham where Gwen and Thomas Jenkinson went. Morley had found it strange entering the modern building, remembering the half-familiar strangenesss from his wedding to Helen in another modern Catholic church. Brought up Catholic, although lapsed in exuberant style at college, her parents had nevertheless insisted on a church wedding and the parish priest on an exasperating series of recruitment-aimed hours of "spiritual guidance" for Morley himself. Brought up in classic English semi-detached Anglicanism, he had inwardly rebelled while outwardly conforming. They had to sign a document promising that the children would be brought up Catholic. This was at least belated honouring of that promise, but he wondered just how much the guitar playing talents of the twins would contribute to the recruitment and retention ambitions of the Twickenham Catholic community. He remembered his old copy of the Electric Prunes' Mass in F Minor, and wondered whether he should be cruel enough to the congregation to introduce the boys to its lysergic liturgical landscape. On balance, they were probably sonically challenging enough as they were, although at least Catholics should already have some concept of Purgatory. He wondered if they were already getting a compensatory discount in confessional Hail Marys.

A Sunday ritual had developed, in which Morley would drop the twins off at Twickenham with Lynette and the kids while he, Gareth and Farquhar would escape gratefully to the river. The boys would be picked up eventually in the evening, after some hours at the church Youth Club, by the sound of it rather holier in principle than practice.

Vizzy, by contrast, still lacked much of a peer group of his own age, and in fact had rather distanced himself from the one or two odd and dysfunctional friends that he used to hang round with. His dress sense had moved out of the Emo mainstream, although still a considerable distance from Topman. He had found various excuses to come down to Putney with his father, then making a beeline for Heidar, whom he subjected to further questioning about Norse mythology. He then managed to startle Morley in his turn, on a Saturday when Dave was bemoaning the late dropping out of his regular babysitter. Vizzy offered immediately, and was accepted by a grateful if surprised Dave. He was even more surprised to hear that Vizzy had not subjected Lucy and Ben to the latest Tarantino DVD, but had watched a series of Disney films with them, and had even cooked supper with Lucy. He was now their favourite ever babysitter.

Heidar dropped round one evening after one of their twice weekly indoor gym sessions, usually dreaded by all. He made his apologies, then said that he wanted to speak to the kids. None took much persuading to come down, and accepted with pleasure when they were offered a half-term holiday job painting and redecorating at Heidar and Margaux's place in Wimbledon.

"Are you sure?" asked Helen doubtfully.

"Absolutely," said Heidar. "I'm taking the week off work and I want some willing helpers who aren't afraid of some hard work. Outside the school environment, I suspect that this is a very good description of your boys. Plus I suspect that they could do with some money to spend unwisely."

So it was arranged. In little over six weeks, a small but important realignment had been effected in all of their lives. Gwen and Thomas were no longer spoken of in disparaging terms, and in fact there seemed to be some genuine bonding going on. Thomas was not only a better guitarist, but could also beat the pants off the boys on the Xbox. With their birthday money they had managed to upgrade to a variant where they could log on on-line, and thus continue battles at all hours of the day and night. Thomas and Alastair in particular used to combine for online battles with various French and Americans, some of whom at least were genuine kids.

Little by little, the four families were becoming intertwined. Helen had begun to enjoy the company of Jane and Lynette when she saw them, although she detected undercurrents of sadness in Lynette and wondered whether she felt threatened in some way by these sudden changes. She noticed that Gareth seemed somehow more relaxed and expansive when away from her, and both Gwen and Thomas were more likely to laugh and lark about while at the Morleys.

The training regime was challenging, even for Morley, who had kept himself in pretty good shape. He wondered how on earth Gareth could cope, but remembered his indomitable spirit from the early days. While he was extrovert in training, playing up his supposed role as fat layabout, he was actually competitive. It was apparent to all that he was catching up fast in the gym and on the ergometer, and was noticeably losing weight. The one month spousal review had been passed, and they had latitude to go on until at least Christmas.

There had been one potential setback. Dave was taken aside by the club captain, and returned slightly apologetically to speak to the crew a few minutes later. "Sorry to mention it chaps, but the captain says that we've got to go official. Joining fees and annual subscriptions etcetera."

They all agreed that this was fair, but were taken aback by Dave's information that this was in the region of £500 per annum. Gareth in particular looked disturbed.

Morley took Dave aside. "Dave, I wish you'd told me first. I think money's tight for Gareth and Lynette. In fact I think that much would be a problem for them. I think that Lynette would jump at the chance to put a stop to it."

"Shit, Peter. I just didn't know. What the hell can we do? Now he knows, he's not going to let us pay for him, even if we could."

It was a difficult issue. A quiet session was held between the other three. Dave, with two children in private school, was not feeling flush, particularly as he did no private practice. The Morley family were just about getting by. Heidar offered to pay for Gareth, although this was turned down flat by the others. They knew that his pay as an academic did not go far in London, and also that they had taken a big financial risk last year when Margaux had left her job as a wine buyer for Waitrose – "all that Australian Shiraz and Chilean Chardonnay. Such an abuse of a proper French palate" – and had set up her own business importing French regionals and carefully selected clarets, not least Belle-Pensée. In the end a quiet compromise was reached, whereby Gareth was informed that the fees were only £200. The others put in an extra £100 each and prayed that he would never find out. The four was still on the river.

The outings were improving, despite having to use the oldest boat in the club. They were now undertaking racing pieces, occasionally surprising themselves with the speed. For the main part it was the long grind of "steady state", at half to three quarters pressure over periods of up to one hour. They turned down as premature the chance to race in the Fours Head in October. They did however pay attention to the result of the Veteran fours for their age group, where Leander were more than twenty seconds ahead of Upper Thames and Nottingham, with London-Thames a further few seconds behind.

It was going to be a very long hard winter. But they were on the right track. They were getting into shape, Gareth and Farqhuar most obviously. Whether their partners benefited from the promised improvements in muscle tone and libido had not yet been discussed, but probably only because Margaux had not managed to place herself in meaningful proximity to a bottle of good red and the other wives. With their current training intensity that was probably a good thing. At least they were sleeping well.

CHAPTER 17

"Dad, this is crap. Tastes like jam. I hate South African Pinotage."

"Since when, David, did you know anything about South African Pinotage?"

"Since we've been working at Heidar and Margaux's. Margaux is teaching us about wine."

"He's right, Dad. New World wine is just so obvious. All one note."

"You too, Vizzy? Another connoisseur. At least my wine rack's likely to be safer these days, unless I stock it with Belle-Pensée."

"Your wine rack, Dad, is a disgrace. You should be ashamed of yourself."

"Bloody hell! I stand corrected. Thank you, Alastair, for your considered judgement. If only you buggers could have been arsed to make just the tiniest effort for those scholarships, perhaps I could afford to keep you in the quality of wine you feel you deserve."

"Good wine doesn't have to be expensive, Dad," said Vizzy. "Margaux's got some great ones that are dead cheap. Côtes du Frontonnais rocks."

"Come off it, Vizzy," said David. "The Cahors was wicked. Really deep and dark. Like drinking a Sisters of Mercy song."

"Bullshit" was Alastair's thoughtful contribution to the debate. "There's no comparison. That Rasteau was awesome. Rhône wines kick ass. They're the dog's bollocks."

Helen looked around the table in some amazement.

"Such expertise! And you've mastered the language of wine already. Anyway, back to the day job. When will Heidar trust you with paintbrushes? Or will you just carry on using your hair like you have so far?"

"Ha bloody ha, Mum," said a slightly grumpy Alastair. "We're doing really well. Heidar's really pleased. The place is looking great. Anyway, if you think we've got a lot in our hair you should see Gwen."

The boys laughed together, Vizzy joining in as happily as the others.

"So how near are you to finishing?" asked Morley conversationally.

"Well it would have been tomorrow, apart from the bloody duck."

"What bloody duck? What on earth are you on about, David?" asked Morley with a look of bemusement.

"It's not a bloody duck," said Vizzy with determination. "It's a Barrow's Goldeneye."

"Ah, that makes it all clear. A Barrow's Goldeneye," said Morley. "Whatever the hell that is."

"Dad. You are just soooo ignorant. You know nuffink," scorned Alastair, mimicking a television catchphrase and inducing gales of laughter in the other boys. Morley and Helen were bemused.

Alastair had of course never heard of a Barrow's Goldeneye until that morning. Heidar had received an excited phone call from a fellow hobbyist to say that one at had been spotted at the Wetlands Centre. This was apparently utterly remarkable, according to Heidar, who insisted that his five assistants should drop paintbrushes and accompany him to Barnes. On the train he had told them how rare the bird was outside Canada and Iceland. His father used to call them by the Icelandic name of Húsond. He described how he was taken by his father, who loved wildlife, and had spent whole weekends observing the wildfowl while camping with him by Lake Mývatn. He had clearly been moved to remember Kjartan, and had told the kids how the journey they were taking made him feel they were honouring his memory. His passion stilled their sense of boredom, and the excitement had been transmitted to Vizzy at least, who sat motionless for what seemed like ages, training Heidar's expensive field glasses on the big head and striking black and white patterning of the celebrated visitor. All had been amazed at the numbers of other enthusiasts who had appeared within about an hour of the telephone call, some wearing suits and clearly bunking off work. Some of these had cast beseeching glances at Heidar's field glasses, clearly having been unprepared. Heidar was happy to help out, and generously loaned them out to a queue of almost pathetically grateful office escapees. Vizzy noticed that not all the enthusiasts were so generous of spirit.

Alastair was less starry-eyed about it all. "It was ridiculous, Dad. A bloody twitchers' convention. All we needed was Bill bloody Oddie and a mating badger and we could have been on BBC HD by teatime."

"Ah, well. That was Heidar's nickname. Twitcher."

Loyal Vizzy glared at the twins to suppress incipient hilarity. Morley felt obliged to explain.

"It was the early morning outings. Up at 5.30 to get down to Chiswick and onto the water before 7. On a summer's morning, it is the most wonderful thing. Even though you were desperate to sleep in – remember we were students – there was something lovely about it. The river was often still then, and you could get some really good work in. Except for Heidar and his birdspotting. Anywhere within fifty yards of a heron and that was it. No racing until he'd had a really good look, and then he wouldn't go until he'd told us about its natural history and migration patterns. When that man gets enthusiastic, he doesn't do it by halves. Doesn't do anything by halves in fact. Anyway we called him Twitcher for a while, never really stuck."

"What was Gareth's nickname?" asked Alastair, never one to miss a trick.

Morley had to give in. "Mint Sauce," he admitted sheepishly, triggering absolute hysterics in the boys, with even Helen joining in. Morley had to smile, despite himself.

"Oh God. Could you imagine Lynette?" she asked between peals of laughter. "Oh darling, and how's Mint Sauce today? She'd probably wet herself."

They ate on in good humour. Helen noticed how much things had changed in the family since the four had reunited. Now they would sit and chat together while eating most evenings, rather than hold plates on their lap while watching television, before the boys disappeared off after about ten minutes, unless the programme was sufficiently unsuitable to hold their attention.

She thought for a second and echoed one small concern. "Do make sure that you don't trash Margaux and Heidar's place. They won't be used to this. They haven't had kids – they haven't said why and I've never asked of course."

Vizzy shook his head. "You're wrong, Mum. They had Haraldur. I've seen his picture. He'd be doing his GCSE's this year."

CHAPTER 18

Morley was not feeling much Christmas cheer. Cash flow was tight at work, as payment was being withheld by one of his customers. As usual it was a banker, and as usual one whose wife had decided half way through construction on a complete change of design theme. His other piece of unwelcome news had been the appointment of Bateman as club captain. While not as overtly hostile as before, he was no friend of Morley or his crew.

The rain was coming down hard as they boated, and the wind strong. Morley looked forward to this as an escape. Gareth was more than usually glad to be escaping from home. His mother, who had been widowed last January, had arrived for Christmas and was at war with Lynette. They had never got on particularly well, but relationships had deteriorated. Dave was also bemoaning the immininent arrival of his in-laws. Heidar by contrast was quite cheerful, as he usually was for outings in bleak winter weather. Farqhuar also appeared in good spirits and was happily chasing some of the seagulls who were escaping the worst of the North Sea storms along the hard at Putney.

The water was at least rowable as they went at half pressure, the only crew on the river. They passed Hammersmith Bridge, keeping tight into the Surrey bank against the swollen winter stream, carrying odd bits of flotsam and jetsam after the recent heavy rains, which had caused flooding in parts of the upper Thames in Oxfordshire. Apart from traffic crossing the bridge, almost no one was out and about, presumably most were Christmas shopping or huddled up at home. An old man, muffled against the winter winds, walked his ill-favoured mongrel along the towpath. Morley half-recognised him, more because of the scraggy dog who would have appeared more naturally disposed to companionship with a Big Issue seller.

They pushed on, and Morley was really encouraged by the rhythm and pace. Despite the increasingly rough conditions and the old creaking boat, they were rowing well and he was really beginning to become hopeful about their chances. He looked towards the bank, and was pleased to see the dark outline of Farqhuar, faithful companion in the wind and snows. He noticed that Farqhuar had been tending to disappear during outings recently, and suspected that he too had discovered the joys of the Wetland Centre near Barnes.

Despite the weather, they had elected to take on a couple of longer pieces at full pressure. Tideway crews often have an advantage in rough conditions as they face so much of it in training. Calm waters appeared very easy in comparison, and moderate swells that bothered crews from more sheltered rivers were hardly noticed by battle-hardened Tideway veterans.

They turned, fighting the lurching as they turned into the wind and waves. They set off downstream, coping well with the swell and then went for the first four minute piece. It was probably their best ever piece, remarkable in rough conditions. Thoroughly exhausted by three and a half minutes, spray flying as the waves increased in size as they rounded the bend near Chiswick Eyot, Morley tried to take it up as far as he safely could for the finish.

Suddenly, a sickening thud, the boat stopping in an instant and lurching to bowside. Suddenly danger, mid-Tideway, standing waves, high wind, alone on the river.

"What the hell's going on?" shouted Morley.

"Fucking railway sleeper," shouted Gareth in return.

He was right. The culprit, a massive piece of flotsam, presumably originating from somewhere in the docks, or even brought in by the tide from the North Sea, continued its slow passage along the side of the four. Already they were lower in the water, clearly holed. Morley noted with a chill that water was flooding down beneath his stretcher. Their boat, possibly the oldest in the club, did not have any of the anti-sinking structures of more recent boats.

"Heidar, quick! Paddle on. Three strokes. Then ten together, quick!"

Heidar tried, with difficulty as the bows were already down. The swell was lurching them nastily side to side. They attacked the strokes. It was hopeless, the bows already submerged. Gareth shouted urgently.

"She's going down. Get out and hang on!"

She was. They did, suddenly realising they were in mortal danger in these conditions.

One thing you must never ever do, unless the boat goes down, is to leave it and head off on your own. That's how rowers drown. They knew this and clung to the boat, clearing the oars from the rowlocks and turning it over. Kicking together for the shore, they made a little headway, but were battered by the waves and getting horribly chilled. The boat was also sitting lower in the water. No hope of rescue, now no chance of making it to the shore. Morley made a decision.

"We won't make it with four of us. I'm the best swimmer."

Without waiting for a reply, he pushed away, ignoring the cries of "No!!". He began to make some headway, although being pushed away from the boat. He lost sight of them in the swell, pushing hard for shore, the cold a gnawing sapping presence that seemed to infiltrate and subvert every fibre. He pushed past another piece of driftwood, too small to help but big enough to hinder. A feeling of hopelessness began to pervade him. His confidence was sapping, now he wasn't sure he could make it. He redoubled his efforts, knocked back by some of the waves, much bigger than they had seemed from within the boat.

Where there had been assurance, then wary hopefulness, then alarm increasing to abject fear, there was now hopelessness. The shore, possibly only fifty yards away, might as well have been several miles. His body temperature dropping, he was on the point of giving up and resigning himself to the river's designs. He felt another piece of driftwood nudge him, adding blunt insult to cruel injury. It nudged again. Then again, then pushed itself under his shoulder. Rather unexpectedly, it then slobbered in his face.

"Farqhuar" - the blunt statement of fact, was about all the breath he had left for words. Something, perhaps the contact or the warmth, perhaps the sharing of will, perhaps something altogether higher in origin and outside his belief systems, something pushed and inspired him. Together, a floating transient symbiosis of elemental canine and human survival instinct, they made some headway, the waves becoming less predatory as they inched to shore. Morley did not dare to test the depth, knowing that he might find difficulty regaining his swimming position if it was too deep. Still they inched. Surely here was shallow enough – too risky. Finally, at last, he tried exhaustedly to gauge his depth. He felt the suck of the Tideway mud, then worried about getting embedded, drowning by malign default as he was sucked down. Half swimming, half walking, dragging and being dragged by Farqhuar, they gained the bank and climbed exhausted, grasped back from the edge of oblivion. He sat, miserable, cold and worried as he just clasped Farqhuar to him, not even noticing the shower of spray as Farqhuar shook himself dry after Morley's grasp lightened.

Breathing still painful, he fought the desire just to lie down and sought the others. He prayed, deeply and fervently, that they too had made it. They were likely to be further downstream, judging by their initial parting. He trudged in cold and silent distress, Farqhuar by his side, and spotted the upturned hull against the Surrey bank. Thank God. There were three figures beside it. Moving, and then waving as they spotted him.

They hugged silently. Both Gareth and Dave had tears in their eyes. Heidar stroked Farqhuar, eventually speaking. "Peter. I know they say never to leave the boat. But you did, and it was the bravest thing I've seen. You saved our lives. We were going down. No chance with my swimming, Dave's not much better. We only just made it as it was. We all thought you'd gone. How the hell did you make it?"

Morley shook his head, still in wonder. "I just don't know. I nearly didn't. Some strange synergy between the good Lord and a fat dog." He ruffled Farqhuar's fur. "OK, Farqhuar. You're an honorary crew member now. Steak for you tonight."

Dave was sensible, practical, shivering. "Come on now. We'll freeze to bloody death if we wait here. We've lost all the wellies in the bloody drink, so it's barefoot. We'll keep warmer carrying the boat and won't go any slower. Anyway, we can't leave it here."

No words were said on the long, cold and emotional walk back. They saw no one, carrying the boat on their shoulders like a coffin, like the coffin it might have been.

As they came past the old Harrods Furniture Depository, now clearly turning its back on the Parker-Knoll's to reinvent itself as yet another upmarket riverside housing development, they passed the old boy with the ill-favoured mutt, thin old coat buttoned tight, muffler round his neck. He looked impossibly ancient, he too apparently kept going solely by force of will. He gave them a sardonic glance, surveying their wrecked boat.

"Ey up lads. Been torpedoed?"

No one had the inclination to reply. They walked on, miserable. The old man shouted after them.

"Hey, is that your bloody dog? That bastard's shagged my Sadie four fucking times this month."

CHAPTER 19

"You bunch of bloody amateurs. Look at it! A bloody write-off."

Bateman was not happy. "If Mr Blobby over there had bloody well looked round once in a sodding while, I wouldn't have to explain this to the Committee."

Morley reddened angrily. "That is no way to describe a bloody good oarsman. How many Henley finals have you got to? OK, I accept that we made the wrong decision going out alone in those conditions. We all recognise that, and we put our hands up to that. But there was no way anyone could have spotted that sleeper. Remember the UL eight in the 70's? They were coxed, did exactly the same thing – you just can't see those sleepers when it's rough. UL were bloody lucky they were out with a launch then. Do you realise how near we came to drowning? There's no excuse to have a boat without buoyancy aids these days. Remember Leo Blockley?"

Morley had a fair point, which even Bateman had to concede. Leo Blockley had tragically drowned during a training camp in Spain with the Cambridge University lightweights, his eight swamped by two foot high waves. The lack of buoyancy aids in the boat had threatened to sink it outright, forcing the crew to take to the water and leading to his death only 50 metres from the landing stages. His parents had campaigned tirelessly for governing bodies to make flotation aids mandatory, and thanks to their efforts a government sponsored rowing safety review was at last under way. The talk on the Putney towpath was that these safety devices would become mandatory in the next couple of years, but for the moment there was no legislation. The boat that Morley's crew had been using, the oldest and least desirable in the club, so shot by nearly two decades of heavy use that even the Under-15's had rebelled against using it, would probably be scrapped by then anyway. Never any chance for buoyancy aids. Never any thought that they might be needed.

Bateman's face hardened. "I don't care what your excuses are. I'm not putting any of our other boats at risk so you bunch can arse around reliving your bloody college days. This is a top class boat club for switched-on rowers with professional attitudes, not the set for Brideshead Revisited 2."

Even Dave, smooth, urbane Dave, now bridled. "Hang on. That's way out of line. Where's your professionalism? Too young for the Princess Alice and you throw all your toys out the cot."

Heidar weighed in. "You must be the biggest jerk I've met in rowing since that arsehole at UL. I walked then. We walk now. But, Mr Bateman, I tell you two things. One – we will beat the pants off your four, very publicly. I don't blame them, they're nice enough guys. But we will do it, just so that you can feel the jerk you are when your committee realise what you lost for the club. Two – we get our fees back for the rest of the year. No boat, no fees. Tell that to your committee. Guys, come on. We have some decisions to make. Duke's Head, now."

Second pint in, they sat planning a way ahead. Bateman had been variously described as a git, bastard, wanker, arsehole and a criminal waste of oxygen. While offering some small satisfaction, this had not really got them any further. They had been grateful for the support of the other Thames oarsmen and women, many of whom had come to like the spirit of the crew they had nicknamed Dad's Navy. There had been a lot of genuine shock about their near-drowning, and Bateman's hard line would not have been widely supported. He was not proving a popular captain, but he had the power at the moment.

They discussed the idea of going en masse to one of the other Tideway clubs, or possibly to Kingston or Molesey. The East End clubs such as Lea were just too far away to be realistic, given their working schedules. None seemed to fit well, and they thought that the chance of getting a decent boat would be slim. Not, they recognised, that the one they were using could be classed as such. They had been hoping that good early season's results might persuade the club to allow them use of one of their better boats. That hope had appeared to vanish when Bateman had taken over.

Gareth took a phlegmatic and philosophical view. "He may be a wanker, he may just be bitter and jealous. Whatever, he's done us a favour. Forced the issue."

Dave nodded thoughtfully. He looked at Gareth appraisingly. "I know you well enough to know when those Welsh grey cells, all three of them, are working on something. Come on then, spit it out."

Gareth simply laughed. His laugh, as always, raised the spirits. "Caught out. Yet again. Simple valleys boy, just not cut out to fox you metropolitan intellectuals. Well, point is, see, we need a decent boat if we're going to have any bloody chance at all. So I've been looking into it. Reckon thirteen or fourteen grand should see us straight."

"Thirteen or fourteen grand!" exploded Morley. "Where the hell are we going to get thirteen or fourteen grand? Pass Heidar the Grecian 2000 and get him working Picadilly as a rent boy? Don't be crazy. None of us have got that kind of money to spare."

"Unless," said Gareth unfazed and doggedly persistent, "we go for the Empacher option, when we'll need seventeen or eighteen. Two problems with that. It is getting a bit pricey, I admit. Plus my colour therapist says I don't do yellow. Can't let my public see me in a boat that looks like a banana on steroids."

Heidar, calmer than Morley and more astute, picked up on this. "OK, Gareth. You've been putting your finely honed mathematical brain to work on this. I suspect in Twickenham Council's time, but we should let that pass, perhaps?"

"There are only so many traffic light sequences that a mortal soul can programme in one lifetime. I simply cut down on the time emailing clips from YouTube and dodgy jokes to my co-workers. This represents a complete withdrawal from local council life, as I'm sure Peter remembers. However I shall make it up to them in the New Year - it's one of my resolutions. But my main one, which I fully intend to keep, is to get one of those shiny Henley medals. We thus need a shiny competitive boat, courtesy of Messrs Janousek, Sims or Stampfli. We get our own boat, we're in control, we're serious."

Morley looked at each in turn, then shook his head and laughed. "This is one bloody expensive mid-life crisis. Why couldn't we just stick to shagging the secretary like any normal middle-aged gits."

Dave looked taken aback. "You mean it's either-or? Now that's taking things way too seriously."

CHAPTER 20

The day after Boxing Day is often an emotional low point. Morley was at rock bottom. Gareth had called, utterly deflated. Lynette had put an absolute ban on him taking out a loan towards the new boat. They had still entertained hopes on Christmas Eve when they met at Dave's house. He was the only one of the four who had his own ergometer, and they took it in comradely and competitive turns. Jane was charming, although Morley knew that she had taken the probable loss of their planned skiing holiday hard. She hugged each of them in turn, saying that she was so glad they were alive, even if they were a bloody expensive luxury. She was looking forward to New Year's Eve at Heidar and Margaux's, where the new décor was having its first major social outing. Lucy and Ben were excited about this already, even with Christmas so close to hand. Ben insisted on watching the Daddies on their gruelling interval sessions, putting a damper on their linguistic responses to the pain.

None of them had found it too easy to raise the money. A new set of tyres and a replaced camshaft on the Volvo had damaged Morley's already ailing credit balance, even before the Christmas spending began. Helen had been very supportive. This venture had brought them, and indeed the whole family closer. "Darling, just cash in the bloody ISA. Some things are more important."

He affected reluctance, but knew there was no alternative. He was moved when Vizzy interrupted. "Dad. I want you to have Grandpa's money. I really do."

His father had left each of the boys a nest-egg of just over two and a half thousand pounds, which he insisted should be wisely invested and not spent before they were eighteen. The twins thought that no investment could be wiser than a Gibson Les Paul, and were making detailed planning visits to their favoured guitar shops. Vizzy had been talking about driving lessons.

"No, Vizzy, son. That's so wonderful and thoughtful. But it's for you, and anyway you can't touch it until next year."

"But you can, Dad. You've got to. You've been loads better since you started with them again. You don't swear at us so much. You've got a real aim. And I know we won't see Heidar and Margaux. You'll say you will, but I know you bloody well won't."

Morley sensed the pain behind the truculence.

"Vizzy, I'm proud of you. And so, I suspect, are Heidar and Margaux. Whatever happens with the rowing, they're back in our lives. And you'll be in theirs. I have absolutely no doubt."

Whatever happens, he thought, we bloody well will keep up contact. But if this all falls apart, goes sour, what kind of contact? They'd embarked on something, full on, that needed intensity and commitment. Without that, with just regret shared, it would inevitably change. He felt awful for Gareth, who had clearly been mortified to make this confession.

He wandered quietly from his study to make coffee. Searching the net had turned up no decent second-hand boats. Next thing had to be a trawl round the other local boat clubs. Maybe one would be happy to take on a bunch of maverick oldies on a mission. Returning with his coffee, he noticed how quiet the house was, with the kids out at friends and Helen braving the Oxford Street sales.

The doorbell rang, distracting Morley from his hunt for new rowing web sites. Expecting one of the kids' friends, he was taken aback to find a small elderly lady with a large handbag and a small poodle, the latter in a tartan coat of sufficiently comical appearance to strip away any residual feelings of self-worth that the artistic aspirations of the groomer had inadvertently left.

"Hello," he said, in the wary tones of one expecting to be handed the latest edition of Watchtower or a petition against a new off-licence. "Can I help you?"

"I don't know about that, Peter Morley. But I hope I can help you" said the strange old lady, in the strongest Welsh accent he had heard for years. "Put the kettle on then. You English. No sense of hospitality."

Brain working overtime, Morley suddenly made the connection. "Mrs Jenkinson! Hello. You caught me on the hop. I wasn't expecting you."

"And I wasn't expecting to be visiting unannounced. But I gather we have a crisis. And one that's not going to be solved by keeping a poor old lady on the doorstep and in need of a good cup of tea. Assuming you English are capable of a good cup of tea, that is."

Morley apologised for his inadvertent rudeness, and took her through to the kitchen. Farqhuar stirred lazily.

"Oh, such a fine dog, Peter. I do love labradors. Bit fat, perhaps, but probably none the worse for that. Doesn't seem to hold Tom Jones back now, does it. Anyway, I'll leave Blodwyn here while we talk, if I may. She's very good around the house usually, but best to be sure."

Seated in the living room, perched somewhat uneasily on the other end of the sofa, Morley made small talk while waiting to hear the purpose of the visit. "A biscuit, Mrs Jenkinson ? There should be some digestives. Possibly even some Hob Nobs if the boys haven't sniffed them out."

"Hob Nobs, now that's what I call a biscuit. They were Eifor's favourite, never said no to a Hob Nob." She sniffed slightly, then rallied. "Never mind. Life goes on. Hob Nobs or no Hob Nobs. Oh, and Peter. It's Gladys, not Mrs Jenkinson. You make me feel like I'm ninety, and I'm not a day over eighty two. Well, maybe a few days, but that would be telling. A girl needs a bit of mystery."

Morley smiled. A small silence fell.

"Well, Peter. I suppose I'd better get to the point. And the point is, I'm worried about Gareth."

"I wouldn't worry, Mrs Jen .... Gladys. I think he's fine at the moment."

"And that, Peter, is just my point. Fine. At the moment. Point is, you didn't see him two years ago. Oh, he took Eifor's illness bad. Well, we all did. Big strapping lad like him, finest athlete in the county when we were courting, sitting in his armchair with a bloody oxygen bottle. Please excuse my language, Peter, but it was. Bloody. That oxygen bottle. How he hated it. Lungs shot from the coal dust, you see. He worked his life in those mines, and he gave as good as anyone. And what did he get in return, when he paid the price of his health? Nothing, absolutely nothing for years. One slippery politician after another, making big promises then moving on to Transport or the Home Office without a backward glance. Then, two years ago, they announced with a bloody big press conference that they'd be giving compensation. Like it was a big and generous thing. And the doctors crawled all over him. And he was weighed in the balance, and found worthy of £21,000. For his life, and his lungs, and for ten years of gasping like a fish. £21,000. Well. I can't pretend it wouldn't have helped. But he didn't live long enough to enjoy it."

Morley did not quite know what to do. He muttered that he was sorry.

"Oh I know, Peter, and I do appreciate it. You do remember Eifor, don't you? When he was well."

Morley did. A visit to see Gareth during their second summer vacation. The slow train from Cardiff station, moving from one small community to another, the valleys already showing signs of malaise years before Mrs Thatcher's coup de grace, evidence of financial hard times biting where the mines had closed one by one. The small house in the squat terrace, impeccably neat and proudly maintained. The tiny living room, sole decoration pictures of relatives past and present, a school photograph of Gareth and a few small ornaments. He was utterly humbled to find, in prominent pride of place atop the mantelpiece, a picture of their four in the second round at Henley, two lengths clear of University of California, whose trip they had spoilt. Gareth was reserved initially, with the slight defiance of a man both proud and slightly ashamed of his origins. This had settled after a few beers at the local, particularly when they became competitive about the respective merits of Welsh and English beer. Eifor had indeed been a good man, already then looking older than his years.

"My Gareth, see. My special boy. Over twelve years we waited for him, Eifor and I. A fine boy, as you know. But not the same as he used to be. Oh, I think that Gwen did wonders for him, making him pull his socks up. Proper spirit, that girl. But, if I can be frank, Peter, that Lynette had sucked the life out of him. Just sucked the life. Oh, she's not a bad girl, at least she wasn't. But now, so joyless, drains any enjoyment for everyone. Now, when I heard that he was rowing with you again, I was overjoyed. And I heard his voice on the phone, and I knew he'd changed. My Gareth. Coming back again. Then you all nearly drowned. And now it might have to stop."

"Don't worry," said Morley, feeling out of his depth. "We'll get something sorted."

"No you won't, Peter. No you can't. And you know it. You may all have very fancy lives compared to the one we had. But with your school fees, and I don't blame you in the slightest, socialist that I am, when I hear of those London schools. And your complicated city lives. You can't find that sort of money in a flash, I know. And that's why I'm here."

Morley felt sick. "No, Gladys, no."

Too late. She handed him the cheque, made out in his name. £5,000, to the account of Mr P Morley.

"Before you say a word, young Peter, you listen to me. I'm not doing this for you. I'm not doing it for Dave or Heidar, nice though you all are. I'm not doing this because I love rowing. Damn silly sport, if you ask me, no ball in sight and heading backwards down a pond. I'm doing this for my only son. I don't know what you've done, but you've brought him back. And I'm not letting him go again."

Morley didn't know what to say. He said as much, asked what he could do.

"Keep going. Keep him going. If you can, win. If you can't, try like buggery. But give my boy back his pride. Make that Lynette see what a jewel she has. Give him back the balls to kick that job with the council. Don't get me wrong, Peter, it's important work. But it needs people who think it's important, and not some slow death sentence. That's no good for him – no good for anyone. I know he wants to run his own business, like I hear you do. He told me how much he admires what you did when you left the council to start on your own. For him to do that he needs pride. Help to give him that."

Peter, emotionally spinning, still wasn't sure. "But think of all the things you can do. We can't have all that."

"This, Peter," she said, fingering the cheque, "this was my trip to Australia. I always wanted to see Australia. Sydney, the Barrier Reef, Ayer's Rock, though I think they call it some other name these days. This spring, after poor Eifor passed away – he was too sick, mind, for ten years or more to even think about going even if we had the money - my sister Rose was going to go with me. Holiday of a lifetime, and my God I think we needed it. Two weeks before the off, she went in to the Heath in Cardiff, deep vein thrombosis she had. She's fine, but no chance now. My long haul days are over, Peter, before they started. No loss, if you think about it. But I do want to come and see you at Henley. A new dress, the Stewards' Enclosure, some of that Pimm's. And, who knows, maybe some nice man who knows a nice pair of pins when he sees them. A girl can dream, eh?"

Peter smiled, rather overcome. "Gladys. If I can track down a chap who likes a nice pair of pins, I promise to point him in your direction."

Not much more to be said. Morley followed his benefactor to the kitchen, holding the door open for her. She gave a gasp of surprise when she looked towards the door. A politician such as Peter Mandelson might claim with seeming conviction that Farqhuar was considerately trying to restore the feelings of self-worth that Blodwyn might have lost at the hands of the groomer. A more spin-free assessment would be that he was giving her an almighty rogering, small patches of fluorescent tartan intermittently visible beneath his impressive bulk as he shunted her round the kitchen floor. Morley was mortified, apologising profusely and offering to get the hose from the garden. Gladys was having none of it.

"Don't worry now, Peter. It's just nature, after all. How about you get a bottle from that nice wine rack, and you and I go and have a chinwag next door. Let's leave the poor things too it. Moments like this are to be treasured in this vale of tears."

Glass of red in hand, Gladys settled herself into the sofa. She looked wistful.

"Lucky girl, that Blodwyn. It must be nearly three months since I had a good seeing-to like that."

She raised her eyebrows and smiled. "Don't you look at me with those big blue eyes like that, young Peter. If you don't join in, life will just pass you by, and before you know it it's gone. A girl's only young once."

Chapter 21

The snow promised for Christmas was finally arriving, although fitfully. The taxi firm had made their traditional New Year's Eve call, apologising that they might be an hour or two late because of overbooking. Thankfully Helen had answered the phone. They decided to drive, and review their return options later. Morley had two bottles of good champagne from the fridge and Helen some flowers. Remarkably, judging by their form of the last couple of years, they had three boys happy to be with them. They had to be discouraged from taking Farqhuar, now putting back the weight lost on the towpath.

The roads were busy, and Morley had to concentrate as flurries of snow would suddenly appear, catching the glare of the headlights. Although slow, they got to Wimbledon without incident, and were able to park within about fifty yards of the house, which looked welcoming, bright light emerging from the side windows. A traditional holly wreath adorned the door. Morley was quietly surprised that they did not have the traditional Scandinavian inverted-V Yule lights in the window.

They rang at the doorbell and were let in by a jovial Heidar, who expressed particular gratitude to the boys for coming, Margaux following behind and giving them all extravagant kisses. "I am sure that you have much more nefarious things to be doing on a New Year's Eve. We appreciate the honour."

The twins surprised their parents. They handed Heidar a small package, its shape betraying its contents despite the inexpert wrapping. "Happy Christmas, Heidar," said David, adding, as it was unwrapped to show a CD, "we saved some of your paint money. We got you the Sugarcubes – they had one in Icelandic at HMV. Isn't that great? We saw you had all Björk's solo stuff."

"Boys. That is wonderful. You know I saw them in '86?"

"Sorry, Margaux," continued David. "They wouldn't sell us any wine in Oddbins. Bastards."

"And you wouldn't thank us for anything from Dad's wine rack," added Alastair. "All Chilean and South African. He won't buy wine from a country unless it has a history of human rights abuse. Luckily we all saw this documentary on what they did to Aboriginal kids in the 50's, so I reckon we're good for some Australian reds next year. Either that, or," he shuddered dramatically, "Chinese."

Morley winced, remembering his long struggles over the morality of South African wine. One particularly mortifying moment came to mind, his student protestations against the suggested Cape red in a Bethnal Green off-licence being loudly approved by the large shaven-headed thug just behind him in the queue.

"Good on you, son. You stick to it. Bloody black feet tramping them grapes. Not right."

Rather more shyly, Vizzy presented his own CD, which turned out to be by another Icelandic band called Sigur Rós. This was received with great delight by Heidar. Morley had never heard of them, but was immediately taken by the strange beauty of the music when Heidar insisted on putting it on.

He recognised some, but not all, of the gathered party. Dave and Jane were already there. Vizzy and the twins were approached at high speed by Ben and Lucy, Ben in particular high with excitement. Morley was surprised and quite pleased to see Heidar's mother and stepfather, both looking older and thinner but well. He had always enjoyed talking to Sula, his mother, although finding his stepfather Mike rather dull and politically too right wing for his tastes.

Margaux, looking wonderful, was chatting animatedly. "Look, everyone, it's Vizzy, my saviour. He makes the best roll-ups I have had since I was at University. Vizzy – you must be careful. If Heidar sees me smoking again, I am in big trouble. When he is out of sight, you must make me another just like Henley. And one for your mother."

Helen snorted. Vizzy defended. "Mum doesn't smoke."

"That shows how little you know. Unless she has become a little churchmouse again, which is always possible. You'd never believe that she used to be a good quiet Catholic girl. I had to work very hard to convert her to enjoyment of a rich and full life, and would be very sad if she's slipped back into good ways. Can't have that now, can we Bernard?"

She pronounced his name in the French manner. Once spoken, it was quite clear that this was entirely appropriate. Probably early 60's, grey short-cropped hair, something about his style indelibly marking him as French. His clothes shouted 1960's left bank café culture, his right index and middle fingers stained with nicotine. He toasted Margaux silently with his glass of red, and smiled generously before replying in a strong Parisian accent. "My dear Margaux. My prodigal parishioner. Not so saintly, perhaps, but maybe not quite as wicked as she'd like us all to think."

He turned to Helen and made a bow of slightly old-fashioned courtesy. "Bernard Portier. Margaux's priest. She honours me with her hospitality sadly more often than I can get her to accept mine. Despite the fact", he said with a look of mock admonition, "that Sacre-Coeur de Londres is less than fifteen minutes by car on a Sunday. But I will continue my work, and maybe, one day, God willing, I will also persuade that good but sadly misguided husband of hers to join us. He is far too good a man, my dear Margaux, to be allowed to stay a heathen."

Margaux raised her eyes good humouredly. "Bernard. If you can persuade that stubborn Viking to do anything he does not wish to, you will have an outstanding career in politics ahead of you. I'm sure the Communists are due a comeback."

Bernard smiled indulgently. "It was Paris, my dear. It was the 1960's. You children of the 70's and 80's do not know what you missed."

"Only a truckload of weed, Bernard. And a lot of Chlamydia."

"Touché, my dear. Augustine was always my favourite saint."

Both Helen and Peter were surprised to find a priest at this particular New Year's party. Heidar and Margaux had unusual depths. And apparently unusual clerics.

Morley was delighted to see the arrival of the Jenkinsons, and intrigued to see the twins make as rapid a beeline for Gwen and Thomas as the little ones had made for them. He noticed that both boys had glasses of wine in their hands, and decided to keep a closer watch on them. Both Lynette and Gladys were behind, the latter tipping him a stage wink. Gareth was not his usual self, and had yet to be told that they had raised the money. He was not to be told how.

Vizzy had not followed the twins to see the new arrivals. He had listened to Father Bernard intently, and had then become quiet and thoughtful. Before Margaux and Helen could begin their conversation, and after Bernard had gone in search of some more wine, he turned to Margaux. "What Bernard said about Heidar. Being a heathen and that. Was that true?"

"Well, yes. I suppose so. I can get him to go to church sometimes. But, at heart, he is really a pagan, just like his father. And his mother."

"His mother?" Vizzy was amazed.

"Sure. Go and speak to Sula. She'd love to talk about it. Get her away from that boring old Mike for a minute. Heidar's sorting out the drinks and food. You won't get any sense from him at the moment. But don't leave it too late. It's New Year's Eve, and you'll get even less sense from him the nearer to midnight we get."

Shy Vizzy no longer, he cut across the room towards Sula and Mike. Helen noticed that the latter was showing the body language of someone unused to the company of Emos. Within seconds, Sula was holding court with animation. Helen noticed her husband signal to his crew-mates, and they withdrew to a huddle in the far corner of the room. Gladys was in deep conversation with a group that she didn't recognise, and had dragged Bernard into what was clearly a hilarious conversation. Helen was glad to have Margaux to herself.

"Do you have this sort of do every New Year?"

Margaux shook her head, her face complex and unreadable. "No darling. It's very special. And I have to thank you all, and your wonderful children, for giving us back our happiness on this day. It's normally just us, Sula and Mike, and my saviour Bernard."

"Your saviour? Margaux, you always manage to surprise."

"Helen, I promise you. Truly my saviour. Without him, I would have taken my own life. A sin, I do know, but sometimes grief and guilt leave a person few choices."

Helen looked at Margaux, whose face remained unreadable. "Margaux. Please. Let's talk in the garden. I don't want to be interrupted."

"The garden. Good. Raid your son's pockets. We both need a cigarette for this story."

Flurries of snow and a pervasive cold. Two women, old enough to know better, lighting now-forbidden roll-ups in the suburban garden, Old Holborn providing aromatic Proustian evocation of their younger selves. Quiet thoughtfulness induced. Several lengthy draws and exhalations before Margaux spoke.

"Vizzy told you about Haraldur." A statement. Margaux nodded.

"He would be seventeen now. Seventeen today."

Helen clutched her arm. Margaux stopped her before she could speak. Shook her head.

"IVF. Third try. Details – not important. We could not believe, at last, our luck changed. My father, away from Bordeaux at Christmas for the first time, celebrating Christmas with us, as excited as we were. Insisted we try Estephe's latest venture. Silly boy with his big ideas. Had seen the shop of Jean D'Alos in Bordeaux. He's the famous affineur. Sells the best cheese you can get. Well the joke is that no one in Bordeaux makes cheese – all wine. They say the cheese of the Bordeaux region is Edam, they really do. Well, Estephe, always thinking big. He decides to get some cows. Gives up a small field where the vines needed replanting. Makes our own cheese – going to take it to Jean D'Alos in the New Year, make lots of money, the first cheese from the Médoc."

She paused. Took three long drags, hands slightly quavering.

"That Christmas, no wine. None. But, and I will punish myself until my dying day, I tried some of Estephe's cheese. My father's face fell when I turned it down. Estephe's big hope, maybe his. I knew I shouldn't, but it felt important. So I tried some. Not bad, not so good, maybe. But my father was happy. Then five days later, it started. Slow at first, a few pains. Then on New Year's Eve, bad, bad pain. We knew what that meant, but not why. Then. And the hospital sent me to St George's, where they have the baby unit. And our little Haraldur was born, 850 grams of perfect sweet baby. Strong, so strong, despite all the tubes. Then the spots, no-one knew why, but they did all the tests and put antibiotics into a tube in his hand. And then the question from the clever doctor that cut me like a knife. Heard my accent and asked if I had eaten soft cheese. Listeria, bloody damn Listeria. Bloody damn Estephe and his bloody damn cheese. Papa heard the news – back home by then – took his gun and shot all three cows. Poor things, not their fault."

Margaux had tears in her eyes. Helen hugged her.

"And my strong little boy. What a fighter. And he fought, and he got better, and his brain – they said it was fine. They put this thing on his head, and you could see his brain on a screen. They said it was perfect, a miracle. And he started to breathe on his own. No tubes, and I could cuddle him properly. And he grew, and they moved him. You know, they have a room, they call it the Feeders and Growers room. Like little flowers. And my little flower, the biggest feeder – just like his Daddy – and the best grower. Then my milk stopped – little by little. I had been expressing it into a bottle – milked like a cow, a happy cow. I could not wait until the day he could feed from me, but he still needed it through a tube in his nose. Two weeks they thought, maybe three. Then my damn milk was just too little. He needed more, and they started to give him formula – that's milk from cows. One week later, the telephone in the middle of the night. And he was back in the intensive unit when we got in. Tubes again. But his belly – big, dark, dark blue. I had heard of this necrotising enterocolitis. All of the mothers had. I had not feared it, thought he was past the danger time. And they tried. But I knew. He died that morning. Not before Bernard came in to bless him - my strong little Haraldur. And that is why Bernard had to save my life, later, as the guilt and grief ate at me. Heidar, typical man, I don't think he's ever talked about it to anyone. Not once. And so New Year's Eve has been deep and dark and sad for us. And Bernard is always there for us for that night, and also on the day in February when he died."

She paused again for some deep draughts, then shook herself and continued.

"Then one day the children came to paint our house, and brought the magic that children carry with them. It was Gwen who said that we should show off our new decoration – she was proud of her work. And Alastair asked why not New Year? He said it would be less boring than usual. And I looked at Heidar. He just said OK. Just like that. It was. It is. If Haraldur is here tonight, he will have friends his own age. Now, we go back in. We drink good French wine. We have found our best and oldest friends. And some special young new ones. We will have a good New Year's Eve."

Which they did. They returned to find Gladys in full flow, surrounded by most of the children, whose uninhibited laughter rang loud and clear as her almost caricature Welsh tones rose in pitch towards the climax of her story.

"So, your bloody Dad, he just stands there like a lemon. Paralysed he was. You'd think he'd never seen dogs at it before. Then what do you think he says? He only offers to get the hose in from the garden! He'd have been in your Mam's good books, wouldn't he? Don't worry the kitchen's under two feet of water, dear, at least the bloody dog's behaving!"

This launched a thoroughly delighted Alastair into yet another of his apparently hilarious exposés of his father's many foibles.

Heidar sat by the kitchen table, guitar in hand, with his other crew members in attendance, ready to play. Margaux pulled Helen's arm. "Well, that will cheer everyone up. One of his Icelandic folk songs. Nothing better than a bit of rape, pillage and painful death to get a New Year's party going. Come on, let's get a top-up and join the girls. Find out what's really going on in the world."

Heidar's voice rang clear and true. Although none of his listeners understood a word, save Sulla who materialised immediately he started, they felt the emotion of the song and a sense of the cold harsh environment from which the music sprang. He sang a second song, receiving soft and genuine applause. He put down the guitar, the group about to settle into conversation. Morley was amazed to see Vizzy pick up the guitar and start to play. He knew that he had Helen's old acoustic in his room, but had not known that he had been practising, clearly much more surreptitiously than the twins.

Not only did he play. He sang, his voice deeper and fuller than his father could have expected. His choice of music, *Wonderful tonight*, was beautifully sung and affecting. Vizzy tailed off, unaware that he had the rapt attention of everyone in the room, including the awed respect of his younger brothers.

Margaux broke the silence, with a look of deep happiness. "My, what a wonderful song, Vizzy. A man of many talents. And celebrating an exceptional woman. You know Patti Boyd had two other great songs composed for her – *Layla* and *Something*. Three great songs. Two more than even the luckiest woman can hope for. She must have been dynamite in the bedroom."

"Or made a particularly good cheesecake," said Helen, raising laughter. She elaborated, "The way to a man's heart."

"Even Dave's," said Jane, provoking even more laughter.

"Especially Gareth's," said Lynette, with the first genuine and easy smile most had seen.

Margaux looked at her watch. "Come on now, break out the champagne, only five minutes to midnight. Bernard, if you think you'll have a clear head for Mass tomorrow, you have another think coming."

There is something about champagne. There is something about that moment on New Year's Eve, ancient and pagan. The world holds its breath, knowing it significant.

"Happy New Year," shouted most in unison.

"To you all, a blessing," said Bernard.

"To Henley," said Heidar firmly. "To the Princess Alice."

"Amen," said Bernard. "Now where's that champagne ? One glass is never enough."

"Oh no!" said Vizzy. "Alastair's got the guitar - he's with David. Not *We will rock you*! Bloody hell. What have I done?

CHAPTER 22

Morley reacted quickly. "We can't stop here! Alastair - do it out the window. Vizzy, open it quick for him, for God's sake! ...: Phew - thank God for that. Well done Vizzy."

Helen looked behind. "Oh, poor cyclist."

"Well he shouldn't be out on a bike at this time on New Year's Eve. What the hell does he expect? Anyway, it's probably good luck."

"I don't think he thinks so, darling. He's shaking his fist a lot."

Morley was not as sympathetic as Alastair felt he should be. "How much bloody wine did you drink? I told you not more than one glass. I trusted you. No! Out the bloody window!"

"Dad," slurred David, "I think there was something in that beef. I don't feel well either. The car's spinning round."

Vizzy was more in control, debating whether he dared ask his father whether he should really be driving. The decision had been taken when the calls to a number of taxi firms went unanswered.

Helen decided to divert the conversation away from drunkenness and vomiting. She turned back towards Vizzy. "So, darling. Did you like Sula?"

"She's great. She showed me her tattoo."

"Darling! That's pretty good for a first date. Especially with an eighty-year-old."

"Don't be funny, Mum. It's true. It's called a Valknot. She says Heidar's got one. Is that true Dad? Does Heidar have a tattoo?"

"Now you mention it, he has. On his arm. Funny thing with three triangles twined together. Thought it was some 70's rock band thing. Never really asked him about it."

"She says that you only have a Valknot if you've pledged yourself to Odin. So that the Valkyries know where to take you."

"Sounds frightfully Wagnerian, dear," said Helen lightly.

"I'm not joking, Mum. It's also called the knot of death. Honestly. I only asked her because that French guy said Heidar was a heathen. Well Sula says he is and so's she. She says they're Ásatrúar. Believe in the old Gods. Loads of people still do." He paused. "Mind you, I don't think Mike does."

"Did you ask Heidar about it, dear?"

"I tried. He said he'd tell me some other time. He said tonight was for a double celebration. New Year with his friends and a special birthday party."

Helen's back stiffened. "Do you know whose birthday, dear?"

"Sure. It's Haraldur. He told me all that weeks ago."

CHAPTER 23

A boat is not an inert thing. It has a spirit. It has foibles and oddities. For those with sensitivity to detect it, it has a feel. To get the best out of it, it has to be appreciated. Honoured. A new boat needs ceremony, quiet or formal. The cracking of a champagne bottle across the bows of a liner honours not just the builders but the soul of the boat and provides appeasement in turn to the spirits of the water it must cross. God bless her and all who sail in her. Not empty words. Heartfelt ancient invocation dressed in modern clothes.

A champagne bottle at speed, even if dispatched by a more senior member of the Royal family, would not be a good thing for the finely sculpted bows of a brand-new Stampfli. In any event, its blood red livery was better suited to the gentle libation with Belle-Pensée, poured from a bottle held jointly by all four oarsmen, applauded by their families. The label faded through storage. The year 1983. No boat could have received higher honour.

A boat must have a name. This had been the subject of lively debate. Morley's suggestion of *Old enough to know better* was rejected by the others, on the grounds that half the boats in the Princess Alice would be named something like that. Dave's suggestion of *Water under the bridge* was better received, and favoured until Gareth suggested that maybe an Icelandic phrase might be most appropriate, given that theirs had been quite a saga. And so Alastair had the honour of suggesting the name, watching in pleasure as the boat was carried out of the boathouse to the waiting trestles for the ceremony, reading the italicised words as the bows emerged.

Icelandic ... Saga ... Holiday.

Compared to their previous boats, the Stampfli looked like something from the future, glorious clean lines, aerofoil wing riggers. The new Croker racing blades. It was exciting for all four. Like taking delivery of a new supercar, you could just sit and look at it.

Unusually for a racing boat, Icelandic Saga Holiday received a proper blessing from a proper priest. Bernard sensed the importance of the venture for the happiness of Heidar and Margaux, playing down the significance on the grounds that he would never knowingly miss the chance of a glass of Belle Pensée. Slightly crestfallen to see the 1983 running to the floor, he proclaimed himself satisfied with the 1988 presented to the humans present, then wistfully sotto voce, "One day, Margaux. One day, the quatre vingt trois."

"I've told you Bernard. My funeral." With a smile, adding, "You've only yourself to blame that you've never had it."

He smiled and nodded in return, appreciating the oblique gratitude.

To the applause of the families on the shore and the obvious excitement of Farquhar they set off for a ceremonial paddle to Chiswick Bridge and back. Not the first outing in three weeks, as Heidar had managed to secure use of one of the QEC fours during the Christmas holidays. It had been strange and initially dispiriting to return to their old stamping ground in Chiswick. The squat whitewashed 1930's façade of the University of London Boat Club on Hartington Road looked unchanged, but the air of neglect and penury inside was a sad surprise. The old changing rooms, dark wooden lockers in neat rows, had been cut in half to form a dilapidated gym. The old sitting room, where tea and sticky buns used to be sold at a counter and inscribed oars honouring international crews and Henley winners had lined the walls, now looked like the aftermath of a particularly devastating student party in a condemned towerblock. Their spirits, quietly sunk by this, were only lifted by the youthful exuberance of the current UL squad.

With permission granted to Heidar by the college to boat from there and store their new four, this made an important financial contribution. He had promised in return that they would row under the aegis of the college old students' club. Alastair had typical opinions. "Queen Elizabeth College Old Students. Will you be called Old Queen's then?"

"No Alastair," grinned Heidar. "Elizabethans. Same old colours. Same old crew. Longer for your Dad to cycle. We'll be even fitter."

The twins heard with enjoyment the teasing given to Gareth, whose mathematical mind had gone into overdrive with the multiple possibilities afforded for adjustment of the new boat. Nadging, as it was called by the crew, is an arcane art whereby the position of the gate in which the blade is placed can be adjusted in just about any direction. For the determined fiddler, the slides can also be altered forwards or backwards. All of these may affect the arc of the stroke and the mechanical efficiency. In the past, crews raced with wildly variant options, although more consensus now applied. For the less secure oarsman, a princess and the pea mentality could ensue, with minute adjustments demanded on an infuriatingly frequent basis. The most severe cases would demand to boat with a rigger jigger, a double headed spanner sized to fit the moving parts of the rigger. A good coach could squash such eccentricities, but the four were currently micromanagers of their own destiny.

Thomas and Gwen laughed to hear their father's foibles teased. David, who took after his father in enjoying maths, wanted to hear more from Gareth. "I thought you had to be a nerd to do maths. You don't seem like that."

Ignoring calls of "he is" from Gwen, Gareth explained with the good humour that Belle Pensée always blessed. "Obviously some are nerds. I mean, your Dad did a maths module. But it's great. Maths affects everything. And you get a better class of joke."

Alastair the maths-hater scoffed, denied that there could be any jokes in the dreadful subject.

Gareth laughed and said that there were loads. Challenged immediately by Alastair he came back. "OK. How can you tell an extroverted mathematician? He doesn't look at his shoes when he talks to you – he looks at yours. OK, fair enough, that's crap. Now, you know there are only 10 types of people? Those who understand binary and those who don't. You don't get it? OK. I give in. I'll own up. The only equation I've really managed to prove. My lifestyle calculation. Hopefully now in the past. Pie arse squared."

"Thank you, Gareth. I think you've just inspired all the kids to a career in Mathematics."

"Only if they promise not to end up in traffic planning," said Gareth ruefully, directing a look of genuine pain towards Lynette.

CHAPTER 24

Winter training. The very name enough to make old rowers shudder. Long bleak outings on short bleak days. Gym work, painful enough before invention of the ergometer, now quantified, relentless and unforgiving. Dull repetition and extensive duration needed, building muscle strength and aerobic capacity, painfully acquired platform for later speedwork. Days cold enough to freeze water droplets on the oar shafts. Wet enough to soak every last stitch. Windy enough to add sharp cold aqueous insult as waves crash onto backs. Responses narrowed through oxygen debt to the rower's linguistic Swiss Army knife, *fuck* covering well enough the full range of emotions evoked by this sport, uttered sharp and short as fingers crack against cross struts with boat lurches, long and decrescendo after painful racing intervals, fierce and exhortatory before the next and just occasionally triumphant with hopeful rising pitch after a piece where things just clicked. This is the time that makes or breaks your summer.

All were aware of the need to avoid injury, recognising that the days of youthful rapid healing were behind them. The bonding between them grew, each trusting the others. Gaps in personal histories filled between outings, as men do, raised eyebrows and shrugs the male shorthand for deep thoughts and emotions, little inner landscape revealed in detail but topography well enough grasped. All deeply committed, deeply engaged. All more dependent than they recognised on generously-given familial support. All now less engaged in home life. Men with new shape, new direction to their lives. On a quest, almost mediaeval, almost adolescent. In a new boat that gave them pride and pleasure each time they boated. For better or worse, returning to the men they used to be.

CHAPTER 25

There are no recognised units for quantitating misery. Rain dripping down his neck as they sat by the bank waiting to be called, Morley sat miserably trying to rectify this. Perhaps one unit per hour watching Piers Morgan or two per root canal filling. Whatever unit he chose, he was currently scoring high marks, and wondering why they'd thought this race a good idea in the first place.

Molesey Veterans' Head. Their first racing challenge. Short as head of the river races go, just over 3,000 metres and usually a reasonably gentle introduction to the racing season. Not this year. Veteran C fours the hottest for years, all with eyes firmly fixed on Henley. Fine in theory, and a great spur to winter training. But chill early February winds and a badly timed cloudburst had left all waiting crews at risk of hypothermia. Even the quips from Gareth at bow had quietened.

They had been going well. The new boat had taken some getting used to, not as forgiving as their old one but much faster when they got it right. The buoyancy aids and safety features, important in their final choice, gave them a feeling of real security, although no chances were now taken with really bad conditions. The only sadness about boating from the UL boathouse, apart from lingering regret over its neglect, was that Farquhar could not get far along the towpath to follow them.

At last they could see the crews ahead of them begin to move, and they followed in their turn. Crossing the river by Sunbury Court island, they tried to warm up on their way to the turning point. Morley could see some very professional crews heading down the course. The home crew from Molesey, containing at least one former international that he recognised, had gone off fast ahead of the pink blades of Leander. Leander looked very strong, and he had private doubts whether they could ever match them. Even as he watched, they seemed to be closing on Molesey.

Their turn came quickly enough. Marshalled to turn around towards the start, they heard the crew ahead of them called to go. They were instructed to paddle on, then got their call in turn. Chilled as they were, they all felt the excitement. Half a minute in and it felt quite good. Morley had deliberately gone off rating one or two strokes higher than usual, all gasping hard, then striding down to a rate of around 33 strokes a minute to allow them to settle. It worked, and they felt unhurried and in control. They seemed to be pulling away from the crew behind, and Morley could see the puddles from the Kingston crew ahead. Rounding the first bend, which turned towards bowside, he could just see the stern of the Kingston boat. By the time they reached the island called Platt's Eyot, they had cleared Kingston and were going well as they closed in on another crew. Things then began to get a bit ragged, the challenge of the slower crew ahead causing some steering problems. They finished fairly happy, now hardly noticing the rain.

There was the usual wait in the clubhouse, long queues at the bar, while the results were sorted. Gareth returned from the throng around the results board nodding with some satisfaction. "We're third. Out of 21 fours. Not bad. 9 minutes 27. Notts City did 9-23, Leander 9-14. Oh, and London-Thames 9-31. Yes!"

Morley and Heidar exchanged looks. Good to beat the London-Thames crew. Good to be in the frame after such a short time. But 13 seconds down on Leander despite a good row. Still a lot to do. An awful lot.

CHAPTER 26

Bernard was exasperated. "Heidar. You cannot be teaching this sort of nonsense to the young people. As history, maybe OK. But not as fact. They are young and impressionable. And it is Easter."

Heidar shrugged. Vizzy, exasperated in turn, countered. "Father Bernard. We're old enough to make up our own minds. And even if it's not true, it's a great story."

His brothers nodded in agreement, as did Gwen and Thomas. Margaux tried to make peace. "Come on, Bernard. Come and try these – Belle-Pensée and Lynch-Bages 2002. I think we're better. What does the Church think?"

Bernard appeared mollified and followed Margaux across the room.

Heidar still looked combative. "I don't think he gets this. Just calls me a bloody heathen. Hasn't bothered to find out anything about Ásatrú. Anyway, where was I?"

"Odin's ravens," cut in Gwen, just ahead of the pack.

"Huginn and Muninn - Thought and Memory. They are Odin's eyes on Earth. They fly out each dawn and bring news back to him each evening."

"And it's Odin, not Thor, who's the important one?" asked David, with a slightly surprised look.

"Yes indeed," said Heidar in reply. "Everyone thinks of Thor when they talk of Norse Gods. But Odin is his father, the leader of the Gods. Odin, not Thor, will lead his warriors in the final battle on the Vigrid plains against the forces of darkness. We call it Ragnarök – the end times. He is called *The father of the slain* because he gathers great warriors to fight alongside him, the Einherjar. To be selected Einherjar is a great honour, only the very best. Odin has swan maidens, Valkyries – you may have heard of them – who choose warriors amongst those slain in battle, sometimes even before. To see a Valkyrie, a warrior knows he is chosen. They appear in dreams, sometimes giving wisdom, sometimes warnings of battle, sometimes even of death. A chosen man would be happy to die, knowing he will join the Einherjar. Odin's chosen were sometimes called Berserkers – you know the term berserk? They fought like men possessed. Battles seemingly lost would be won. When a chosen man dies in such a way, the Valkyries take him across Bifrost, the rainbow bridge, to Valhalla. There he will practice fighting each day, so that he is ready for Ragnarök. You know that the Northern Lights are reflections from the armour of the Valkyries as they train the Einherjar? And each night, the Einherjar drink mead from the udder of Heidrun, Odin's goat, and feast on meat from Saehrimnir, his boar."

"Cool," said an appreciative Alastair, the others also nodding.

Vizzy was troubled. "Heidar, I looked this up on the net. Some really horrible sites talked about all this. Racist, white supremacist."

Heidar looked saddened. "Vizzy, I know. It's sick, and it's wrong. You'll find that even more of these groups do the same with Christianity. Stealing the clothes of good and devout people to dress up their inadequacies and hate. The Íslenska Ásatrúarfelagið – the Icelandic Ásatrú – is a proper recognised religion. It just means true to the Æsir, the old Gods. In Norway the old religion was persecuted. Olaf Haraldsson, Olaf the Stout – tortured and burned alive anyone who would not convert to Christianity. I don't think even Bernard could be too pleased that he was made a saint – I always laugh when I see schools called St Olave's. In Iceland the change came later. It was peaceful and based on trade. So the old religion never went away, and people sometimes practised both at the same time."

Vizzy now looked rather happier. He asked Heidar how he had chosen such an unusual religion.

"My family, Vizzy. Kjartan, my father, used to like traditional Icelandic music. You have heard me sing some. There was a man, Sveinbjörn Beinteinsson, who was a poet and singer of rímur, these ancient epic poems. A true historian, who preserved and brought alive our heritage. He persuaded my father to convert, then my mother – you've met Sula – then finally he persuaded the Government to recognise it as an official religion. It was around 1972 – I still remember my father's excitement."

"And do you really believe?" asked Gwen. "Really truly believe? In Odin. In Valkyries?"

"I do Gwen, I do. Truly. I've seen a Valkyrie."

"No!" Shocked, awed expostulation from five young people, almost in synchrony.

"Twice," said Heidar, nodding his head towards them to emphasise the point. "A long time ago. In my dreams. Sígrun, I knew her name without her having to say it. Once, a dreadful night before our final at Henley. I was going to walk out – you may have heard the story. She told me that I must stay, and I must fight more bravely than I had ever fought. At the end, to lose like that...."

He tailed off, shaking his head. Asked about the second time, he nodded once, then continued. "A cold wet night in an Italian barn. Sheltering from storms, my motorbike misfiring worse than usual. With a cold and very wet Margaux. The first night of our new life. I was asking myself what crazy thing I had done. And Sígrun came to me and told me it was my destiny. Which is why, I guess, that I have ended up living where I do and doing the job I do. And why we are here today. I don't think it was chance that Gareth sent those emails. The Welsh, they sense the spirit world in a way you English don't."

"We're not just English," said outraged Vizzy. "Our grandmother's Irish and Mum's grandfather came from France. Troyes."

"Well then," said Heidar, "you should put away those looks of disbelief when I tell you these very personal things. Maybe one day you will see a Valkyrie. At least now you'll know who she is."

Having decided by the time the call came for lunch that they were quite interested in this, the young people planned different approaches to take their studies further. Thomas and the twins were discussing animatedly a forthcoming Xbox game called *Battle for Asgard*, working out the chance of scoring sufficient pocket money to get it or whether they would have to trade in one of their other games. Vizzy and Gwen were taking a more academic interest and deciding to research it further online and in the library.

"Funny that," said Alastair as he entered the kitchen to see Margaux and Bernard standing with all of the other parents. "Claret. A real grown-ups magnet. Are we allowed any, Margaux?"

"It depends, Alastair," came her slightly amused reply, "whether you are truly repentant about New Year's Eve. My wines are too good to be drunk until you make yourself sick. You broke our trust. If you remember, you have been banned from any until you are repentant."

"Margaux, I'm really sorry. But I don't think it's fair. It's three months now."

"Then your sorrow is remorse, but not yet repentance. Have a think about it. When you truly repent, then you will have earned some more claret. Bernard here knows more than anyone here about repentance. He repents of a whole decade. Though perhaps not so much remorse."

CHAPTER 27

Speedwork. The very name exciting to the rower, redolent of lengthening evenings and the end of winter. The pain different, sharper but shorter. Sessions of fartlek, Swedish for speed play, though more work than play as the bursts of high intensity lengthen. Designed to equip Swedish endurance runners to cope with the challenges posed by Paavo Nurmi and his outstanding generation of Finnish athletes, its bursts above race pace provided both cardiovascular training and exhilaration.

Self-coached, Morley and colleagues relied on experience and maturity to hone their technique and deal with problems that inevitably arose. Gareth, mathematician and self-confessed rowing nerd, scoured journals and training schedules, rigging manuals and technical handbooks. Each brought something different to the crew, each now better able to appreciate the unusual synergy that they had. The children, sometimes annoyance, sometimes catalyst, played a role in shaping the ethos of a venture that went beyond four men in a boat. Families enmeshed in a common venture.

Planning for the summer, they had mapped out a racing schedule. To avoid the feared Qualifying Race, it was important to do well at key regattas. They chose Nottingham City regatta at Holme Pierrepont in early May, and Metropolitan and Marlow regattas in June. The former was at Dorney Lake near Eton, the latter still on the Thames. All had memories of sinking conditions at Holme Pierrepont, built on some old gravelpits previously planned as the site for East Midlands airport but turned down because of its tendency to be afflicted by high winds. The National Water Sports Centre. Very British sports planning.

The joy of lengthening evenings was enhanced by the ability to go out on the water after work, rather than to the gym. Morley was still caught up with the ever-changing whims of bankers' wives, dreading the calls for last minute changes in design plans that followed each new edition of House Beautiful. Dave had been able to alter his on-call rota, to avoid clashes with regattas. Heidar was feeling liberated after completing the Research Assessment Exercise submission, where the apples of Nordic Studies would be compared with the oranges of Astrophysics for the benefit of a government who didn't much care what type of fruit they bought so long as it didn't cost too much and generated some revenue.

Escape from their troubles and cares came rapidly on the water. Escape from most of their other neural activities came about a minute and a half into racing pieces, especially when Morley tried to take them off above 40 strokes a minute. They liked the definition of a veteran as an oarsman no longer capable of rating his age, and Morley seemed intent on denying them that status.

It is odd that rowing is still considered a posh sport, and certainly now it is largely untrue. It is undoubtedly a legacy of history, as for many years the sport was dominated by the alumni of Oxbridge colleges and the well-heeled members of Leander Club in Henley. Leander itself has been reinvented as a high-tech centre of the international rowing scene, although its quaint nursery colours and society underpinnings remain. In full Leander summer plumage, with matching baby pink socks, tie, cap and pocket handkerchief, monogrammed gold buttoned blazer and white flannels, a gentleman might be mistaken for the legendary sixth founder member of the Village People. Leander's baby pink, which they claim rather hopefully to be a shade of cerise, lulls visiting American oarsmen into a false sense of amused security. Their unusually camp sporting colours probably have some historical basis other than covert support for Oscar Wilde during his hearing, but this has been lost in the mists of time. Their emblem, an overstuffed pink hippopotamus, also reeks of one of the more languid Victorian public schools. Their boats, however, by and large go extremely fast and their oarsmen are of such a size and disposition that one is wise not to go on for too long about the pink business.

CHAPTER 28

"Next Saturday then. Santé. Cheers. Bottoms up, as you English say. Always mixing your pleasures," said Margaux. "But please excuse us if we don't trip up the M1 to watch you. I remember those gales at Holme Pierrepont from '82. I thought you were mad. The sad thing is that it has taken me twenty five years to realise that I was right."

"Cheers to you, Margaux," said Morley. "To you all. And to Dave and Jane for asking us all round. And of course to Lucy and Ben. Never before, in the field of human endeavour, have so many twiglets been brought round so often by so few. Well done and thank you."

Jane smiled. "You owe me one skiing holiday, Mr Morley. It may be a very nice boat for you boys, but there's not been much in it for me."

"Particularly with the amount of training Dave is doing."

"Thank you, Gareth," said Helen. "Do you have to be quite so predictable?"

Morley shifted the subject. "We're going to need to hit your cellar hard, Dave, if we're to survive the concert later."

"Don't be unfair," said Heidar. "I thought they sounded pretty good."

Morley raised his eyes. "Gareth's two are. Gwen has a lovely voice and plays keyboards well. Grade 6, she says, but prefers doing pop tunes. Sounds like her musical taste may be a bit more refined than the others."

"If Duffy and Christina Aguilera can be described as refined, I think we've just moved to a parallel universe," interjected

Vizzy, these days happier in adult company than with the younger ones.

Morley persevered. "Thomas is brilliant on the guitar, absolutely brilliant. It's our two. Sonic torture awaits. Worse still, they're on this sing for Jesus kick. Sorry Lynette, no offence meant but I don't think Him upstairs will feel desperately honoured by David and Alastair's contribution. My Sweet Lord with feedback. I don't know though, Heidar, maybe Thor would?"

Lynette did not take offence as Morley thought she might. Deep in conversation with Dave, she looked unusually animated. The conversation lulled naturally and Morley caught a sentence or two. Dave was working, in clinical mode, and Morley could see why he was so popular in his profession.

"I hate feeling like this, Dave. I hate arguing with his Mum. I know she means well. I just feel tired all the time. I'm just not the same person I used to be. The doctor keeps giving me iron, but my blood count's always low. And my digestion's just not right."

Dave looked focused. "Lynette, can I ask you a personal question? Do you have any bowel problems? Sorry to ask such a question, but you'll know that I have form in that department."

Lynette looked taken aback. "No, I wouldn't say so. No."

A voice from behind Dave. "Mum, you're such a fibber. You know we have to evacuate the first floor when you go."

Lynette, aghast, almost tearful. "Gwen, for God's sake."

Dave looked at both. "Lynette, I think that Gwen may have done you a big favour. Don't go away. I'll be back in a couple of minutes. I've tracked something down in Boots that might just be helpful. Peter, if you have the resources and stamina to keep my glass of red out of the clutches of your predatory sons, I would be grateful."

After he had left, the others exchanged glances of bemusement. Lynette simply looked embarrassed. The moment was swept away in gales of laughter as Alastair emerged with water dripping down his shirt, shouting, "I don't believe it. Dave's got a bionic toilet!"

Lucy looked at him with all the contempt of a knowledgeable seven-year-old. "Don't be silly. It's perfectly normal. And it has a remote control."

Jane smiled. "That bloody lavatory. That was *last* year's skiing holiday. God knows what he'll come up with next year. Well, if any of you want hot water up your jacksie and a nice pelvic airdry, be my guest."

A large and happy throng gathered round Dave's inner sanctum, marvelling at the remote control that summoned forward a tube with an upward pointing spout, presumably the source of Alastair's wet shirt, then laughing uproariously at the hot air dryer that emerged at the touch of another button.

"So at regattas," said Gareth, laughing and shaking his head, "if they've only got these tents and a hole in the ground, how can we keep his poor little bottom in the style to which it's become accustomed? Will we need a hairdryer, or should Heidar and I just have to lie beneath and blow hard?"

Dave picked the wrong moment to return. Deluged by laughter and ribald comment, he took it in good part. "Unless you've had IBS, you haven't lived. And in answer to your question, Alastair, no I don't put hair gel around my bum."

He nodded to Lynette, who followed him. They didn't get away with it quietly. Gwen and Thomas, flanked by David and Alastair, watched with rapt attention as he opened a small test kit and read the instructions, then used the small lancet it contained to get a drop of blood from her fingertip. He filled a small capillary tube from the box with the blood drop, then transferred it to a small vial containing liquid. He dipped a test strip into this and waited for some seconds. There was a silence as he waited, then he looked up and nodded. "Lynette. I think I've found the problem and I think it can be fixed. Looks like you might have Coeliac disease. We'll need to get this checked. But if so, a gluten-free diet might just change your life."

CHAPTER 29

Victory. Sweet victory. Their first victory. Worth the long trip to Nottingham. Crossing the line first at the National Water Sports Centre, concrete 1970's temple honouring the Anemoi and sundry minor wind Gods. Breezeblock-built shrine to Boreas, Notus, Eurus and Zephyrus. Standing waters breaking over riggers into the boat, they had cause to thank their boat's buoyancy-aids as Holme Pierrepont displayed once more its dark side. Racing not yet cancelled, but clearly sinking conditions. They handled it better than all others, inflicting their first defeat on the powerful Nottingham crew that contained three former Henley winners. It might be a different story in flat conditions, but for the moment they were happy. No Leander here, no chance to assess relative speed. But on target. In the frame.

Discussions cheerful on the way home, all four in Morley's old estate, the boat safely de-rigged and tied firmly to the UL trailer. A decision taken. A month of increased training intensity, of ergometer sessions, possibly a decisive month.

Gareth more cheerful than usual, even for him.

"Dave, can't thank you enough. Lynette feels great – didn't relish the gluten-free diet to begin with, I think we all dreaded it. Thomas has a bone to pick with you, mind. Poor sod's been found to have it as well. He didn't feel so bad, not so pleased to have his biopsy. Tell you what, though, his teachers have noticed a difference already."

Dave was modest, glad to have helped, intrigued to hear that Lynette was now getting on with Gladys. Morley was pleased to hear this, quietly grateful to Gladys for her extreme generosity. She had sworn him to secrecy from the rest of the crew, and he had honoured this. He also intended to honour her request to come to the regatta, and suspected that Farqhuar might hope to make Blodwyn's journey worthwhile.

Now began the planning in depth of the critical month ahead as the elderly Volvo and its even older passengers ploughed steadfastly though the Sunday M1 traffic.

CHAPTER 30

"What do you mean, cancel the outing? For a flipping duck?! Heidar, you've lost the plot. I don't care if it *is* a bloody Harlequin duck. I wouldn't give a toss if it was pink with bright green Adidas racing stripes. I don't care how bloody rare it is. You can't be serious. It's six days to Metropolitan Regatta. You can't do this. Oh bloody hell," he turned towards Helen, "he's rung off. Bloody stupid twitcher."

"Dad, let me speak to him," said Vizzy. He dialled. "Heidar, are you really missing the outing for a duck? What - an Icelandic Harlequin? Possibly even a pair? Near Bisham? When are you leaving? Can you drop by and pick me up too?"

"Bloody traitor," growled Morley.

"He said you'd understand it better than anyone, Dad. Its proper name's *Histrionicus histrionicus*." Vizzy beat a hasty retreat, heading to the cloakroom to get his coat.

Vizzy had never been on a motorbike before, and knew that he wouldn't have been allowed to go on one with anyone else. The noise was tremendous, the backfiring random and capable of turning heads across the street. The passenger seat was not particularly comfortable. Heidar explained that this part wasn't original from when the bike was first built in '67, and said that it had been a real test of love for Margaux to travel across Europe on it. It didn't seem the ideal transport for a bird-watcher, as all but the very deafest avian would probably take to the wing when he got within half a mile.

Initially clinging to Heidar's back for dear life, it took Vizzy several miles to begin to enjoy the experience. He was startled to see Heidar take the flyover to the elevated section of the M4 near Heathrow, somehow never assuming they would actually go on the motorway. Eyes wide, he was half-terrified and half-thrilled by their speed on the motorway, Heidar riding expertly but prone to undertaking the odd outside lane blocker. He had never felt such speed in his life, more alive than ever before but half-praying for the journey to end. After Heidar had left the motorway and finally turned off the fast dual carriageway, Vizzy saw another side to biking as they roared down small country roads, through shadows cast by the warm May sunlight. Eventually Heidar slowed, and Vizzy saw a surprising number of parked cars and vans for a small road. Heidar turned and shouted above the engine's growl "See Vizzy. You've got to be up early to beat the twitchers."

Standing by the parked behemoth, Vizzy pulled off the helmet that he'd been loaned, still shaking from his experience. "Why are you – sorry, they – called twitchers, then?"

"I'm not really sure, Vizzy. It's a term you British use. The real twitcher loves keeping lists of rare birds he's seen – not so often she, as you'll see. His hand's meant to be twitching to tick off another on his list. In the States it's just called chasing. It's different to being a birdwatcher or a birder – that's just a full-time birdwatcher without a social life. Twitching is something you only do when you know there's a rare species sighted. It's like a club, a big club. Thousands of twitchers sometimes appear if it's really rare – it gets in the papers then. It relies on generosity – if you see a rare species you are honour bound to let others know – it's called suppression if you don't and viewed as really low. I've got the contact numbers on my phone in case one day I'm the first, but I'm not really a proper twitcher. It's only birds that may have come from Iceland, and I've usually seen them before with my father. I'm honouring them for their journey, not ticking them off on a list."

They crossed the meadows leading down to the river, joining a throng of over a hundred like-minded enthusiasts. All now seemed to have field glasses, the advantage of a Sunday sighting. Heidar was asking others about the Harlequin – a few had caught a glimpse, but none had yet heard its odd squeak. "Like a mouse," said Heidar, who had heard them by the River Laxá as it flowed into Lake Mývatn. "Never in England. Never. Always by cold streams, fast flowing. Waterfalls sometimes – maybe it found the weir at Marlow. Maybe blown from Iceland, maybe even North America or Siberia. Chances of a pair – no, I don't believe it likely."

There was movement about a hundred yards down the bank. Some started running, being hissed at by others to slow down to avoid scaring off whatever they were going to see. Vizzy saw at last what the fuss was about, at first just a very duck-sized duckish bird, until he got a good view of its darkish blue colour with contrasting red-brown sides and numerous white patches. It was striking, and he was finally caught up in the others' enthusiasm.

After about half an hour of desultory conversation with some others, all excited to see the Harlequin so far from home but a little disappointed that there was no female, Vizzy and Heidar returned to the Harley. Vizzy was wasting no time in filling the gaps in his Nordic knowledge. "So this Valkyrie. The second time. Why were you wondering whether you'd done the right thing? You'd ridden across Europe, you must have made your mind up already. I don't understand."

"Vizzy, life is complex. This is a long story. Not best told on the back of a Harley. Particularly with a petrified passenger – yes, you don't fool me. Never been gripped like that by a male before. You can tell I didn't go to boarding school."

He kick started the beast with some difficulty, the roar clearly upsetting the new arriving twitchers. "Come on. Time for your next challenge on the Bike of Thor. Helmet on. You don't want to be standing next to this without some ear protection."

CHAPTER 31

Silence. Just silence. Boat back on the racks in silence. Sitting on the grass in silence, the drizzle hardly noticed. Heads shaking. Dave was the first to speak. "Three lengths. Three lengths over a thousand metres. We've been kidding ourselves, haven't we?"

The first day of Metropolitan Regatta, brainchild of Charles Dickens. The lake at Dorney flat and calm despite the rain. The final of Veteran C fours a disastrously bad row for the Elizabethans after the promising heats. Fourth of six, within a length of Nottingham and just a canvas down on London-Thames, but two lengths of clear water down on Leander. Heidar banged the ground with his fist. "No. We haven't. We just rowed like a bunch of amateurs. Tomorrow, it all starts again. 2,000 metres. We see then. Now come on. We won't go any faster tomorrow if we get hypothermia in this rain."

Little was said as they changed and headed for home. Morley was tetchy and difficult with the twins when he got back. Helen did her best, but ended up stomping angrily upstairs after getting the rough edge of her husband's tongue. Vizzy, now engaged and interested in the crew, had come down when he heard his father return, and tried the risky tactic of asking him about the day.

"I don't know, Vizzy. When we get it right, we're miles better. I don't know what we need."

"Dad, I know. You need a coach. I was watching this programme about the Olympics today. Everyone needs a coach if they're going to get to the top. Why don't you ask George again?"

"You don't understand, Vizzy. You really don't."

"That's where you're wrong, Dad. I really do."

Morley looked at his son. He nodded with lips pursed. Little by little, Vizzy was growing in maturity, and so was their relationship.

"Dad. Can I come and watch you tomorrow? I want to see for myself."

And so Vizzy, travelling voluntarily and without coercion, listened to the old engine turn over before it caught, settling in for a less adrenergic trip up the M4 than his last. It was also less adrenergic for Morley than his last car ride with Vizzy, who had been at the wheel for his third driving lesson. It had been decided that future lessons would be conducted by Helen.

Sixteen crews in Veteran C for Sunday, most aiming for Henley. Three heats, with just the first two crews from each reaching the afternoon final. The draw tough, six crews, including both Leander and Nottingham. The Heat of Death, as Gareth insisted on calling it. At least the sun was out today. They were getting to know the Nottingham crew, tough competetition but open and friendly, exchanging some good natured banter. Leander were above such commonplace exchanges, not returning nods of greeting, their strokeman Heyward particularly prone to dismissive looks. Nerves were taut, and taughtened further just before boating by Dave in time honoured fashion. "Where the hell is he?" shouted irate Morley. "As if we didn't know. He's having another of his bloody Miruts Yifter moments." Yifter had won a bronze in the Olympic 10,000 metres in Munich, but was thrown in jail on his return to Ethiopia after missing the start of the 5,000 metres in a stadium toilet. His nickname of Yifter the Shifter was earned later, happily rather more conventionally, following coruscating turns of speed to win gold in both races at the Moscow Olympics.

"For God's sake, Dave," Morley shouted at the apologetic returnee, joining them on the landing stage after Vizzy had helped the other three get the boat out.

"Don't stress, Peter," chipped in Gareth, trying to defuse the situation. "Boat's two pounds lighter."

"I wish," said an unhappy Dave.

The row to the start of the heat too hurried for anyone to think. Only just time to turn for the start. Despite all this, a good clean start, all six crews level. By about 250 metres they were in second, half a length down on Leander. The other three crews kept pace initially, but were falling back well before 1,000 metres. By this stage, Leander were out in front by around two lengths, but Nottingham had crept through into the second qualifying place. Morley put in their planned burst and was pleased to see the Nottingham sternpost move further into his peripheral vision. In the final 500 metres he attacked early, then built up the rate. Nottingham were struggling, then started to fold as Morley raised their rate further. He noticed puddles coming past on his left and realised that they had come right back at Leander. A close second, and through to the final.

A happier four. They sat down on the grass to talk, discussing their chances against Leander in the final. Vizzy, sitting by his father, shook his head. "Not rowing like that. Honestly, trust me. I don't know much, but I could see they were taking it easy. I can't put my finger on it, but it's just not quite right."

"You wait and see, you cheeky young pup," said Gareth, good humour belying his words, as he gave Vizzy a mock cuff.

But Vizzy was right. Gloves off, the final, Leander three lengths clear by halfway, pegged back to just under two lengths at the finish. Disconsolate, defeated, slumped in the boat. Second in the final out of sixteen entrants, a result they would have been pleased with six months ago. The magnitude of their defeat was what hurt.

By the boat racks, Morley turned on his son. "OK coach, what was wrong? What should we do?"

Vizzy pondered. "Well, you're dashing forward, dropping in six inches short. There's hurry through the whole boat. Dave, your timing's out at the catch and your blade's going in too deep. Heidar, you're washing out at the finish under pressure.

Gareth, you're looking round too often, and you too are washing out. Plus your timing's crap."

They looked at him in amazement. Morley snapped "Well thank you, Jurgen bleeding Grobler."

Heidar looked thoughtful. "Vizzy, you're absolutely right. I couldn't put my finger on it. How on earth could you see all that?"

Vizzy shrugged. A deeper voice came from behind.

"He didn't. I did."

All four heads turned. Gareth was quickest off the mark. "George!"

CHAPTER 32

"This is the second vindaloo you've forced on me, Morley."

"Dave, after this morning's performance, we've decided you need all the help you can get. We had several thoughts about medication – this is the only one that's not on the banned list."

Still rather stunned, the four become five - in fact six if Vizzy was counted - they sat in the Windsor curry house. George was in good spirits, clearly happy to be back.

"So you have to thank Vizzy. Never thought I'd be back near the water. Least of all with you lot. Well, Peter, your son is a born saleman. And not to be trusted with other people's mobiles. You made a big mistake, Gareth, leaving him yours to look after while you raced this morning."

"If he used the frequent contacts, he probably dialled three massage parlours first," said Dave to laughs around the table.

"I did," said Vizzy. "Then I realised I'd got your phone."

"So why," asked Gareth in more serious vein, "did you give us the bum's rush last Christmas?"

"Well, complex. Firstly, it's not the honeymoon fiasco. We dined out on that for years afterwards once we'd got over it. So, no hard feelings, Dave. Not that I could have any for weeks afterwards. Anyway, Gareth, I'm sorry I was curt. In fact downright rude. Just couldn't face a meaningless social do. Especially at Henley. Never once won – never happy going back. Plus my life was in a bit of turmoil."

He looked around, making a decision, then spoke.

"You'll all remember Angela. Well, I guess you won't, Vizzy. Married in haste, repented at leisure, really. Kids all grown up now. We realised last Autumn that we wanted different things.

She got what she wanted, my money, mainly. I got what I wanted. My new partner."

He paused for several seconds. "Gavin."

Another of the silences the crew were getting used to. Gareth, as usual, lightening the tone. "Well, so long as he's a good cook."

Heidar smiled. "George. I think I speak for all of us. We are pleased and honoured that you've agreed to coach us. We need it, but with your help I think we can do it. And we look forward to meeting Gavin. Margaux has just got hold of some wines from the Languedoc she's getting excited by. I'm sure she can be prevailed upon to air them for such an occasion."

Gareth again, happy. "And it's our turn to host it. Next Sunday? I'm sure Lynette would be happy. If you're feeling masochistic you can hear them play at church first."

"These wines of Margaux's, George," put in a concerned-looking Dave. "Promise me one thing? Don't get plastered."

CHAPTER 33

"Dave, you've changed our lives more than you know."

"Lynette, I'm just glad to have helped. Any doctor would. Surprising how common Coeliac disease is. I know because I see a lot of it at work, as it can affect fertility."

"Yes, you bastard. You didn't mention that," cut in Gareth. "Gwen is not best pleased with our news on that front."

"Ah. Oh dear. Whoops. Well, *you're* obviously not training hard enough."

"The economic impact's not helped by the fact that I chucked in my job last week."

Lynette smiled and shrugged. "It's the right thing. You've got to be brave. Your finance prediction model's worked really well so far – even in these difficult times. If you'd actually invested rather than had dry runs we'd be off to the Seychelles this summer. Not that I've got anything against Gower, but the kids are getting fed up and I don't want them to stop coming on holiday with us. Particularly now they're having to come to terms with the new baby. So, your big chance. Our big chance. And you've got talent, and a civil service pension to fall back on if all else fails. Of course, your Mum's money helped."

She looked questioningly towards Gareth, who nodded and she went on to explain. "We found out she had £16,000 left over from the compensation money that Gareth's Dad got a year before he died. Dear Eifor. He was such a lovely man. Well, apart from one holiday, they never touched it. She always wanted Gareth to have a chance on his own. I must say, now I think about it, I agree. Bless her. We'll be alright. And that's something I never thought I'd say two months ago in these circumstances."

Margaux breezed across, glass in hand. "Lynette, darling, who's that gorgeous young man over there? Now, if I were twenty years younger."

"That's Gavin, dear. I know just what you mean, even if it is only ten years for me – sorry, darling." Margaux smiled and stuck out her tongue. "However, I think you might need more than youth on your side."

Morley felt relaxed. Relaxed in the company, all having engaged in pursuit of a common aim but finding enrichment along the way. Relaxed in his relationship with Helen, each seeing the other with renewed eyes. Relaxed and happy about his children, the twins directing their considerable energies in more constructive directions and complex Vizzy beginning to find the calm and happiness that had eluded him for so long. He, and all his colleagues, delighted to have George back and coaching. Differences made already, in three outings. All seemed comfortable in their own skins. All had taken easily to Gavin, who had a wry wit and sense of humour, although none yet had started to tease George. Morley suspected that would come, and come first in a Welsh accent. Remembering that George had been the first to call Gareth Mint Sauce, he suspected that he'd cheerfully give as good as he got.

Ben came rushing in, shouting – "They're starting! They're starting!". All moved indoors and crowded into a room upstairs that had been the children's old playroom, now converted into a home recording studio, with old duvets lining the walls and a computer terminal attached to a keyboard. Several leads snaked across the floor from microphones, arranged on either side of a large old drumkit. Morley was impressed by the setup, but apprehensive about the likely contribution of the twins.

He noted with some relief that Thomas had the lead guitar, and that Alastair picked up the bass. Gwen sat on a stool behind the keyboards while David climbed behind the drumkit.

After one loud false start they kicked into a song. Morley was amazed. Away from the lead guitar, the boys had achieved a level of some competence. Gwen played neat keyboard piano and had a good clear voice. The twins, cutting in for the choruses, could not be described as natural vocalists, but over-all it was a good effort and earned deserved applause. The young band sang two more, competent but rather forgettable songs with strongly Christian lyrics. All in all, the members of the Twickenham Catholic community appeared to have been treated to an almost biblical deliverance from the threatened Morley musical onslaught. For the second time in a few months, Morley had pause to wonder whether there really was a Lord who liked to move in mysterious ways. Certainly some-one seemed to have performed wonders with the boys.

CHAPTER 34

There is nowhere, absolutely nowhere, like the upper reaches of the Thames on a bright June morning. Scintillae of early morning mist clearing as the day begins to warm, the stretch at Marlow looking like a picture postcard, coots and ducks paddling on intermittently urgent business, contrasting swans with patrician disdain for rush. The water under Marlow Bridge accelerating imperceptibly towards the weir, with just the occasional bedroom curtain yet opened at the Compleat Angler, presumably by early birds keen to take in the scene, bid sad farewell to mistress or recover from last night's second Calvados. The air crisp, still little traffic noise. The small town awakening slowly to a big day. Marlow Regatta.

Boat trailers congregated in fields, some hardy crews camped out overnight, the smell of frying bacon on the air. Cars arriving, one or two initially, inhabitants often joining the campers for breakfast, then many others on more pressing business. By 8 o'clock, queues waiting to park, directed by yellow-jacketed parking attendants. Crews emerging from the changing tents, one or two taking short outings, others rigging boats. Officials, some nondescript in dark suits, others resplendent in Oxbridge blazers and white flannels, reporting for duty armed with little more than pen, field glasses or hipflask.

Morley parked the Volvo, pleased to have Vizzy's company if not his CD collection. He was upset to see the disdainful glance shot in Vizzy's direction by an older man in a faded Oxford Blue blazer as he emerged from a carelessly parked Land Rover Discovery. The bottle green car was distinguished by several hunting stickers and a large and rather dangerous-looking metal bonnet ornament of a retriever with gamebird in its mouth. The intrepid hunter looked rather more approvingly at Farqhuar, happy to be released from his incarceration in the back of the estate. Morley thought he recognised the man, who was making for the Umpires' tents. Then the penny dropped. "Bloody hell. That's Bennersley-Panton. Thought he'd died years ago."

Sir James Bennersley-Panton had yet to recover from losing his two Oxford-Cambridge Boat Races in the mid 1950's. Thankfully, as a High Court judge, he had a useful outlet to vent his feelings of residual anger. He had made the tabloids on several occasions, not only because of the exemplary severity of his sentencing policies but also because of his florid and intemperate descriptions of the personality flaws he perceived in those who ended up before him. He had been one of the more notorious umpires at Henley in the 80's. It was rumoured even then that his judgement would shift from merely autocratic to downright lunatic after his lunchtime imbibations, which were apparently heroic even by Henley umpires' standards. Luckily for Bennersley-Panton, it would be difficult to pick two career paths more tolerant of advancing age, misanthropic temperament and Herculean lunchtime drinking than High Court judge and Henley umpire. Morley hoped that he wouldn't be given any of the coxless races.

Vizzy appeared oblivious to the looks he had received from Bennersley-Panton, and merely remarked to his father about the unusual old buffers the sport appeared to attract. He pointed towards the large receding shape now stomping towards the Umpires' tent and said, "Twenty years, Dad. That'll be you. Be very scared."

Their first race was at 9.45, with semi-final and final to follow. The river was wide enough for three to race abreast, only the winner proceeding to the next round. They had a relatively straightforward first round, the other two crews having finished several lengths behind them at Metropolitan. George nevertheless sat them down and went very precisely through the race plan. "Never underestimate the opposition, guys. Never." It had always been his mantra, and it had stood them in good stead over the years. It helped on this occasion. Stalked by a happy Farqhuar, and remarkably a running Vizzy, they were able to cruise home comfortably in front.

They now knew their task. Leander, equally comfortable in their heat, faced them in the semi-final. Only one to get through. The third crew, a Scottish composite, good heat winners but likely to be outgunned in this company. Nervous chatter before boating, Dave present in good time on this occasion. Elizabethans drawn in the inside lane by the North bank, the Scottish four in the centre and Leander outside them towards the South bank. They boated, did their warmup pieces and progressed towards the start. Morley looked up to see Vizzy walking along the bank in company with Farqhuar, stopping to throw the labrador's much slobbered tennis ball for him to fetch. As they turned before the start, they got their first acknowledgement from the Leander crew, a mocking "see you at the finish, chaps," from their two man. That was the moment that Morley's feelings towards the Leander four changed from slightly awed respect to dislike and a burning desire to beat and humiliate them. Mocking your opponents is never a very bright move. Whatever other qualities Leander possessed, brightness did not appear to be their defining characteristic. An opponent who hates you is a more dangerous opponent than one who fears you.

They waited to be invited to the start. Morley heard a peremptory barked order, accent hued in deepest plum, telling them to come along now. He looked towards the bank. The unmistakeable figure of Bennersley-Panton, already with the slight swaying motion that spoke of a good lunch. As he gave the instructions to the three crews in a slightly slurred voice, Morley saw two fours pass up the course past the start. There was the not unusual sight of a sudden flurry of ducks near to the bank, as one of the bowside blades took the catch in what appeared to be the middle of a family group. One of the ducklings, looked to have been hit hard and was obviously hurt, small wings flapping ineffectively, head at an unusual angle. Morley was always saddened to see this sort of thing, which only tended to happen when there were broods of young that could not fly off or get out the way in time. He dismissed it from his mind and sat forward in the start position. He heard Vizzy shout from the bank, unexpectedly not a shout of support but of warning and alarm.

"Hey, Heidar, look! Quick!"

The response from the two seat was rapid. "Mr Umpire, we must stop the race! It must be stopped!!"

Bennersley-Panton was not impressed, giving a slurred and dismissive query. "Equipment failure, Elizabethans?"

When Heidar replied no, but that the race must be stopped, Bennersley-Panton shook his head, which seemed to increase his angle of sway. He delivered his next message in no more than five seconds with a dramatic sweep of his starter's flag, the drama of the moment enhanced by the induced forward stumble.

"No time for delay. All crews – Get Ready .... Are You Ready .... Go!!"

A catastrophic response from the four. Heidar, unprepared, agitated and inattentive, missed the first stroke entirely, the boat thus slewing towards the bank. Morley shouted "Heidar! Wake up!" Heidar rallied, joining the others in their second stroke, the boat still lurching. They were now heading towards the bank at increasing speed. Gareth, rudder full on, tilting the boat further, had to take two half strokes before having to miss completely a third to avoid hitting the bank. Almost a complete restart needed, the four now careering in the right direction but close to the bank, having to make another emergency course correction to avoid ploughing into an eight paddling up to the start. The next tangent in their bizarre geometric progression was then across the course towards the far bank, behind their two fast disappearing rivals. By the time they had achieved some kind of alignment with the river, they were bumping along in the wake of the Scottish four, who had at least a length of clear water over them. Viral rush had over-come them, their rhythm short and panicked, not helped by a series of megaphoned yells from an enraged Bennersley-Panton, waving his flag like an Ark Royal flight deck marshall trying to land a Harrier flown by Mark Thatcher.

"Elizabethans!!! Steering!!"

"Elizabethans!!! Look ahead!!! Back in lane!!!"

"Elizabethans!!! Get back in your bloody lane!!! Damn you!!"

"Elizabethans!!! Get!! Back!! In!! Lane!! Now!!!!"

"Elizabethans!!! Back in lane!!! This is your final warning!!!"

A good strokeman is a leader. Morley led. Angrily shouting "Stride", he deliberately took the rating down by two strokes a minute, concentrating on length and smoothness. Dave followed well, and within two strokes they had regained some composure. Gareth at bow also regained control of the steer-ing, moving them across towards their station and then straightening. This had cost them some distance, leaving them nearly two lengths down on the Scots, with Leander out of sight towards the far bank. Morley sensed that the rhythm was now good enough to risk an attack and called for twenty, a signal to the crew to attack for the next twenty strokes. Within ten strokes they had taken back half a length on the Scottish crew, and all could sense they were moving well. Within a further ten they were almost level with their sternpost, and over the next twenty they had taken the lead. No sight of Leander and Morley did not waste time by turning to see them. He felt that the boat was now going beautifully, dropping the Scots with each stroke, and decided to hold the rhythm stable and hard. He was surprised to hear a shout from Gareth, as they reached the mark showing 500 metres to go, saying they were closing on Leander. He decided to go for it again, and felt real power coming down. The volume of shouting coming from the bank suggested a close race, and he was surprised to see the puddles coming down from Leander out of the corner of his left

WATER UNDER THE BRIDGE

eye. It was hard. It was painful. But they were flying, like they'd never flown before, the refinements brought by George clearly paying dividends.

They finished exhausted, just half a length down on Leander. Morley looked round and was encouraged to see how knackered they looked, the goading two man looking particularly distressed. He managed to shout to them between gasps of breath. His cheery call of "See you at Henley," both challenge and warning.

George pulled them into the landing stage when a place became available. He seemed positive. "Another hundred metres, you'd have had them. You've scared them, no doubt. If it hadn't been for that bloody awful start. What the hell happened?"

Between pants for breath, standing on the landing stage, Heidar spoke up. "Down to me, George. Sorry to you all. But there's a crisis. We have to stop the Regatta. Stop it now."

Morley was first off the mark, also fitting short sentences between gasped breaths. "What the hell do you mean? Stop Marlow Regatta? You're bloody mad."

George, less hypoxic, more astute, recognised that this behaviour was unusual even for this passionate Northerner. He put his arm around Heidar's shoulder. "OK, Heidar. Why? Why would you want to do that in the middle of the biggest regatta of the season?"

They were interrupted by the arrival of a panting Vizzy, with Farquhar about twenty yards behind. He gasped at Heidar. "Did you see? Did you see?"

Heidar nodded and spoke, forceful hand movements emphasising the passion behind the words. "Harlequin ducks. A breeding pair. Never before in England. Never. We must stop the Regatta. One duckling killed already. Come on Vizzy."

They marched towards the Regatta offices. A large man in Lycra. A thin boy in black. And a fat dog.

CHAPTER 35

This time it was Heidar's nose that was broken. Negotiations hopeless and ill-tempered. Courtesies nevertheless maintained until the return of Bennersley-Panton. Remarkably, despite the slurring and swaying, he had an effective right hook.

"Ha! Not landed one like that since Eton! Bloody bird-watching half-wit. Should be bloody horsewhipped."

Heidar's self control was deeply impressive. Blood running down his face, his nose skewed to port, he fixed all in the room with a dark and determined gaze that chilled all but the judge, too crazed with adrenaline and Tanqueray gin to notice.

"I am sorry. If I cannot persuade you of the importance of this, then I will need help to do so."

They walked tall from the tent. Heidar turned to Vizzy. "I am sorry that you had to see that. Now I need my mobile phone back. I need to call reinforcements."

Vizzy smiled. "Don't worry. I've already done that while you were racing. You showed me the numbers you'd saved last time. Didn't think those pompous gits would listen."

The first twitchers arrived within minutes, making straight towards the start area with field glasses and long-lensed cameras in hand. Then more arrived, then more, then yet more. Then, just as Vizzy wondered whether there could be any more twitchers in southern England, they started to arrive in real numbers.

Morley looked at his son with a bemused expression. The rest of the crew just watched and stared, as yet more continued to arrive in groups small and large.

"Well, Vizzy. You've done it now. Master of the decisive telephone call," said George, also with a look of wonder on his face. They had strolled towards the start, seeing the gathering throng near the bank, all training field glasses or cameras on the small huddle of birds on the water. One of the ducklings daringly left his siblings and moved away from the bank in curious exploration. It would be hard to imagine greater numbers of expensive telephoto lenses flashing intently away at a small dark object unless the paparazzi were to catch Kate Middleton emerging from a Lamborghini when going commando.

Heidar himself looked amazed. "Never so many. Never. There must be hundreds. A breeding pair of Harlequins. So rare. So important."

They walked back towards the start. Morley looked towards Marlow Bridge, traffic now stopped by a stream of anoraked humanity, trendy North Face and Nike marching shoulder to shoulder with classic Barbour and snorkel-nosed parka. Gareth shook his head with a look half bemused, half-amused.

"Bloody hell boys. It's the Day of the Twitchers - the bloody Sparrow March."

Heidar looked appropriately unimpressed. He also looked worried. This was building up into potential confrontation, and there were plainly dark mutterings amongst some of the oarsmen who were being heckled by passing twitchers.

A crew practising a racing start scattered the ducklings. Suddenly it turned nasty. Shouts at the crew. Unwise V-signs in return. An apple thrown from the throng hitting the stroke man on the side of the head, eliciting cheers from the crowd. Leaders emerging, galvanising the normally docile twitchers. Shouting beginning. Some moved reluctantly away, despatched from the vicinity of the birds to picket the landing stages. Scuffles breaking out between lycra-clad oarsmen and anoracked twitchers. Then conflagration.

One twitcher shouted towards the oarsmen waiting to boat. "You stupid thick rowers. Don't you know this is a once in a lifetime event."

One of the oarsmen replied equally loudly. "So's this, mate. My first Marlow final in ten fucking years of trying. So fuck off back to your mummies and your stamp collections, you bunch of losers."

Pitched battle, waged by landing stage and boat rack, stretchable lycra versus breathable Gore-Tex, lightweight trainers versus stout walking boots, toned angered muscle versus enraged ectomorphic scrawn. Five hundred Victor Matures battling a thousand Charles Hawtreys. Soon, in the distance, the sound of police sirens. Presumably hampered by the gridlocked traffic, they did not seem to be coming nearer very fast. Overhead came the unmistakeable sound of a police helicopter. Morley thought that discretion was the better part of valour. "Heidar. You are not going to be popular. Let's stay out of the way in the cars."

Vizzy came running up, out of breath. "That weird bloke in the blazer. He's just decked Bill Oddie. Now he's gone back to his car. He's got out a gun."

They ran to the cars. Bennersley-Panton's Discovery was empty, its rear door left open in haste. Morley could see a gun case, evidently expensive, advertising James Purdey and Sons in gold leaf. There was a receipt for shotgun servicing from their South Molton Street office, lying by a large Purdey carrier bag. Bennersley-Panton had paid an unfeasibly large amount of money to get it serviced. He must be serious about his shooting.

"Bloody hell," said Morley. "He must have been getting ready for the grouse season. The Glorious bloody Twelfth. He'll have been taking the bloody thing back to his country pile tonight."

Heidar was already running. Morley shouted anxiously after him. "For God's sake, Heidar. You'll get shot. He'll blame you. Come back! Oh, bloody hell."

He set off in pursuit, Vizzy and crewmates just behind, Farqhuar lolloping in their wake. As they approached the throng fighting by the start, they heard a large bang, then a second. Most carried on fighting, others stopping at the noise.

A wailing began, and Morley could make out some bloodied feathers on the water's edge. One shot had hit its target. It looked like the other had thankfully missed. Bennersley-Panton stood about twenty yards further upstream, away from the fighting mass. He was cursing loudly as he somewhat unsteadily reloaded. "No one stops Marlow Regatta. No one. Matter of bloody principle. Would be Henley next. Right, where are those damned quacking things? Sort this out."

He swayed upright, the gun barrel wavering across the crowd. The fighting settled as people turned in amazement towards the gun bearing umpire in the Oxford blazer. Shouts of warning and protest stilled by barked command from Bennersley-Panton. "Get back you lot, dammit. I will bloody shoot. Any of you. I've had enough of this behaviour. Disgraceful. If you were before me I'd give the whole bloody lot of you five years. Now stand back! Let me sort these damned trouble-making fluffballs out. Blasted immigrants – even the bloody ducks cause problems."

He fixed his aim at the remaining brood, then was startled by a loud shout of "No!" from close by. He looked round to see Heidar, who was advancing slowly on him.

"Aha! It's that bloody duck-loving Elizabethan. The architect of all our sorrows. Let me tell you now, sir, that nothing would give me greater pleasure than to fill your bloody snivelling Guardian-reading bird-loving posterior with grape shot. Don't tempt me, sir, don't tempt me."

He steadied his aim on the ducks, in as far as he could steady anything after his liquid lunch. He let off one shot, cracking loudly and peppering the water by a passing swan, which hissed in protest and flapped its wings at him. He aimed again, this time rather nearer to the ducklings, which looked pathetically weak and vulnerable, their parents having been startled into flight. A sudden rush of black. Two black figures, one thin and Emo-clad, one fat and furred. They impacted together, Bennersley-Panton pushed backwards into the Thames in mid-shot. A chill down Morley's spine as the crack ricocheted around. Two black figures momentarily still, lying on the edge of the bank. Morley held his breath, fearing the worst. Then one got up, gingerly dusting himself down. His howl could be heard half a mile away when he looked down at the other.

"Farqhuar!!!"

Morley's blood chilled. Better Farqhuar than Vizzy, but still intense visceral spasm of fear. There was no sign of movement from his dog. He could see a stain of blood spreading out beside the prone body. He ran forward, could hear Farqhuar whimpering as he knelt down by him. He looked down at Bennersley-Panton, who was struggling to his feet in the river, directing a look of fury at Vizzy.

"My bloody gun! You stupid ill-favoured oik. Do you know how much this thing costs? More than your parents' house, by the look of you."

Morley boiled over. "You ignorant, overprivileged, self-indulgent psychopath!" he shouted. "You've broken my crew-mate's nose. You've assaulted one of the Goodies. You've shot rare and special birds. And you've killed my bloody dog, you bastard. It was only good fortune that stopped you shooting my son. You crazed old buffoon."

Bennersley-Panton stood as straight as the situation allowed. "I can assure you, Sir, that I regret shooting your dog. However I certainly could not say the same for your son, who I suspect the world would miss rather less. Had I more time, I would have adjusted my shot accordingly."

And so, just as the first policemen finally arrived, Morley had jumped into the Marlow Thames and was vigorously beating up a High Court judge.

CHAPTER 36

It was the first time that Morley had been taken in the back of a police car with siren wailing. He looked across at Dave with hopeless expression. They were making slow progress despite the siren. Morley felt anxious for Vizzy, traumatised to the core by the day's events and sitting mutely between them. He felt anxious for Heidar, who had been singled out by the other oarsmen after Bennersley-Panton's tirade. Despite their dislike of the man, they did not like to see their umpires led off in handcuffs and the cancellation of their regatta. He felt anxious for Gareth and George, who were standing by Heidar's side in what had the makings of an episode of real nastiness. Most of all, however, he felt a gnawing visceral anxiety about Farqhuar, who lay across their laps with a large deep wound across his lower abdomen, making unusual small whimpering sounds.

"Can't we go any faster?" he asked of the police officers sitting in front.

"Sorry, sir," came the polite reply. "No chance with all this traffic. We've got the animal hospital in Bracknell on stand-by. We'll be there as quick as we can."

Farqhuar's blood soaked into his legs. Morley pressed the towel harder. Vizzy sat quietly, an occasional tear quickly wiped. The car sped up, finally out of town and onto a fast road.

"Not more than seven or eight minutes now, Sir."

"Thanks," said Morley, largely by reflex. His hopes were receding. Even five minutes may be too long now. He noticed Farhuar shivering, his previous feeble movements otherwise quietening. He looked at Dave.

"You're going to have to do it."

"Do what?"

"The kiss of life. It's his only chance."

"No, Peter. You can't ask me to do that. Look at that slobber. No way."

"Bloody hell, Dave. You slept with Julianne Robertson. Don't deny it. Since when did you get so bloody choosy. Just bloody do it. Farqhuar needs you. You're by his head. Remember, he risked his life to help us. Vizzy! Hold his bloody head down if you have to."

"Bloody hell, Peter. The bloody things I've had to do for you over the years."

"Good man, Dave. Good man. Well done. Now Vizzy, look away! There are some things a teenager shouldn't see."

CHAPTER 37

"It's BBC Breakfast. Would you be happy to come on tomorrow? Darling, no. I can't say that to them. Shall I just tell them what I said to GMTV?"

Morley grunted irascibly. "Tell them what you bloody want, Helen. Sorry, *darling*. I don't know what all the bloody fuss is about. He's not the first dog to have had his bollocks blown off, and he probably won't be the last."

"I know dear. But he's probably the first dog who's had his bollocks blown off to be on the front page of the News of the World."

Helen was right. Above a large picture showing the inside of a police car, with a stricken Farqhuar stretched out across the knees of his three companions, ran the single word headline *Knackered*. The paper, in common with all the tabloids and most of the broadsheets, was delighted to run a story as compelling as the Battle of Marlow Regatta, at a time when good news stories were thin on the ground. The Sunday Telegraph stayed true to form, with one article deprecating the violence of the clashes and another discussing the results of the racing before the regatta was abandoned. The News of the World had managed to outdo even the Sunday Mirror in its coverage, providing a week's respite for errant politicians and vicars. Eight pages of eye witness reports of carnage and mayhem plus a full two paragraphs, by their standards utterly remarkable in-depth factual coverage, on the usual habitat and migration patterns of the Harlequin duck. He was quietly pleased to read in the Sunday Mirror that the parents had returned to their brood in the early evening. Morley wondered how many statements of potentially unpopular government measures would be quietly released while this fuss continued.

They had managed to read all the papers, after Morley finally escaped the intrigued questioning of the newsagent unwittingly responsible for it all. They had heard from a miserable Dave, still trapped in his home by a dozen paparazzi and journalists. Sadly a teenager with a cameraphone had shot video footage of Dave's canine kiss of life as the car door was opened by the police. This had run on the evening news and was currently the highest hitting item in YouTube history. Although pushed to the second page of the News of the World by Farqhuar's injury, the banner headline labelling him *Dave The Dogging Doctor* would probably bother him longer than any of this would Farqhuar.

The star of the show himself lay convalescing from his surgery at Bracknell, racking up vet's bills at a rate that Morley already feared. He had required transfusion and abdominal surgery but was now off the danger list and expected home at the weekend. Vizzy had managed to create a minor family sensation, coming down for breakfast in a red teeshirt, the first time for three years the family had seen him voluntarily wear any colour other than black. He withstood good-naturedly the ribbing from the twins, telling them that they should write a celebratory song for Jesus. They promised to do so if his AS level results were any good, as it would really mean a miracle. Vizzy chose not to fight back, knowing that his GCSE's had been less than stellar and that the ice was thin beneath his feet.

The media furore continued for the next few days. Bennersley-Panton had suffered the consequences of mistiming, his escapade with the Purdey only two days after the Home Secretary announced a clampdown on gun crime. The tabloids smelled blood and bail had so far been refused. Jeremy Clarkson broke new journalistic ground for him by producing a balanced article, caught between his deep admiration of Bennersley-Panton's Land Rover Discovery 4.4 litre V8 and Purdey shotgun plus what was in his view a long-overdue assault on Bill Oddie's nose, and his children's equally deep disapproval of any man who could shoot ducklings and labradors. Henley Royal Regatta, loyal to the last and concerned lest the Harlequins decided to move in their direction, issued a statement of support for their missing Umpire.

It was fortunate for the crew that their story was rapidly eclipsed by other media sensations. One of Jonathon Ross's more crazed producers had managed to persuade Jim Davidson and Pete Doherty onto the same show, and a politically struggling Prime Minister ignored the advice of his aides that any other show would be a better place to demonstrate his more human side. The ensuing furore ensured that the paparazzi had abandoned them by the time of their Saturday outing, just eleven days before the first round at Henley.

Morley found the letter at the UL boathouse, good quality cream paper vellum with the Henley Royal Regatta crest. He had been entertaining quiet hopes that they would be one of the seeded crews. He broke the seal in front of his crewmates.

"Here goes. …. Fingers crossed." He went quiet, eyes wide. He paused, then shouted. "Bastards. Bloody evil bastards. They're making us qualify."

CHAPTER 38

Complete change of plan. The gross unfairness underlined by study of the Henley website. The Princess Alice had four seeded crews. Fair enough, no complaints. All were likely to be good. Leander. New Haven Rowing Club, USA. Probably Yale alumni. Cambridge Boat Club, USA. Probably Harvard alumni. Trident Rowing Club, South Africa. Former national squad, almost certainly. Other crews entered included two from Holland, one from Australia, one more from the USA, two from Ireland and a large number of British club crews. Nottingham City, the Scottish composite and London-Thames all straight into the regatta proper. So was the crew from Upper Thames that they had beaten four times that year. To punish them by making them row the qualifiers was a mean and vindictive act. Only three crews to qualify for the Regatta from eighteen condemned to the qualifiers. A savage toll, allowing no room for error.

All suspected that Adrian Heyward, the Leander stroke, may have been abusing his position as a Steward to rig the draw. George grimaced. "He always was an evil bastard. I remember him when he first joined the squad. Always ready to knife you in the back. The only Moscow medal winner I really resented. If it hadn't been for my bloody back, I'd have been in the eight. I was really glad for the rest of them. To think he had my place – my medal."

Gareth looked thoughtful. "You know, I think he's scared of us. I think he was really scared at Marlow. When we closed on them like that. I could hear him shouting. They were really going for it. I think he knows that we could beat him. So the thing that scares me – they could rig the timing. We could win that race and be kicked out on our ears. No one ever the wiser."

All looked at each other. He was right. A minute between each of the boats. Easily done. At most thirty or forty seconds between the fastest and slowest crews. Plenty of scope for creative timekeeping.

Morley thought about this idea. Much as he hated to admit it, this had the ring of truth. He looked at Dave.

"Sorry to ask for your help again. Particularly after the last time. But there's only one thing that can stop this sort of dirty tricks campaign. The oxygen of publicity. No good having George and Vizzy with stopwatches. No one would believe it. We need television cameras. And you're the only one who can guarantee that. Dave the Dogging Doctor. Live on GMTV. They're getting bored with their daily Duckwatch specials. You'll be a breath of fresh air for them." He fished in his pocket. "Here's the number."

Dave paled. "Thanks, mate. It was a nice career while it lasted."

CHAPTER 39

"So, before we leave Dave the Dogging Doctor, one more viewer's question. Mr Collins of Sidcup has a question about the ducks. He asks if you have the same feelings for them that you do for dogs."

Dave squirmed under the studio lights. He had just about had enough, knowing that all his clinic staff and half his patients would be watching. He shrugged and put his hand up.

"OK. It's a fair cop. I admit it." He nodded. "Not ducks though. Egrets."

"Egrets?" asked the designer-clad presenter in shocked tones, plainly appalled and delighted in equal measure.

Dave nodded again. "I've had a few." He paused. "But then again, too few to mention."

Whatever else is required of prospective GMTV presenters at interview, a sense of humour ticks the optional rather than essential box. His attempt at levity flew straight over the expensively-coiffed head of the presenter, and he escaped gratefully as the Minister for Overseas Development was led in towards the sofas alongside the Pub Landlord.

He was reassured by the producer that the cameras would be there to film him and his crew at the Henley Qualifiers that afternoon. Dave was told that it would be appreciated if he could perhaps pick up the odd duck or two after they finished, or if all else failed stroke a dog. The programme would try to track down a nice-looking one if it would help. Dave made his excuses and left, planning a painful death for Morley.

The promised camera indeed arrived, possibly the first time that the Henley qualifiers had been filmed by national television cameras. The crew had arrived some time before. For the first half an hour they had simply luxuriated in the scene, the large striped boat tents containing some of the world's most expensive boats, the numerous crews from around the globe, the magnificent sight of the boomed course stretching downstream towards the start at Temple Island. They had registered and weighed in, picking up the number to be put on their boat. They looked around for other older oarsmen, reckoning that a Princess Alice crew would stand out amongst the young fit men and women in the other events.

Morley spotted a familiar face from long ago. He pointed the man, maybe ten years older than them, adjusting some rigging in a blue and green New Haven Rowing Club sweatshirt. "Heidar. Isn't that Greg Houston?"

Heidar agreed. They went over to greet him. Now famous for coaching two US Olympic gold medal crews, he had been the coach of the Yale four that had narrowly beaten them in their 1982 semi-final. Still youthful, and with an open and optimistic air, he greeted them in a friendly manner. Once he had recalled who they were, he appeared utterly delighted.

"Guys, this is just great news. Wow! More than I could have hoped for. You know, I still have annual reunions with that four. Four great guys. Boy, did you give them one hell of a tough race. Still talk about that one. Well, maybe we'll do it again. Who knows? We heard about this Princess Alice event. Annual reunion last Fall, hell, we decided to go for it. I was glad to coach them again. John even moved back to Connecticutt. Not sure his wife was so pleased. Still, you know Henley as well as I do. When this place calls, it sure shouts."

Morley was genuinely delighted. "So, you're the New Haven crew that's seeded for the Princess Alice. That's great. I hope we get to race."

"So do I, Mr Morley – sorry, Peter. So do the boys. We'd heard you were here. Would love to meet up. Show you last time was no fluke. Heard you're going well. Second best English crew, so it seems. Those Leander guys must be favourites, then. You know, I reckon we could give them a hard time."

They nodded. He paused. "So you guys ain't seeded. Seems strange to me. Those Harvard old boys in that Cambridge boat – that's good old Cambridge Boat Club, Massachusetts, not your Cambridge University."

"Actually, we call ours Fen Tech. They prefer it," said Gareth.

"OK. Thanks for the tip. I'll know in future," replied the American coach. "Well, those Harvard guys used to be good, real good. But no form now, far as I can see. Dark horses maybe, but I don't see how they got seeded."

"Probably the same reason we have to qualify this afternoon," said Morley. "Not the most level playing field."

Houston looked shocked. "What. You guys have to qualify? That can't be so. Right?"

"I'm afraid it is so," said Morley. "Think we've upset Leander. Heyward's one of the Stewards now. We're worried that he might even try to rig the results – get us thrown out. We gave them a shock last time. Guess he's worried."

Houston looked concerned and serious. "Now that ain't good. I know that Heyward. Swaggering all over the place at the LA Olympics. Real asshole. Wasn't smiling so much when we whipped his sorry ass. From what I've seen of that jerk, I think you're right to worry. Tell you what, I'll get the guys to shout you on. And I'll time you myself. They won't dare to mess with the results under some good old US inspection. So long as you don't want us to track down any weapons of mass destruction, that is. Or ducks. Hear you guys have a real soft spot for them." He laughed, gave them the thumbs up, then set back to his rigging.

A nervous time waiting to boat, an air of seriousness settling over the boat tents. Almost gladiatorial odds. For most of the crews embarking now, their Henley would be over before the regatta started. They carried out the boat, tracked by the TV crew. As they started to boat, a large Alsation puppy and a cocker spaniel gambolled up the landing stage towards Dave. Morley looked and saw the producer giving the thumbs up to a Barbour clad woman, presumably the dog trainer. Dave, looking mortified, did the decent thing and patted them on the head. The spaniel, obviously trained, licked him on the nose as he got into the boat. The producer gave a cheery wave. "Thanks Dave. Thanks lads. We'll be off now."

Morley, suddenly anxious, spluttered "H – Hang on. What about filming the race?"

The producer smiled back. "Oh, don't worry. We've got all we need now. Great shot, that spaniel licking Dave. We've had a good look round. No ducks anywhere. Nothing else to shoot. Good luck then. Remember to watch on Monday. Bye."

They pushed off. Morley saw the cameraman dismantling his tripod. They set off for the start. They were at the mercy of the timekeepers. Only George and Vizzy's stopwatches, possibly the Americans', to straighten the record if dirty tricks were afoot.

CHAPTER 40

They had raced for their lives. Pace judgement important, easy to go off too fast and burn out. George shouting instructions as they raced past Temple Island at the start of the course. Morley held the rate back deliberately, but not by much. As well as his eyesight would allow, he looked at the stopwatch mounted on the stretcher between his feet. By the time they reached the Barrier, he thought they had pulled away on the crew behind. By Fawley, just over half way, this was definite. He'd then started to wind it up, and they were moving well. Gareth called to say they were gaining on the crew ahead. Morley risked a glance round as they passed the enclosures. The crew ahead were just finishing. They must have caught up at least thirty seconds.

They disembarked at the landing stage. They were relieved to be joined by George and Vizzy, who had timed them at 7 minutes 24 and calculated that they were 21 seconds faster than any of the other crews. Morley was grateful to see Greg Houston come into the boat tent and give the thumbs up. He said that his guys had watched them and timed them somewhere between 7-23 and 7-26.

"Miles ahead, you guys. What was all the fuss about? You looked mean too. Reckon it would be a good race. Hope to see you next week."

Morley frowned. "Greg, we've done our bit. But if they're going to screw us, they will. We'll see at 7.30."

Houston shook his head. "No way. No way would anyone try anything like that. This is Henley. You guys may not have played it straight in the 1760's, but you know how to run a straight regatta."

Morley hoped so. A nervous wait, then a sudden rush to the noticeboard by the regatta offices. None of them could get near for what seemed an age. Morley pushed for a gap, at last able to see the results sheets. "The bastards. The bastards. That's a disgrace."

The man next to him looked round, saw it was Morley. "Bloody hell, mate. You've been robbed. You must have taken twenty seconds off us. And we're through. I'd complain mate. Just so long as you don't take our place."

Morley saw the names of the three crews supposed to have qualified. They had beaten all of them that year, comfortably on each occasion. The times of the slower crews were given. Insultingly, they were not even in the first five, given a time of 7-58. He pulled away angrily to meet the others, standing with Vizzy at the edge of the throng. They all stood, head in hands. Gareth summed up the feelings of all of them. "The dirty, cowardly bastard."

They marched as a group to the offices. Morley barged the door open. A startled man in a blazer jumped as they came in.

"Where's Heyward?", Morley growled.

"What do you mean?" said the man, looking alarmed.

"You know just what I mean, you little shit," said Heidar, with uncharacteristically intemperate language. "You get him now, before we call the police."

The man looked round, eyes swivelling nervously. Morley pressed home the advantage. "You realise this is a police matter. We've got two lots of independent timing. You may not approve of what happened at Marlow, but if you lose Henley its reputation for straight dealing you'll kill it more effectively than a million twitchers armed with bloody bazookas. Now you get Heyward now, or I mean it – the police. And we can get GMTV back in ten minutes. If they sniff double-dealing at Henley, this place is buggered."

The man blinked, looking alarmed. "OK, OK. Hang on." He made a call. A tense wait, lasting for at least a quarter of an hour. Then the door opened and Heyward entered, dressed in Leander blazer and tie, looking calm and confident. He was accompanied by an older man, dressed expensively. He introduced himself as Richard Davenport, Chairman of the Stewards. "*Sir* Richard," chipped in Heyward with heavy emphasis. Davenport looked every inch the smooth patrician, smooth to a degree that Dave could never attain. White silk shirt and blue HRR tie, white hair dressed a little long. His suit a shade that spectral analysis would place between *battle* and *in*, with more than a hint of the vain. He looked round distastefully.

"We get this sort of nonsense every year. Sad. I know it's disappointing to lose out. But frankly, you should take your defeats with a bit more backbone. People get caught out every year by the quality here."

Heyward stood quietly, smirking in a manner that made Morley want to hit him. He looked across at George, attempted an ironic and insincere greeting. George stared him down, then cut in.

"Sir. We timed this. Not 7 minutes 58, it was 7-23. They nearly caught the crew ahead. Elizabethans were the fastest by over twenty seconds."

"Don't be ridiculous," said Heyward. "You had a bloody awful row. Saw you myself. You're just not up to it. Face the facts. You're second rate. Troublemakers. Not content with trying to sabotage Marlow Regatta." He directed a significant look at the chairman, who nodded almost imperceptibly.

"Do you deny that we went over at 7-23?" asked Morley. "Do you really deny that? Is this what Henley is about these days? A charter for cheats and grafters?"

"Dear boy," said the chairman condescendingly. "Even if there had been some unprecedented error, what could we do now? We've offered places to three crews. We can't go back on that now. Right or wrong, you'll just jolly well have to live with it. This regatta is bigger than you are. We can't make exceptions for every Tom, Dick and Harry who think they've had a raw deal."

Morley looked hopelessly at Heidar, Dave and Gareth. He didn't dare look at Vizzy, whose anger he could feel without turning round.

A loud voice came from behind. A loud American voice. Greg Houston's voice. "Then shame on you, Davenport. Shame on you, for colluding in this shabby scam that shames your regatta."

They looked round. Houston stood there with the four tall figures of the former Yale four, their conquerors in 1982. They nodded heads in greeting.

"We may be rowing as New Haven. But we're Yale, through and through. And Yale men do not like cheats and cheating, sir. If this is not sorted out fairly and properly, we pull out tonight. These guys were the fastest by twenty seconds or more, and I think you know that. And I can tell you, sir, if I pull our crew and say why, I will have the rest of the US entrants out by Sunday. I was national coach for five years, they'll listen. And then you can say goodbye to US crews for a generation. Why do you think we come over? We've got no end of good six lane regattas on our side of the pond. If you trade in your stock over one crooked Steward," He paused and looked meaningfully at Heyward. "you have written off a century of tradition. And if Henley loses tradition? Well it's lost the whole damn shooting match."

Davenport looked calm. He was betrayed by pupillary dilatation and slight sweating. He gathered himself. "Mr Houston. You leave us in a position of some difficulty. It would be, hmm, deeply regrettable if you were to pull out. I cannot accept that we did make an error of timing. But, um, if we, um, did – what do you suggest we can do? We can't unselect the crews who got through. We can't have a knockout with seventeen crews."

"Yes you can, sir," ventured the tallest of the New Haven crew. "We would be honoured to race these guys again. Revisit the best race we ever had at Henley. Start of play on Thursday. Winner goes on to the first round proper later the same day. We think that's fair play – the Yale way."

Davenport blinked, shrugged and finally nodded. Heyward looked uncomfortable and unhappy. Morley turned round in gratitude. Greg Houston smiled, patting him on the back.

"Keep your thanks, young Peter. You may not be so grateful when you see what my boys do to you next Thursday. But for now it's Friday. We've all had one hell of a day. I guess the least you boys can do is join us at the Angel on the Bridge for one of your disgustingly warm British beers. Sad to relate, we've developed a taste for your Brakspear's. I guess that's what you guys call going native."

CHAPTER 41

At last, they lined up on the stakeboats at Henley Royal Regatta, the first time in a quarter of a century. Their opposition, now friends, but steely and implacable in a boat. Mutual respect. A cordial shaking of hands before boating, then eyes fixed on the task in hand. No quarter to be asked or granted. Indeed no quarter wanted. The high seriousness of sport. The privilege of competing with worthy opponents. The prize desperately wanted by all.

Vizzy stood at the start, remarkably accompanied by both his younger brothers. Gwen and Thomas were sitting proudly in the Umpire's launch. Greg was standing by the judges' tent with George, two of the few people in the Stewards' Enclosure so early in the day. The first race of Henley Royal Regatta. It was only 8.25 am. Before 8.33, one crew's regatta would be over.

Both crews started strongly, rating similarly and almost level. Both went straight on station, the Umpire in the launch following them untroubled. By the Barrier, feet in it. Already Morley felt the pain and breathlessness. He thought of striding down the rate, then realised that New Haven had crept into a lead of a canvas. He could see their sternpost out of the corner of his eye. No latitude for striding down now, they'd be finished. By Fawley, loudly shouted on by his running sons, Morley was beginning to worry. Now more than half a length down, no sternpost visible, already well in painful oxygen debt. Time for decision. Call a burn now and risk blowing up by the enclosures? Keep it steady and risk being dropped? Heidar made the decision for him. For only the second time in twenty-five years,

Heidar made an urgent call to burn. New Haven must be moving further away. Now or never, then. He shouted for twenty, hitting the catches hard and jacking up the rate by an unsustainable amount. All followed, and within the twenty he now had their sternpost in his line of vision. He felt awful, unsure how he could make it to the finish, but knew he'd put New Haven under real pressure, pulled them from their comfort zone into the land of hypoxic anxiety where mistakes are made. Shouts from the sparsely populated enclosure. The mile post passed, their sternpost now a definite three or four feet behind, the mile and an eighth post, further gain of a few feet. The last desperate twenty strokes, attacking, attacking, closing. Out on their feet, rating higher than he imagined possible, they finally matched and moved up. Now he had their stroke, now level with their three man, now two, now the line. The blessed relief of the line.

All slumped in the boat, gasping. Tradition followed, Morley calling for three cheers for New Haven, gasped in unison. Gasped cheers for Elizabethans in turn. Disembarking on the landing stages. Hand shaking with honourable opposition, shoulder clasping. Greg Houston standing tall, congratulating with honest sincerity. "OK guys. Well done indeed. Never seen a Masters' crew come back like that. You guys are just too persistent for your own good. And I guess ours. So. It's one-all then. Both races way too close for comfort. Therefore, we need a decider. Don't we? Fancy the Head of the Housatonic? Our place, this October. You guys up for that?"

They were indeed. Friendships forged in competition have depth, and they last.

They lay recovering on the ground outside the boat tent. Six hours until the first round proper. Things easier this afternoon, their old friends the London-Thames composite. The teenagers emerged from the direction of the enclosures, wandering over in a group. Vizzy and Gwen were following behind. Morley could have sworn they had been holding hands when they turned the corner, although they were now at least a couple of feet apart as they approached their fathers.

A less welcome visitor. Bateman, blazer-clad, a sad non-competitor this year, crossed the grass towards them. He seemed more friendly than they remembered. "Well. Good result. Take it all back. By the way, like the boat. Anyway, guess you will have the chance to beat our four like you said. Not long 'til 10.40, we'll see then."

Morley smelled a rat. "Hang on. It's at 15.10. Look at the programme."

Bateman smiled. "Didn't you hear? Unscheduled programme change. Our guys were put on standby last night for an early start. Said they'd make a decision this morning. 10.40 it is, so we're told."

They got up wearily, went to the official tents. It was there, in black and white. Revised timetable. Elizabethans Boat Club versus London Rowing Club and Thames Rowing Club, Princess Alice Challenge Vase, 10.40. Heyward's crew's race time also shifted, oddly enough from 10.40 to 15.10. Nothing to be said. No avenues to explore. No room for complaint. "That bastard Bateman did us a favour," said a philosophical Gareth. "If he hadn't come over to gloat, we wouldn't have known about the time change. Disqualified. No way back."

"I guess so," replied Dave. "Trouble is, I'm completely buggered. How the hell can we turn round and boat again in less than half an hour? London-Thames aren't brilliant, but they're good enough. Shit. That sneaky bastard Heyward."

Heidar spoke out. Passionately. "Dave. Gareth. Peter. We want this. We want to show that Heyward what we can do. We cannot do that from the bloody Stewards' Enclosure. Now, come on. Stand tall. And win." The last words shouted.

It is at moments like this that good coaches come into their own. George took them aside, first individually, then as a group. Building up, cajoling, shaking shoulders, patting backs. Adrenaline induced. Fight or flight responses following, exhaustion ebbing.

And they boated with clenched-fist determination. And they raced with clenched-fist determination. And they won with open-handed jubilation. Won clearly. By three and a half lengths. And just three seconds slower than their first race.

CHAPTER 42

Henley Saturday. The first anniversary of their reunion. A lot more water under the bridge. Lives reassorted, like benignly shuffled cards. All somewhere better.

Morley walked towards Henley Bridge, his nostalgic trip up the High Street over. Race today a big one. Tough. The Cambridge Boat Club four, winning Harvard Crew of '85, justifying their seeding with imperious victory over Hollingworth Lake and a rather closer encounter with a tough Australian four. The Elizabethans' second round victory over the Nottingham four had been easier than their first day, though still close until Fawley. Their times had been similar to Cambridge, although both were several seconds slower than Leander in the other half of the draw.

Morale was good. Heidar had been concerned to see the large and unmistakable figure of Bennersley-Panton, clearly out on bail, marching up the towpath in the company of two uniformed officials, each carrying large nets. There were rumours in the boat tents that the Stewards had instituted a duck patrol, ordered to capture and destroy anything that looked remotely like a rare visiting species. No chances were being taken. The Regatta would go on.

As he crossed the bridge, he noticed a row of dark cars cross slowly in the direction of Remenham Hill. Clearly a funeral cortege. He was touched to see an elderly gentleman, dressed in immaculate blazer and flannels, sporting pink Leander cap and tie, standing tall and straight on the pavement as the cortege passed, almost like a guardsman on parade. All the other trippers seemed oblivious to the sight, ignoring the cortege. Morley thought the man quietly magnificent, very English, very decent. As he approached, he saw that the man looked quite affected by the sight, old eyes rheumy and red-rimmed. The cortege passed, and the elderly gentleman turned towards Leander.

Morley was moved by the scene. He approached the elderly man and spoke quietly. "Sir. May I say that I thought that was very fine. So few people show that sort of respect these days."

The elderly man turned towards him, clearly still emotional. "Dear boy. Thank you for saying so. Least I could do, y'know. She was a damn good wife." He sniffed, clearly close to tears, then rallied, straightening himself. "Anyway, must get on. Leander race in the Stewards' at 10.30."

Their race was the last before lunch, starting at 12.50. Ready to boat, fired up by the team talk from George, they had one problem. An old problem.

"Where the hell's Dave? Oh, God, as if I didn't know. I'll go and get him."

Morley went into the vast tented changing room, home to a long series of ancient shower heads delivering the coldest showers he had ever encountered, apparently sourced directly from the depths of a local lake. Behind these, there were about thirty toilet cubicles in a row, zones where the normal social niceties observed in communal toilets are placed on hold. No courtesy flushes, no finely-measured sphincter control, no quiet and surreptitious expulsions here. No. If you tend to extroversion in your defaecation, the Henley crew tent is the place for you. Morley remembered the frightening noises that had echoed round the tent during the 1981 regatta, enough to scare an impressionable child into life-long constipation, sounding like a fight to the death between two grizzly bears, followed by a loud contented sigh as if Brian Blessed had just enjoyed a lengthy massage with a very happy ending. A very large Russian had then emerged, lustily singing the Volga boating song off-key, pausing only to wash his hands before sallying forth to win his heat of the Grand Challenge Cup. That sort of thing tends to linger in the memory.

Morley shouted at the row of cubicles. "Dave! For God's sake! We'll miss the boating slot. We've got to go. Now!"

Dave emerged white-faced. "Oh God. I don't know what to do."

Morley was ruthless. "I'll get a champagne cork from the Stewards' Enclosure if necessary. Let's bloody go."

A very rushed boating. The time window narrowing when crews would be allowed up the course before the racing restarted. One Steward tried to stop them, thought better then said, "Just go. Fast. The Grand's coming down."

They had to race up the enclosures towards the start. Gareth called "Hurry". Morley knew what that meant. If they weren't clear of the course, there would be a head-on collision. The booms attendant had the gap opened, and they slid in, out of breath, no more than twenty seconds before two eights came racing past at high speed. Once the wash from the launch had settled they set off, again at half pressure. They finally made it past the start with just a few minutes left.

And then Dave groaned. "Sorry Peter. Emergency. Just got to go."

"For God's sake, Dave. Where?" barked Morley.

"The bank. Got to be the bank. Pull us over."

"Bloody hell, Dave," called Gareth. "This takes the bloody biscuit."

Less than five minutes until the start of the semi-final. The boat, pulled into the Berkshire bank. The three man, crouched desperately on the bank, lycra round ankles. Surprise for the passing family. Surprise in turn for the three man.

"Mr Hewitson! My goodness." The accent cut-glass, the speaker dressed in her Henley finery. "Darling, this is my gynaecologist, Mr Hewitson. Perhaps best not to shake hands. I must say, Mr Hewitson, that it's jolly nice to see the tables turned at last. It's usually me that has to squat with my legs apart. Anyway, best of luck with your race."

Dave, miserable, had to ask whether they possibly had any tissues with them. He was discomfited further to find that all they could offer were two ten pound notes. His patient's husband, splendid in striped college blazer but frowning in distaste, at last broke his silence. "Queen's head side down, man!! For God's sake!"

His patient turned for one last word as they reboated in haste. "Mr Hewitson. A suggestion. Dulcolax suppositories. That's what you prescribed for me. They're jolly good, you know. Physician heal thyself and all that. Good luck now."

They raced towards the start. The Umpire turned angrily to them. "Elizabethans! Where *have* you been? I should disqualify you! Ten seconds more and I would. I award you one false start. Think yourself lucky."

Morley turned round, fighting the jangled nerves, trying to regain composure. "OK, professional now. We've one false start. No one make a move until I do. Calm. Professional. Got that?"

Nods all round. A quick look at the opposition. Unusual to see a crew named Cambridge in Oxford blue. They looked calm, focused. Morley knew they'd try to jump the start, knowing that their opponents had a false start against them. He would do so himself in their circumstances.

Cambridge did, and got away with it. Elizabethans playing catch-up, and not going so well. Still nervy and disjointed. Clear water down by the end of the island. Morley heard the shouts from the twins, running alongside on the bank until they lagged behind. Even nearing Fawley, no real distance clawed back. He could feel the bounce of the boat as they started to hit the Cambridge puddles. He looked behind, saw that Gareth had them on station. Cambridge were pushing into their water, either by accident or design. Thankfully fair umpiring, white flag raised, shouting to Cambridge a warning to return to station. A good moment to attack, and he took it. The rhythm and timing in fact improved with the burst, and he could feel the bounce from the Cambridge puddles more strongly. While this was offputting, it also meant that they were closing on them. Another warning to Cambridge from the umpire, then a third. They were definitely closing, and he knew that the opposition would be getting anxious about a clash and disqualification. Risking all, he pushed the rate up again, seeing his first sight of their sternpost. Yet another warning from the umpire. "Cambridge, I will not warn you again! Move over!"

Desperate stuff. They were closing and Cambridge were at last returning to their station. He noticed that Gareth was now steering towards the centre of the course, deliberately testing the Cambridge steersman. The umpire was having none of it, quite rightly.

"Elizabethans! Elizabethans!! Move over! Back to your lane!"

Gareth moved promptly. He'd achieved his aim. Cambridge faltered, obviously pushed into overcompensation for their steering, now running too near to the booms. They got back on course but the damage was done. Elizabethans, now just a canvas down at the mile and an eighth post, were battle hardened by their year of racing. The Cambridge crew, outstanding oarsmen all, had not been seeking competition in the same way. Fighting the pain, just wishing to hold out for the finish, Morley took the rate up, seeing them gain inch by inch, stroke by stroke. Passing the Judges' Box by the finish they had nearly a length. They were through to their second Henley final in a quarter of a century.

CHAPTER 43

The picnic in Butler's Field on Henley Regatta Saturday. Bigger than last year. Better. Relaxed and happy. Success to be toasted. Hopeful libation for tomorrow's final. This year, George happily in attendance. And Gavin, engaging and likeable. Perfect foil for Margaux and she for him.

"Margaux, I tell you. That man is just the most stubborn thing on two legs. Such a nightmare. God knows what I see in him."

"No, Gavin. I cannot agree. He's just a beginner. If you think that your George is a stubborn old man, you should listen to that grey old Viking of mine. And such a baby when he thinks no one but me can see him. That broken nose! You would have thought he was the one who'd lost his little *couilles* two weeks ago. Ah, sorry Farqhuar, my brave little warrior."

Farqhuar, recovering well and oblivious to the comically large white plaster still covering most of his underbelly and rump, came snuffling up at the mention of his name. He had lost weight with all his traumas, but was eyeing the picnic in a manner suggesting that it was only a matter of time before that was remedied. Gladys detached herself from Gareth and Lynette to stroke him. She turned to Morley. "Now Peter. If only I'd known, I'd have brought Blodwyn. Mind you. The poor chap might feel some performance pressure, eh? Best to let those stitches heal first."

Morley demurred. "I don't suppose he'd be so interested now, poor chap."

Gladys shook her head. "Nonsense, Peter. Shows how little you know about dogs. Now, be a love. This wine is lovely, and

I've got an empty glass. A win to celebrate, and no better wine I can imagine. Lovely it is. Bottoms up, then. Here's to tomorrow. *Iechyd da*."

Helen came over and hugged her husband quietly. Probably only she and Margaux really understood what it meant for their partners. They determined to take an early trip home, get some rest for the big day tomorrow.

Alastair interrupted. "Before we go, we've got a presentation. Jane mentioned it's your birthday next week, Dave. We kids have clubbed together, and we've got you this."

Gwen, Thomas and David stood by him as he handed Dave a small parcel, beautifully giftwrapped in gold paper with red ribbon. Clearly Gwen's handiwork. Dave was touched. "Shall I save it or open it up now? OK now."

He slowly unwrapped it, revealing its contents. A large box of Dulcolax suppositories. Morley applauded, then spoke on behalf of his crew. "Tomorrow, Dave. Two. No, make it three. And if you don't know where they go, we'll bloody well put them in for you."

CHAPTER 44

Finals day. No Sunday morning more tense. The quiet walk to the crew tent. Recognised now by many oarsmen after their several rounds, receiving numerous wishes of good luck. Now changed and in the area in front of the boat tents, looking towards Henley Bridge and the Leander clubhouse – the Pink Palace as it was known – from which their opponents would embark. Already there were happy winners and devastated losers disembarking after the early finals. Morley recognised the emotions.

Families gathered around them, Farqhuar renewing acquaintance with Blodwyn in new found chastity of spirit. All four tense, Heidar particularly, grateful for the company of family and friends during the nervous final hour before boating. They were humbled to receive a visitation from the New Haven four and their charismatic coach. Greg was on top form, jesting with them, trying to work his magic on their behalf. Another man who knew instinctively how to get the best out of an individual.

Another, less predictable, visitor. The elderly man in the Leander blazer that he had met yesterday came towards them at his slow pace and sought out Morley.

"Sorry to bother you, sir." Morley was taken aback to be addressed in this way. "You were very kind to me yesterday. I wanted to thank you. Giles Handscombe." He put out his hand.

"Peter Morley." Hand out in return.

"You probably think I was a callous old man, coming here rather than to Margaret's funeral. Dear sweet girl that she was.

But my Margaret died years ago. All that was left was a shell. I visited her once a week when they took her to that nursing home – just couldn't cope with looking after her any more at home. You know she didn't recognise me once. In twelve years. The only people coming to that funeral were her blasted relatives, sniffing about for the chance of a legacy. Fat lot of good they were when she was alive and in need. I've said my goodbyes. And I'll do so again, in my own good time." He took out his handkerchief, sniffed.

"You know, my Margaret would have applauded me for doing that. The years we came here together. She used to watch me race – in those days I used to be Leander captain. Margaret saw me win my Olympic medal here in '48. Our first date, almost. Leander first eight. Ended up with the silver, not far behind the Americans. They were just too fast. And too well fed – no rationing for them, lucky devils. Would you believe it, we even had to provide our own kit. They did try to help - doubled the butter ration for us. Best they could do." He paused, lost in reminiscence, then gathered himself again.

"Anyway, won't take up more of your time. I really wanted to say this. And, mark you well, I've never said this before and hope never to have to again. But I hope you beat Leander today. That Heyward is a disgrace to the club. I've heard all about those shenanigans – I'm a Steward too. The oldest and most decrepit perhaps, but still a Steward. And someone who cares about this Regatta from the bottom of his heart."

Both were taken aback to see three of the Leander four coming towards them, Heyward an obvious absentee. They obviously held Mr Handscombe in deep respect. The two man, who had been unpleasantly cocky at Marlow, spoke on their behalf.

"Came to wish you good luck. Let you know we respect you. You've done well. Still plan on beating you, don't get me wrong." He looked towards the older man. "And we came to apologise to you for the way you've been treated. We heard last night. It wasn't right. Not what Henley's about. Not what

Leander's about. We just wanted you to know that this didn't come from the whole crew. Don't want to say any more, but the three of us felt we should come and shake hands before the race."

"That's good of you. Much appreciated." Morley meant it. He was pleased to see Handscombe nodding in approval as the Leander three went off to speak to his crewmates.

Handscombe put out his hand. "Must be going then. Good luck, Mr Morley." He shook hands, started to walk off. Morley, deeply affected by this good and honourable man, unsure what to say. Not usually a man for inspiration. Nevertheless, inspiration struck today. He ran after the elderly man.

"Mr Handscombe. Please forgive an impertinent question. If it's inappropriate in the circumstances, I apologise. I just wanted to ask you ... um, something on behalf of a friend." He blanked, then blurted "Are you the sort of chap who likes a nice pair of pins?"

Slowly, imperceptibly, a smile creased the corner of Giles Handscombe's mouth. He snorted, then threw his head back and laughed out loud. His face looked ten years younger. "Capital, Mr Morley. Capital. Yes indeed, but it's been rather a long time."

"And do you have any objection to Welsh accents?"

"Dear boy. Now we've moved this to the personal, I don't mind telling you that I had the most wonderful night of my life on VJ Day, with a rather racy young lady from the Rhondda. 'Fraid it was all downhill from then. Though of course Margaret did her best, poor dear."

"Sir, I hope that you wouldn't object if I introduced you to a good lady friend of mine. Name of Gladys Jenkinson. She's just there by that rather strange looking poodle. I think she would deeply appreciate it if you could show her some of the sights of the regatta."

At last, the moment of destiny. Icelandic Saga Holiday, resplendent crimson racing shell carried down to the landing pontoons amidst applause. Stopping for a second while Bernard anointed the bows with holy water, new and unusual go-fast tactics. Bernard smiled at Heidar. "I'll have to leave the lightning to your lot."

Heidar returned a tense smile, preoccupied. They continued to the water's edge, flipped up the boat and put it on the water. Vizzy acted as their boating assistant, taking shoes and surplus tops. He turned his head when Dave suddenly shouted "Oh, bloody hell. No."

Marching to the end of the pontoon came the unmistakable shape of Bennersley-Panton, wearing hunting Barbour over blazer, brandishing a large net on a pole. He stood and shook his fist at them.

"You bunch of bloody oiks. It's a disgrace they've let you go so far. No sense of tradition. What you did at Marlow was unforgiveable. And I'm not going to let you do that to Henley. The chaps and I found those bloody Harlequin ducks down at Remenham this morning. Managed to scare them off, before you get any fancy ideas. Did bag one though."

He withdrew a small fluffy object from his pocket. Heidar and Vizzy gasped.

"Just so you know what I think of you and your birds, Mr Twitcher. Banned from guns now, damn you. Well, sometimes a mallet is just as good."

He put the duckling on the ground if front of him, removed a tent peg mallet from his other pocket and bent over the defenceless bird, arm raised to strike. Vizzy was rooted to the spot in horror.

Suddenly a dark flash and a loud howl. Bennersley-Panton turning side to side, shrieking to the heavens, with a fat Labrador firmly attached by its clenched jaws to his buttocks, hanging on tight whatever movements he made, comical white bandage flashing first one way, then the other.

Vizzy dashed, rescuing the small bird and taking in back to the landing stage. A crowd gathered, unsure what to do. Greg Houston was first to venture an opinion. "We ought to help this guy. What he was going to do to that bird was sure not nice, but back home we've a tradition of helping folks in need."

Giles Handscombe waved dismissively. "Nonsense, dear boy. You are American. Your country hasn't got traditions yet. Just habits. Anyway, that brute deserves all he gets."

Vizzy looked at the four, all shocked in their own way by the scene. "Good luck, Dad. Good luck everyone."

He looked closer at Heidar, seeing something in his eyes. "You saw her again last night, didn't you?"

CHAPTER 45

There is no more intense and serious moment for an oarsman. The final of a regatta that means the world to you. Olympics. World Championships. Henley. The very peak of your season, possibly the culmination of several years. The difference between victory and defeat something that will last a lifetime. The nerves, building up all day, inhibiting appetite, pervading all sensation. That feeling again.

Morley nervously removed his T-shirt, stuffing it into the well behind his foot stretcher. He looked over towards Leander. No mocking calls from them now. Still favourites. Four seconds quicker than Elizabethans in their semi-final against Trident, the strong South Africans pushing them to a length and a quarter. More importantly, six seconds quicker to the first mark at the Barrier. Morley knew that they might not be able to rely on the same scrupulous umpiring they had in the semi-final. Heyward had shown his ability to manipulate the regatta on enough occasions.

They had arrived in good time today. They were in better shape than yesterday. He knew that if they could keep in touch during the first half, they had the strength to come through. He had a hunch that Heyward knew that too. So, now, the test. He had wished good luck to all three crew mates, looking each in the eye as he turned. Each had met his gaze, Heidar with unsettling intensity. Not the gazes of middle-aged men, accustomed to ironic detachment in the face of life's buffets. Young men's looks. No irony. No self-protection. No excuses.

A moment of significance, long to be remembered whatever the outcome. They sat forward on the start, waiting for the

Umpire to begin his litanic countdown to the off. He could see the nervous movements of the Leander bowman to his right, could feel the jiggling of the boat as one of his own crew members did the same. No devout Christian, he nevertheless uttered a quiet prayer, hoping that all spiritual as well as physical bases were now covered. Hopefully Heidar could invoke Thor as well. Deep breathing, concentrating. No shallow nervous gasps. Prepare for the battle in hand.

Temple Island, a place of quiet magic. There are river deities here. You can feel this if you sit here quietly for long enough. In his nervously heightened state of awareness, Morley took in the details of the scene, one he suspected he might not see again. Difficult to see this consuming folie a quatre becoming steady backdrop to middle years, quixotic quest mellowing to quaint hobby, their chances diminishing year by year as they aged and younger men became eligible. No Harlequin ducks that he could see. He noticed some moorhens darting near the bank of Temple Island, three white doves flying to land near a couple of unusually large ravens standing still by the trees, and a magpie on the Berkshire bank, strutting around with characteristic perky yet somehow combative gait. He warded off evil with a "Hello Mr Magpie" under his breath. He had always disliked seeing them singly since a child, the old country saying fixed in his mind since its use in a children's television programme. *One for sorrow, two for joy.* No second one to be seen. He hoped the sorrow would be Leander's.

The umpire lifted his megaphone. "Come forward."

Final small shuffles. Blades flat on the water. Last small shudder felt from movement behind.

"Leander, ready?"

Blades squared. Hand raised by their bowman, calling "No!" One tiny touch taken by his blade. Hand down again. Old rower's trick. More to unsettle the opposition than alter direction.

Umpire calmly repeats. "Leander, ready?"

No hands raised this time.

"Elizabethans, ready?"

No call from Gareth at bow. Blades buried. Still, quiet, intense moments pass.

"Both crews. Get .. Ready!"

Long hold, urge to jump fought.

"Go!"

Flag sweeps down. Both crews hit their short first stroke. Henley final under way.

As good a start as they have ever done. Level after ten strokes. Level after twenty, then Leander moving up slightly. Noise from the bank ignored. Call of *Stride* from Gareth. Morley deliberately settled the rate, concentrating on length and smooth powerful finishes. Settling well. Their best racing, best rhythm. Somehow calm, although Leander now moving up on them, their sternpost dipping rhythmically in Morley's peripheral vision. Heyward calling for twenty – surely too early. Barrier passed, Leander moved up, but still less than a length. Never so close before at this stage.

No change during another intense minute. Still in control, oxygen debt mounting but brain still in charge. No calls from Gareth, steering fine, rhythm fine. Approaching Fawley Lock, classic time for mid-race burst. No call from Morley, all pre-planned. Wait for Gareth. Spot on timed call – simply "Now !" They went together, the twenty big strokes, the twenty fast strokes, the overdraft extended, the twenty strokes that may break an opponent. He heard Heyward call again. They were closing. Leander sternpost now level with his eye, now six feet behind. This was their moment. They were coming through to take the lead against a crew they'd never led. Surely. Yet somehow Leander hold on, feet ahead.

Pain now intense, lungs and muscles screaming protest, willpower battling weasel thoughts of self-preservation, capitulation. Barrage of noise from the banks to their right, increasing as they approached the enclosures. Heyward calls again, big decisive effort by Leander. Sternpost again moving out of peripheral vision. Past the mile and an eighth mark, Leander now moving away stroke by stroke, must be half a length. Nothing can be done, now. Battle lost. Rhythm beginning to crumble. Willpower spent. No way back now against Olympic medalists.

A roar. Inarticulate. Feral. Atavistic, ancient battle call. A roar from Heidar. And power. Such power. And yet more. Galvanising. Influence spreading virally, men transported to places few have been. The rate driven up. And up. The rudder tweaked, Gareth having to invoke physics to hold course against Heidar's might. Another roar from Heidar, his puddle larger than Morley had ever seen, ruptured water spun and frothing in shocked protest. The rate driven up again. The Leander sternpost now in sight, now level. Now half their canvas gained. Surely too late: ten strokes left, no more. Intense noise from the bank, drowned by third, awesome, terrible, yell of war from Heidar. Rate pushed up, impossibly up. Morley now level with Heyward, now three, now two, now bowman. And the line.

Boat lurches. Push to hold level with blades, little consciousness left even to do this. Beyond exhaustion, vision faded, lying, some hunched forwards, some lying back. Both crews. No differentiation in pain yet. No punching of the air. No showboating. No roars of triumph. Silent. Spent. Applause from the Enclosure still loud. Morley vaguely aware of the result announcement, seeing four wives jump as one within the Umpire's launch. No strength yet to acknowledge Leander, who had fought like tigers. Pat on back from Dave. He turned, grasped his hand and held it. Nothing yet from Heidar or Gareth, lying flat on their backs in the boat.

Twenty, thirty seconds, slight easing. Acknowledgement to Leander, exhausted reply received. Movement from Gareth's blade, signs of sitting up. Just one long drawn-out "Shit!" to signal his return and encapsulate feelings. Morley ending his journey to the Princess Alice as he had begun it, the "Fuck!" this time long, drawn-out and decrescendo.

Heidar was still struggling, exhausted by his efforts. Superhuman. Morley had rowed for many years, but had never seen such an effort. Unbelievable, extraordinary, berserk.

Dave was worried first. Heidar still in difficulties, grey from the extreme exertion. Signalled to the safety boat, who came over. Oxygen mask to his face, Heidar was lifted from the boat into their launch and taken quickly to the St John's Ambulance tent ashore. They paddled in as best they could, just the stern pair, and were pulled onto the landing stage by the jubilant twins. George and Vizzy were already by the St John's tent. Morley was relieved to see a thumbs up from George. They were ashore. Their wives running towards them after disembarking. They were champions. Henley medal winners.

CHAPTER 46

The last ice-cold shower of the week, scalp muscles contracting in protest as shampoo rinsed. A deep complex feeling of, what? Joy, satisfaction, vindication, quiet sorrow that the saga was over, their course complete. Turning towards Dave, enduring his own icy challenge in the shower to his left, putting thumbs up. Smile in return. Gareth singing loudly in Welsh to his right. The prizegiving to come.

Morley hoped that Heidar would be back in time. Health and Safety regulations. More than the St John's ambulancemen's jobs were worth to spare him the checkup in hospital, his pulse still high after half an hour. Margaux upset, swearing when not allowed in the ambulance. Helen calming her, offering to drive her in the Volvo as Heidar had insisted on the Harley for Finals day. Vizzy's pockets raided once more, calming roll-ups needed. Vizzy wanted to come along, but was dissuaded by Heidar. "You don't want to miss your Dad's big moment. They could spend hours messing around in the hospital. I don't need a presentation ceremony. I think your Dad does. And I think he'd like you there, just in case your Mum's not back."

The walk to the Stewards' Enclosure now the walk of champions. Recognised by other oarsmen, genuine warm congratulation. Less stressful trip to the Regatta offices, asking to be late in the prizegiving, giving Heidar as much time as possible. A rather better reception. And an odd request.

"Her Majesty asks whether you might bring your dog if he's with you."

Morley was taken aback. He didn't know that the Queen would be presenting the prizes this year. Usually only jubilee years and other special occasions. He found it somehow reassuring to think that she might read the News of the World. He realized that he'd forgotten about Farquhar, last seen embedded in a High Court judge's rump. Vizzy reassured him. "David's got him. Didn't you see them on the towpath? We thought it better that he lay low for a while away from here. Didn't want that psycho to get his gun again."

And so Farquhar had the unique distinction of being the first non-working dog to be admitted to the Stewards' Enclosure. White bandage catching the late afternoon sun as his tail wagged, he was fussed and petted by a number of unusually well dressed News of the World readers. There also seemed to be a lot of GMTV watchers, and Dave endured celebrity rather greater than the average Henley winner.

They congregated near the Pimm's tent for their final celebratory drink. Dave went to get the round in. Morley was delighted to see that Gladys was still escorted by Giles Handscombe, talking animatedly to Gareth and Lynette. He got a big hug as he approached and bent down to receive a kiss on the cheek. She whispered in his ear. "Well, Peter. You did it. Everything. You won your cup. Helped my boy get his new job. I cannot thank you enough for that. A year ago, he was broken. A man staring defeat in the face. Now he's not so flexible. Excuse my awful joke, Peter. Now you know where he gets it from. The life we had – well, if you didn't find a way to laugh then you'd cry. And, Peter. You did it. You got me — a nice gentleman. A very nice gentleman. Who has always wanted to see Australia. Haven't you Giles dear?" Mr Handscombe nodded, then bowed more formally towards Morley, nodding his own quiet understated thanks. No doubt, at least ten years younger. Gladys was full of the joys of the day. "And an Olympic silver medalist. I expect nothing less of my men."

Gareth raised his eyes and smiled. "And how many other Olympic silver medalists have you known, Mum?"

She looked back at him with a hint of annoyance. "Just the one, Gareth. Just the one. Eifor. Your father. The four by one hundred metres relay. Wembley Stadium, 1948. Three years before we married. Didn't like to shout about things, did Eifor. Sold his medal when you were little. Wanted to help the Aberfan fund. I was prouder of him that day than when he won the damn thing."

A toast all round. To Heidar. Dave said it all. "Never known anything like that. If anyone deserves that medal it's him. Where he found that energy. Just amazing. I was completely buggered. Had it. Now it looks like he'll be late."

It did. Five to six. Time to gather near the presentation stand. Morley felt strangely torn. He'd waited over half his life for this moment. But no Heidar. And no Helen. He had wanted to share the moment with her. His victory he knew owed to her as much as his crew mates. He was pleased at least to have his sons with him. And proud of them, deeply proud. They had grown up in this last year. So had he.

The winning crews called up one by one after the short well-chosen speech by Her Majesty. The National Anthem had been played, the Band of the Royal Marines in attendance today. The standing to attention almost universal, even Vizzy swept up by the moment and standing like a guardsman, albeit a rather long haired guardsman with somewhat more stubble than would pass muster even in lesser regiments.

The vast Canadians came back down the carpeted steps with their prize of the Grand Challenge Cup, the greatest award that Henley had to offer, their strokeman lifting the large heavy trophy above his head with an ease that few normal mortals might show. And at last, after all other prizes had been awarded, they were called by the Chairman.

"And finally, the Princess Alice Vase for men's veteran coxless fours – Elizabethans Boat Club, London." The applause was the loudest of the entire ceremony.

Four walked up to receive the trophy, three winning oarsmen and a fat labrador with a large white bandage containing rather less than he might ideally have liked.

Her Majesty, as always, was gracious. And, as always, rather better informed than might be imagined.

"Mr Morley. I am very pleased to meet you. And your crew. I always find it rather nice when the teams named after me win. I'm very sorry that your Mr Kjartansson is indisposed. I saw your race. Forgive me for pointing out that he was perhaps the outstanding sportsman. Please do pass on my congratulations to him. Thank you also for bringing your famous dog. Fine fellow by the look of him. A bit fat perhaps, but that's not always a bad thing. It didn't seem to hold dear Mr Churchill back. As you know, I am rather fond of dogs. Perhaps not as fond as Mr Hewitson? Please forgive me, Mr Hewitson. I think that you've been rather unfairly treated by the media."

"Thank you, your Majesty," said Dave, making a small bow.

"I rather like GMTV, you know. I know one is expected to listen to the Today programme. I leave that to my assistants, for the most part. For the dog lover, I think there's no substitute for GMTV. The number of clever chihuaha's that I've seen over the years. Such devoted trainers, I think, such patience to teach them those tricks. Very decent people, I have no doubt, but they might just struggle with some of the questioning they would get from Mr Humphrys on Radio 4."

She paused, just as she was about to distribute the medals. "Please excuse me asking, Mr Morley. I hear your dog's injury was unfortunate. Most unfortunate. Can I perhaps ask whether he was the sort of dog who would, how can I put this, notice the loss?"

"I wouldn't have thought so a year ago, your Majesty," said Morley. "But since then, I think he might indeed have some cause for regret."

"I always think that a good quality in a male dog, I have to say. I have had a great number over the years. I still miss my dear sweet Bertie. He used to be particularly fond of Mrs Thatcher, used to look forward to our weekly meetings immensely. After we'd been served our tea, dear Bertie always liked to pleasure himself against her leg. We monarchs no longer have absolute power. My husband maintains that's rather a pity, and some days I'm rather tempted to agree with him. But moments such as that do make it all seem worthwhile."

And so the Elizabethans and their faithful dog descended from the podium to ringing applause. There were prolonged hugs all around. Morley was honoured to receive a firm handshake from Giles Handscombe, and pleased that three of the Leander four were gracious enough in defeat to give their congratulations. He hugged the twins, hugged Gwen and Thomas. He was delighted to see that the Stewards had allowed Lucy and Ben to enter the hallowed sanctum, against the rules, to see their father pick up his precious medal.

Morley noticed that Vizzy was not present to share their moment. He wondered about this for a moment, then saw the explanation. A clearly distressed Vizzy was running towards them at some speed, pursued by one of the more menacing attendants. He arrived panting, clutching his mobile phone by his ear. Morley tried to calm the situation, asking the attendant to hang on while he sorted things out. Vizzy, tears running down his cheeks and breathless, tried to explain.

"Dad. It's Mum. From the Hospital. It's Heidar. Odin took him."

Morley still didn't get it.

"Vizzy, speak in English. What do you mean, Odin took him?"

"Dad, just listen. Please. Heidar's dead."

Morley froze. Numbed and immobile, he could hear gasps from the others around him.

Vizzy continued, speaking rapidly and urgently. "His heart just stopped. Suddenly. Mum was there with Margaux. He was speaking, Mum says smiling. Suddenly slumped, the alarm went off. Doctors came running. Mum says they're still trying in the emergency room, but it's forty minutes now. They won't let Margaux back in. It's Odin, don't you get it? Heidar knew. I'm sure he knew. I should have guessed when I saw his face this morning."

CHAPTER 47

The day they had been dreading had started badly. Vizzy, regressed in behaviour since the weekend, in deep trouble. Morley had found the Volvo parked three spaces down from where he had left it.

"I don't care how bloody upset you are, Vizzy. That was bloody dangerous. You've only had four lessons and you're still a bloody menace on the road. I'm sorry. That's you grounded for a month. You could have bloody well killed someone."

Vizzy sat, mute and miserable, eyes dark rimmed from grief and tiredness. It got worse. A shriek from Helen upstairs. "Where the hell's my bloody makeup? Which of you kids has taken it? Was that you Vizzy? Vizzy!! Not even Emo's need that much!"

She calmed down when she realised that little Ben was standing behind her, open-mouthed to hear her shriek like that. They had a full house. Gwen and Thomas had come to stay, taking the pressure off her father when Lynette had to be admitted two days ago with bleeding, possibly brought on by the shock. So far things were stable, and she hoped to be allowed out for the funeral this morning. Lucy and Ben had heard of the sleepover and campaigned against their unfair exclusion. Helen felt in the circumstances that it would probably be helpful for the children to be together and had agreed. All had appeared reasonably well, and they had been allowed their choice of takeaway pizza or Chinese last night. Helen had been preparing for this afternoon's reception and did not want extra cooking or washing up. Both she and Peter had been glad to offer to hold the reception at their house, wanting to take pressure off Margaux.

The doorbell rang, Dave and Jane arriving to help the little ones dress, both already in black, their eyes as red rimmed as Morley and Helen. Apart from little Ben, excited to be in the Morleys' house with the big ones, the other kids seemed tired and grumpy. All were finally dressed, and eleven black-coated humans and one black-coated dog trooped out to the two cars in good time. Fights broke out between the children for the honour of sitting with Farqhuar in the back of the Volvo estate, Ben being allowed to win. He took up his special position in the rear facing seat with such obvious pleasure that no one begrudged him this.

Funerals are awful things. For a young healthy person there is an added sense of bleak unfairness. Bernard did his best, welcoming them at the rather ornate entrance to Sacre-Coeur de Londres, a special greeting to all those he now knew. Gareth and a rather pale Lynette arrived about five minutes before the start, Lynette giving reassuring nods to the other girls. Margaux, striking and tragic in black with traditional French veil, walked down the aisle to hug her.

The service was dignified, restrained. It felt very French. The stained glass windows were beautiful in the summer light. There was an air of calm Christian peace. All were tight lipped. Quiet tears. Grief rending but somehow contained.

On behalf of the crew, Morley read the words from Bishop Brent, Anglican Bishop of the Philippines. Words they had found the most apt and apposite for such a man as Heidar. Words that encapsulated their hopes and feelings. He read them well.

"What is dying? by Charles Henry Brent

I am standing on the sea shore
A ship at my side spreads her white sails to the morning breeze and
  starts for the blue ocean
She is an object of some beauty and I stand and watch her
Until at last she fades on the horizon

Then someone at my side says
"She is gone"

Gone where?
Gone from my sight – that is all
She is just as large in the masts, hull and spars
as she was when she left my side
The diminished size and total loss of sight is in me, not in her

And just at the moment when someone at my side says
"She is gone"
There are others who are watching her come over their horizon
And other voices take up a glad shout:
"There she comes."

And that is dying.
An horizon and just the limit of our sight.

Lift us up, Oh Lord, that we may see further."

And Morley returned to his pew amidst deep silence.

Bernard was eloquent and in his own way magnificent. He did not skirt the issue of Heidar's faith in his humane and well judged address. He described his many conversations about faith and spirituality with Heidar. "He was a man of deeper spirituality than many regular churchgoers. A man who had a deep sense of right and wrong. A truly moral man. While he may not have chosen a Catholic, indeed Christian, funeral service, I am sure that he would have been very pleased to support Margaux, his devoted and devout life companion..." He paused, himself fighting back the emotion of the moment. "To support Margaux in this choice of his final oration, and his burial in these hallowed grounds where so many of her countrymen lie in the peace of our Good Lord, Jesus Christ. And so I ask you to rise with me and to sing our final hymn before we commit his earthly remains to their final resting place – a place that I hope you will

take the time from your busy lives to visit. You will always find
a welcome here at Sacre-Coeur de Londres. "

After the last strains of the hymn had died, Morley, Dave,
Gareth, David, Alastair and Vizzy carried his coffin on their
shoulders, strange symmetry with a cold dark walk carrying a
fractured boat half a year ago. Similar feelings of intense misery
and loss, awareness of mortality.

As the coffin was interred and Bernard intoned the words of
comfort and commitment, Morley felt strangely detached,
unmoved by the ceremony. Not comforted as he should be,
despite the hallowed words. He knew Heidar well, knew his
complex northern ways as well as anyone. He did not sense
Heidar here. Perhaps already gone.

The drive back to the house in silence. All arrived together.
Margaux, in the second car with Bernard, summed up the
mood that all of them felt. "God. I need a drink."

Vizzy already had a cigarette rolled for her.

Another landmark reprised. Lunch at the Morleys. A world
apart in mood. More people. Sula, intense and tightly coiled.
Accepting from Vizzy her first cigarette in two decades, already
on her second gin and tonic. Gladys, glass of red in hand standing by ramrod-straight Giles, their first joint engagement a sad
one. Margaux, tight-faced and brittle. Dave, Gareth and
Morley exchanging glances. George and Gavin looking shell-
shocked. A red-eyed George turned down with a shake of his
head Margaux's offer of Heidar's Henley medal. Margaux
nodded, then spoke to the room.

"I can't say much. Can't say much at all. Please excuse me.
I need to keep this brief. I want to thank you all. Peter, Dave
and Gareth, thank you for taking Heidar on his last great journey. I mean that. It meant the world to him. Life and death.
Literally. For a small medal. Oh, I know that it was more than
that. But that medal symbolises this quest and venture, and
symbolises Heidar. I don't want it. I have my memories, my
pride in his many achievements. I think I might come to hate
that piece of metal. Think it stole my man from me. That

wouldn't be fair on him, on you, on what you all did. I have asked George to take it, and he won't. I don't think that Farqhuar would appreciate it, though he probably lost more than anyone in your quest. So I have decided. I would like to do something that I believe that Heidar would wish. I would like to give Heidar's medal to someone who would honour it, and will always honour him. To someone I hope would have been a friend to Haraldur if life had turned out less mean and bitter for him. To Vizzy."

Vizzy's eyes out on stalks. Lost for words again. Margaux's special ability to ablate Vizzy's powers of speech. Overflowing, beyond overflowing, with emotions of a richness and complexity that he could scarcely comprehend and only just endure, Vizzy took Heidar's precious Henley medal and clutched it to his chest.

The red wine exerted its own magic. People who had thought earlier that they might never have appetite again, now queuing for casserole or chilli, salad, poignant summer pudding. Little Ben asking if they had any ice cream. Helen calling her husband.

"Darling, can you get some of the Ben and Jerry's for the little ones. I've put them in the chest freezer in the cellar. Bottom rack."

Ben looked a little alarmed. "But that's where Heidar is."

Conversation stopped. Margaux smiled, saved the moment.

"Oh the poor dear boy. He's confused by it all." She saw that Ben was near to tears, mortified. "Darling, give me a hug."

Ben went off with Morley, glad to escape the scene of his shame. He returned at some speed thirty seconds later, shouting at the top of his voice. "See! I told you so! No-one would believe me!"

Morley, one step behind. Purple faced. Wall of Death moment in polite company, his voice echoing round the room and startling Farqhuar.

"Will one of you bloody kids tell me what the fuck is going on?!"

CHAPTER 48

Vizzy shook the sleeping figure. "Alastair, wake up. It's time."

David was already out of bed. He looked at Vizzy. "Did she come back tonight?"

Vizzy nodded, then headed quietly downstairs. Gwen and Thomas came quietly down the stairs in his wake. Probably no need for such quiet. Helen and Peter had ploughed through most of the second bottle by bedtime, steeling themselves for next day's funereal ordeal.

Next day was already here, albeit in very early form. They gathered by the door, Vizzy in the lead. Thomas was concerned, reluctant. "Are you sure we have to do this? Won't we get into trouble?"

Vizzy looked round at them. "You all knew Heidar. Knew what he believed in. What he wanted. A Christian service would be meaningless for him. I didn't know what we should do. Then Sígrun came to my dreams. Just as Heidar had described. Long dark hair. A dark cloak, really thick material – it looked old. Ancient. Shiny armour underneath. You could see it when she moved. And her face. Amazing. Really beautiful. But fierce. I wouldn't want to be on the wrong side of her. And she's told me what we must do. So first we've got to rescue him. Either that or dig up the grave. It's better if we do it this way, so they'll have to cancel the funeral. Then he can have his proper one. Are you all agreed?"

Quiet thoughtfulness, then nodding from all. They moved towards the door. Suddenly, a voice behind them, startling them all. "Where on earth are you lot going at this time of night?"

Gwen answered first. "Lucy. Go back to bed. It's very late."

Lucy was unimpressed. "No I'm not. You're going to get Heidar, aren't you. I heard you say."

"Then you shouldn't listen behind doors," said outraged Vizzy.

"How else can a kid my age find out anything?" asked Lucy reasonably.

"Well, you've got to go back to bed. This is no business for seven-year-olds." Stern Vizzy, the leader.

"I'm not going, so. Not! Anyway, I'm nearly eight. So I'm coming with you. And if I can't, I'll wake your Mummy and Daddy up. It's not fair. You big kids get all the fun."

"Lucy, this isn't going to be fun. We're going to get a dead body," said Alastair, doing his best to dissuade her.

"I know. It's just like Scooby-Doo. Exciting! I'm not going to miss it. I just need to get my outside clothes. And if I find you gone..." She soundlessly mimed a scream, shaking her hands over her head. Her face was set in determined mould.

Gwen looked at Vizzy, shrugged and raised her eyes.

Vizzy grunted. "Well, don't blame me if you have night-mares for a month."

"She won't be the only one," said a rather frightened look-ing Thomas.

David snorted. "And that's just Vizzy's driving."

The Volvo started the first time. Lucy had insisted on sitting in the middle seat behind Vizzy and Gwen in the front, so Thomas was relegated to the rear-facing child seat in the back. Vizzy was rather taken aback by driving at night, taking a while to master beam dipping and getting flashed by a number of cars. He missed several gear changes, inducing groans from his brothers. He resisted their calls to jump red lights. Gwen supported him. "For God's sake, you two. We do not need to get stopped by the police. Think about it, dur-brains."

The small Wimbledon side street found, the car parked inexpertly nearby. No space immediately by Harrison's, the windows of the small premises bearing the proud label of

Family Undertakers. The twins provided the expertise in casing the joint.

"Thank God. No alarm," said relieved Alastair.

Thomas was not so sure. "They may have infra-red beams. Like in Mission Impossible 2."

David snorted in amusement. "Sure. And trained Ninja assassins if you get through the door."

Thomas looked thoroughly frightened, eyes wide in the dim reflected glow of the distant streetlight. Gwen came to the rescue. "Don't be silly. There's nothing like that. And don't spook the younger ones. It's scary enough as it is."

"It's not scary," said Lucy. "It's fun. Like being in a story."

Thomas was still uncertain. "But why do we have to do this? Can't he just be buried like anyone else?"

Vizzy was implacable. "No. He can't be. Sigrun told me what we must do. He needs us to help him finish his journey. Come on, Alastair. How do we get in? You're the expert aren't you?"

"It's a bit more difficult than the sweetshop door at school, Vizzy. Hadn't expected that," said a flustered Alastair.

"Look," said Lucy. "A tiny window. Up there. I could get through that."

"Don't be silly," said Gwen. "How are you going to find your way through a strange place full of dead bodies?"

They were stuck. All avenues explored. Vizzy looked up at the small window. Gwen spotted him. "No! Vizzy. No way!!"

"But I want to go," said a determined Lucy.

"I think that Sígrun would protect her," said hopeful, desperate Vizzy.

"And if she gets stuck in there, we can just call the police" nodded David sagely.

"The police?!" Wide eyed Thomas out of his depth.

"Yeah. Don't worry. Easy after the first time," said Alastair. Seeing Gwen's look he found need of a rider. "But never since we found God, honestly Gwen. Hardly touched dope at all, have we David?"

So brave and fearless Lucy was hoisted up on Alastair's shoulders, Alastair's feet in turn on Vizzy's. A small call of "It's fine, it's a toilet," then worrying silence. Finally, shuffles from behind the door. Scratching as several keys were tried. Then at last, triumphant Lucy found the right key. Still no joy when the door was pushed. Vizzy looked at the door.

"There's a second one, Lucy. Probably long. Big key."

Finally, more scratching from within and the door at last opened. Beaming Lucy hugged by all. A strange place. Stranger in the thin light from the Morleys' kitchen torch. A desk, small office computer in the front office. Dark furnishings. Small well-furnished room to the side. "That's where I went with Dad," said Vizzy. Margaux had been grateful for Morley's help with arrangements. The small door at the back of the room had been hidden by a pair of large crimson curtains by day, now pulled back. This door too was locked, the key eventually tracked down in one of the desk drawers. Inside, a number of coffins, mostly large. One tiny one, spotted by Vizzy. "Like Haraldur," he said, a catch in the throat. Gwen and Thomas made involuntary Signs of the Cross, the twins not especially swift to follow them.

"We're looking for big fridge cabinets, like filing cabinets," said Vizzy. "At least that's how it is in the X-Files."

Through another door at the end of the room. A dark space, without windows. Safe to switch on the light. Long strip lights flickered into life, resulting in a harsh unflattering glare. A row of five grey-doored cabinets lay at the end. "Here goes then," said David. He pulled a drawer open. "Oh, that's gross. She must be ninety."

Thomas was standing back, looking grey. Alastair an unlikely companion in the unwilling rearguard. Vizzy and Gwen determined but unhappy, close behind David and Lucy at the front, unmoved and interested. They finally found Heidar's body in the fourth of five cabinets. "Oh God," said Vizzy. "What have they done to him?"

David was steely. "Vizzy, he's had an autopsy. What the hell did you expect when a guy below fifty keels over like that?"

"But we can't take him with all these cuts on him. That stitching looks horrible."

Gwen's turn for determination. "Vizzy. We've got a task. Just get on with it. We'll deal with the cosmetic stuff later. Your Mum will have make-up."

"Make-up!" squeaked thrilled Lucy, on the night of her life.

Poor Heidar, his mortal remains propped between the shoulders of two strong fifteen-year-old twins, one cold arm round each neck, dragged like a Glasgow drunk on New Year's Eve with feet trailing behind. Propped up in the second rear-facing child seat for his trip. His seat belt fastened by well-trained kids. The lights in Harrison's switched off and doors closed. Brave Lucy locking the door from the inside and retracing her steps to the small upstairs toilet, jumping from the window into Vizzy's arms below.

They drove off, streets now quieter. So near home, then just the one misjudgement. Wrong car to flash with inadvertent main beam. It flashed back, then turned, switching on a blue flashing light. Vizzy pulled over as ordered. Window wound down. The policeman's head appeared by the window. The dreaded "Excuse me, Sir," to a frozen Vizzy.

The day again saved by Lucy. "Please Mr Policeman. Please can we hurry. I've got a very sick tummy. My uncle is taking me home quickly. It hurts so.." She moaned pathetically, worryingly. "And I need to get to the toilet fast. My doctors say I have to. Even my teachers let me go. Oh, please!"

And she cried. Tears that would melt a heart of stone. Racked with sobs. It would take a brute to deny her. And the policeman, decent sort, was no brute. Vizzy was on his way with no more than a verbal warning about dipping his beam.

Alastair was deeply impressed. "Where the hell did you learn to act like that?"

Lucy looked at him. "Alastair. You don't know Miss Potts. She's an absolute ..." she paused, thinking. "Dragon! And if you forget your homework she's really horrible. She's on Tuesday mornings. Every Tuesday. I hate Tuesdays. And if you need to take a Tuesday off school, and your Daddy is a doctor, you need to be very very good. I'm teaching Ben. I'll teach you if you want."

They arrived back at Trinity Road, negotiated the streets back to the Morleys'. Heidar carried down to the basement. Gwen looked at his face in the light. "We need to redo these stitches. Where's your Mum's sewing basket? And get the make-up. No, Vizzy. Don't bin out now. Come on. We need help."

Lucy looked at Gwen and rolled her eyes, giving her considered opinion. "Boys! They're all the same."

Chapter 49

Not a good start to the day in Harrison's either.

"Mr Dakins! Mr Dakins! Number Four's gone!"

"What the hell do you mean, Number Four's gone? Go out back and see what he's up to, Jim. Bloody work experience kids. That flipping sixth form college."

Jim left his tea with some reluctance, folding his copy of the Sun and shoving it into his overall pocket. He shouted back twenty seconds later.

"Bloody hell, Bert. He's right. No one there. He was there last night, I checked them all."

"Bloody hell. Not again. Bet it's one of those bloody Scandinavians. Always happening to them. Anyone ending in Son with a double S. God knows how or why. Maybe they beam them up to some spaceship, maybe they're from the future. Maybe they've found a way to come back from the bloody dead. Like Abba. Or the bloody Swedish football team. They're always dead and buried by half time. Then they always come back from the bleeding dead and stuff England."

"That's 'cos half the bloody England footballers are brain dead."

"That's true. Lot of bloody money to pay someone brain dead though. How they gonna spend it?"

"Oh, they don't spend it. It's those bleeding wives and girl-friends. Now they can bloody spend – for England."

"Guess you're right, Jim. Spend for bleeding England. And still look cheap."

"So what we going to do, Bert? Hearse is due in twenty."

"Same as last time, Jim. Same as always. Sandbags are out the back. Get the work experience lad on it. Could do with the exercise."

And so, twenty-five years after burying her mother, Margaux buried her husband. Two major differences. The cask antiqued pine and not wine-steeped oak. The contents silicon rather than carbon based.

CHAPTER 50

Bernard was apoplectic. Enraged. Eyes bulging. Shouting. Vizzy was giving as good as he was getting. Gwen was standing by his side, the twins on his other side. Thomas was crying, cuddled into his mother. Lucy and Ben were interested spectators, out of the line of fire.

Margaux was sitting on the sofa with Helen, both clutching large glasses of red and openly smoking Vizzy's roll-ups. "The least you can bloody do," Helen's sole contribution so far.

"So you thought – *you* a seventeen-year-old boy, *thought* that you knew better. That you could deny him the sacraments, the benefits of a Christian burial! *You thought* that you knew best! You have no idea what you have done. That was utterly wicked and sinful. And you intend putting poor Margaux through another burial service once we've got poor Heidar out of the deep freeze?"

"Not another burial service. That's not right. It's not what he believed. He was Ásatrúar. Not Catholic. Not Christian. Ásatrú. Worshipped the Æsir. The old Gods. Not Jesus. You have to allow him to have the funeral he would have wanted."

"And you think you knew him better than Margaux? His wife! His confidante in all things. You arrogant boy! You tell me one thing, just one thing that that poor man told you that no one else knew better. Just one!"

Defiant Vizzy jutted out his jaw, the room otherwise still silent. "He didn't fear dying. He had dedicated himself to Odin. He had his tattoo, the Valknot."

"Well, I think everyone knew he had a tattoo. That's hardly novel enough insight to justify body snatching."

"And he saw the Valkyrie. Sígrun. He saw her again the night before the final. I think he knew he was going to die. I think he didn't mind. How do you think he rowed like that at the end? Everyone said they'd never seen anything like it. Berserk. Like one of Odin's Berserkers."

Vizzy looked round, defiant and strained. He looked at his father. "And you only won your precious Henley medal because of that. They'd beaten you. You know that. You won because Heidar went berserk. You were all brilliant. But you only won because he had pledged himself to Odin. And you have to honour that pledge."

Morley cut in, softer, gentler than he might have done a year ago. "Vizzy. I know you're upset. I know you cared deeply for Heidar. But there are no such things as Valkyries. This is all ancient history from the Dark Ages. We've moved beyond that now. Become civilised."

"Dad. There are Valkyries. I know because I've seen one. Sígrun. She came to me twice and told me what we had to do. And we did it. For Heidar."

Margaux got off the sofa. She came and gave Vizzy a hug. He hugged into her, fighting back tears. She spoke, softly. "Vizzy, dear. I know you meant well. I know you care. But, I promise you, I knew Heidar better than you. And I think he would be content to lie in that place. Knowing one day I could lie by his side."

"No he wouldn't be. No he couldn't be. He told me things he'd never told anyone else. Important things he'd never even mentioned to you."

Margaux started. Eyes widened. "Such as what, Vizzy?"

Vizzy looked back, miserable and defiant at the same time. "I'll tell you quietly. Just the two of us."

"No you won't, Vizzy. You'll tell us all. I don't want people thinking I have shameful secrets."

Vizzy cornered, desperate. "No. Only you."

Margaux defiant. "If you decided to steal my husband's body without my permission, why do you bother about my feelings now?"

But Vizzy insisted, whispered quietly in Margaux's ear. She stiffened visibly within seconds. Her eyes widened, her face otherwise frozen in extremity of shock. She dropped her wine glass and staggered, actually staggered. Vizzy clasped her arm to steady her. She turned to him, facial musculature tight, eyes bright, water film catching the afternoon light from the window. She spoke in a hoarse cracked voice, quiet but crystal clear.

"He knew? He knew?"

Vizzy just nodded.

"He knew all through the IVF? When Haraldur was born ...died?"

Vizzy nodded, face etched in desperate seriousness.

"He knew about that July?" Her voice trailed. "M ...my abortion?"

Helen gasped. Otherwise shocked silence. Bernard the first to speak, stern-faced but soft-voiced. "Margaux. I have taken your confession for twenty years. You didn't mention this once. It might have been better for you in so many ways if you had. I would have understood. You have borne alone a load that could have been shared."

Margaux hardly seemed to have heard, her face still shaped by grief and shock. But no anger.

"Vizzy. How? Nobody knew. That was my shame, my secret. Nobody knew. Apart from my mother, and she took that secret to her grave. Not my father. Not you, Bernard. I'm sorry for that. Sometimes things are better held in. Believe me. But not Heidar, never. How did he ever know?"

Vizzy, intense, compassionate and serious, looked at her. "In a barn, Margaux. In a wet barn in North Italy. That night he rescued you on his motorbike. You were chilled. And feverish, he said. You sought shelter from the storm."

"God, I remember," said Margaux. "I thought I was going to die. We only had money to buy petrol, needed to get back to my father's house. So we found a barn. I remember lying on the straw. Then nothing. Then I woke up at home. Heidar said it was two days later."

Vizzy explained. "Heidar told me you had a fever. And started talking. And didn't stop. Although he wanted you too. Told him about all your lovers, one at a time."

"God. I must have been out for a bloody long time. The poor man."

"Then you told him about the abortion. Didn't know if the baby was going to be his or Dave's. He told me you'd gone for it the day after their first Henley final. You didn't think he would understand. He told me he'd never forgiven himself for sending you away that time. Especially when Haraldur died."

Dave now had quiet tears. Jane saw this, then held him and stroked his arm.

"He said he didn't know what to do. Thought he was out of his depth. Had made the worst mistake of his life. And that was the second night he saw Sígrun, the Valkyrie. And it was her who told him that you were his destiny. And he stayed because of her. And later he won his medal because of her. And we should honour her commands, and his wishes. He's been chosen by Odin. And he can't go to Odin unless he has the right funeral. A Viking funeral."

Sula broke this silence. "Like his father had. Like Kjartan. He was chosen too. He saw Sígrun. She woke him. That was how he saved those children in the storm on the lake. Odin took him instead that night. There is only the one proper way to honour those chosen by Odin. Only the one funeral."

Margaux straightened her shoulders, pulled back her head. "Then that is what we must do. He should be honoured."

Sula turned to Vizzy. "And you have really seen Sígrun twice? And she has advised you twice?" Vizzy nodded.

"Then you too are chosen. An honour to your family. You are a true Viking, Vizzy Petersson."

That was the moment that the boy Thomas Morley became the man Vizzy Petersson. Yes, *that* Vizzy Petersson.

Bernard now the one in a corner. "So, you're suggesting that I speak to my Bishop? Get dispensation for faking a burial? God knows what was in that coffin. It seemed heavy enough.

Then ask him for permission to go to a heathen funeral? Any virgin sacrifices I need to let him know about? We'll probably need a different form."

Vizzy stood tall. "We're not asking you to come as a representative of the Catholic church. We're asking you as a friend of Heidar's, to honour a great life. And to toast him with the only thing fine enough for the occasion. Chateau Belle-Pensée 1983. That OK, Margaux?"

She nodded, slowly at first, then vigorously, exultantly. "Yes. The '83. It has to be the '83."

Bernard exhaled. "Why on earth did you not say so in the first place, you foolish boy. You could have saved us a lot of theological debate."

CHAPTER 51

Temple Island, a place of quiet magic. There are river deities here. You can feel this if you sit here quietly for long enough.

Tonight the magic felt strong, quiet river deities honoured to welcome greater forces. A stillness in the air. No sounds now that the motor launches had gone. All standing quietly on the island. All aware of the atmosphere, sensible of the honour. Even the dogs. Farqhuar, nose to beak with a large raven. Both standing still as if sharing quiet conversation.

The children, rigging up cables and putting amplification in place.

"Do you really think that Heidar would appreciate you lot?" asked Morley.

"Yes Dad," said Alastair. "I know he would."

Vizzy nodded. Morley grunted. "So long as you don't do something like Jesus wants me for a bloody sunbeam."

Gwen reassured. "Don't worry, Mr Morley. We've changed."

"Changed?" asked puzzled Morley, obviously behind the times.

"Yes," said David. "And not before time either. We said we'd try a year of bible bashing with them, then we'd show them the rock and roll lifestyle for a year. Then we'd all decide which we wanted for the band."

Lynette raised her eyes. "The rock and roll lifestyle, Gwen? That's a development. A year ago I'm not sure I'd have coped with that. You and I need to have a few words. About how a girl needs to look after herself if she fancies the rock and roll lifestyle."

"Oh, Mum! Gross! He doesn't mean that kind of lifestyle."

"Then you don't understand my boys half as well as you should," said Helen.

The evening light fading slowly, Morley, Dave and Gareth undid the corks on several bottles of the sacramental offering, an entire case of Margaux's '83 in reserve under the trestle tables to cope with thirsty guests in numbers. The small but quietly grand building behind, built as a temple for fishing rather than religious observance, offered genteel and pictur-esque backdrop to the proceedings. So far, a quintessentially English lawn party in a pretty riverside setting.

The occasion different in every respect from Heidar's first funeral. Many passions blunted after the cathartic last days, this provided comfort to all. Bernard was so far untroubled by his inaugural foray into paganism, the 1960's excepted. Sula showed a look of quiet fierceness, with Mike rather bemused by her side, seeking foolish solace in gin and tonic rather than Belle Pensée.

Five honoured guests, returned from Connecticutt. Greg initially serious, then relaxing as atmospheric and bottled magic mingled.

"Just knew you'd find some way to duck the Head of the Housatonic rematch. Guess it'll stay one each for ever now."

The New Haven strokeman spoke up. "Guess it's pretty extreme to come all this way for a funeral. But it sounds a pretty extreme funeral. Can't think of a better way to go, myself. Well, we talked about it. Reckoned this is a once in a lifetime occasion. And some more Brakspears. Never too much of a penance. Hey this wine's real good. You sure it's not Napa Valley?"

Gladys and Giles were holding hands, looking towards Henley Bridge in the distance as the last rays of the sun sank.

"You know my dear, I think I'd like a send off like this. Just here. When my time comes. Hope it's not for a year or two yet, bit of luck."

"Time for a bit of fun first, eh Giles? Like last night?"

The final disappearance of the sun hid any blushes. The evening cooling, as the twilight deepened. Cardigans sought. An owl hooted, first of the evening. Ducks and moorhens now ceasing aquatic exploration. Quiet calm settling over this quiet part of the Thames. No wind. Still.

Conversation settling, all sensing the atmosphere. Hushed contemplation. Morley and Gareth now lighting the long rush torches they had previously laid in lines towards the end of the island. Electric lights in the Temple extinguished. Drinks slowly finished. Toasts made. Heartfelt and deep. But accepting of fate and not miserable. Bernard quietly thoughtful, nodding in appreciation of the unexpected dignity of the moment.

Now dark. Dark night with clear sky and crescent moon, low in the sky. Venus and Mars visible in the heavens. A night of significance. Night sky dark witness to human ceremony. As it was. As it will be. All aware of the charged moment, ancient emotion no differently perceived despite veneer of modernity. The funeral rite. Unchanged in essence since the time of the bear and bison, the time of caves and flints. There must be honour. We are all part of something bigger.

Vizzy had wanted music, had chosen it, found the CD's. Had turned down Morley's suggestion of Pärt's Cantus in Memory of Benjamin Britten, fine music that it might be for such an occasion. The music must spring from Iceland, from the cold, from the dark, the land of lakes and fire.

To the sounds of a Rímur poem, familiar yet strange song construction, sung by his father's spiritual guide Sveinbjörn Beinteinsson, Heidar's defrosted body was carried forward on a wooden board, borne on the shoulders of the same six who had carried his sandbagged coffin, before this was laid near the water's edge on trestles. His face, a tribute to the make-up talents of Gwen and Lucy, caught sudden glimmers from the torches. All came up in turn to say their respects, Vizzy last and longest, before Margaux approached. She bent into his neck, staying still for some time. She then stood back and nodded.

The music was changed. Also Icelandic. Intensely appropriate. A song about a rowing boat, by the Reykjavik band called Sigur Rós. *Ara Batur.*

By the flickering light of torches, some embedded in earth, some held in hand, the body was carried on its board towards the water's edge. One boat here. His boat. A red Stampfli. A boat not naturally suited to Viking funerals, but the only appropriate vessel for the trip of such a man to the rainbow bridge of Bifrost and then on to Valhalla. Gareth and Dave had laid paving slabs over the aerofoil riggers and Morley had built up layers of kindling on top, architectural skills again invoked as on that bright late summer's day a year before. And then, with full ceremony, the body was lifted up and lain reverently on top.

Then, a moment of deep poignancy. Vizzy returned his most intensely precious possession to its rightful owner, its winner, placing the medal in Heidar's cold right hand, before clasping both Heidar's hands together over his chest.

At a signal, Morley applied the torch, and all three pushed the boat into the stream. The flames flickered quickly, then seemed to settle. And then, as they started to worry, it caught. And as the music swelled it blazed. Blazed against the night, light reflecting off the still Thames and the undersides of leaves.

Smoke on the water. Fire in the sky.

Helen grasped Margaux's hand. And as they watched, it began. Swooping down across the bows of the blazing boat, two snowy owls. Then ten, twenty owls wheeling around Heidar's pyre. Then Barrow's Goldeneyes, big heads and white patches catching the reflected firelight. Twenty, fifty, maybe more. Then barnacle geese, greylag geese, common scoters, red-breasted mergansers, shelducks, scaups, black tailed godwits, red-necked phalaropes, purple sandpipers and wigeons, kaleidoscopic against the night sky, wheeling and dipping, in and out of the glow from the fiercely burning pyre. And lastly, what seemed a thousand Harlequin ducks, their mouselike squeaks echoing around Temple Island.

They sat in silent wonder for some time after the last Harlequin duck had disappeared into the night, a final faint squeak just audible as it headed North. Bernard finally broke the silence.

"I do think we've jettisoned rather too much of our ceremony. Must have a word with the Bishop."

And then it started. The band. The band you'll know as Viking Funeral. Unless you live in a cave. Their first performance a cover version. Nothing unusual in that. The sound deep and dirty. Mainly loud. Loud enough to be heard in Henley High Street. Loud enough to be heard in Valhalla. Bloody loud.

And so, loud enough to delight Thor, to impress Odin and to terrify his opponents on the Vigrid fields even at the height of Ragnarök, the newborn Viking Funeral burst forth in fierce pagan exultation.

DUM DUM DUUUUH, DUM-DUM-DI-DUM,
DUM DUM DUUUUUH, DUUM DU-UUUUM
der-der-der
DUM DUM DUUUUH, DUM-DUM-DEE-DUM,
DUM DUM DUUUUUH, DUUM DUM-DUUUUM

Thomas played lead guitar like a man who'd spent twenty years in the world's meanest rock clubs, rather than most of his fourteen at genteel schools in Twickenham. Alastair fingered his bass and Gwen her keyboards like seasoned professionals, David assaulting his drums like Bonham reincarnated, entirely possible on such a night. And Vizzy – shy Vizzy no more, quiet Vizzy no more, complex Vizzy no more. Standing tall and confident, playing the dirtiest rhythm guitar, he sang loud. Sang like an angel. Assuming angels spend time in those sorts of clubs. And drink those sorts of drinks. And mess around with those sorts of women. And smoke those sorts of cigarettes. And gargle with diesel oil. Vizzy sang. My, did Vizzy sing.

And there stood Margaux, fierce tears of pride, joy and sorrow running down her face, punching the air in time with each chorus and singing along at the top of her voice. And she was not alone in doing so.

No warrior for a thousand years had entered Valhalla to such ceremony.

None before with a Henley medal.

And none to such loud, visceral accompaniment, enough to gladden the heart of Thor and stiffen the sinews of the Einherjar.

Tomorrow he would fight with sword and axe on the Vigrid Fields, preparing himself for the days of Ragnarök. But tonight was a different matter. Every person on that island knew that tonight Heidar would drink mead from the udder of Heidrun, and that he would feast on meat from Saehrimnir. And, without a doubt, sit by Kjartan in the place of honour at Odin's side.

Epilogue

The Northern Lights late that summer were the most remarkable in living memory. Scientists thought that they were probably the most dramatic since the Great Geomagnetic Storm of 1859. As far south as London people would marvel as the evening sky flashed green, red and blue. They were so spectacular that a normally cautious editor broke with tradition, allowing a large colour photograph to take up the entire front page of the Sunday Telegraph.

Thanks and acknowledgement

I wrote this book in difficult times. In such times you really find out who your friends are, and I have been blessed. So many friends and colleagues have stood beside me and provided support – thank you all.

I will always be grateful to Sue Hutchinson, Franco Torrente and Camilla Salvestrini for their unstinting support and generous hospitality. Much of this book was written while staying in their homes, and I will remember their many kindnesses all my life. Thank you also Camilla for your insights into Tuscan life.

I have been helped so much by other friends who read early drafts and made suggestions that improved this book. Many thanks indeed to Carolyn and Charlie Kimpton, Owen Wyrley-Birch, Clare Haxby, Roy and Maureen Kay, James and Belinda Neuberger, Ghislaine Bowden, Sally Dickinson, Lynne Hilton, Tina Low, Sarah Murch, Martin Murch, Rosy Murch and William Bedford Russell.

I am grateful to Virginia Bovell and Leah Schmidt for initial support and guidance. Looking further back, I thank my great friends from University College & Hospital Boat Club all those years ago. If we had finally managed to win that elusive Henley medal I guess this book would never have been. One of the longer deferred silver linings I've encountered.

I hope that rowers may feel that this honours the spirit of the sport. I also hope that none recognise too much of themselves in the characters – none are based on any individual person. As I am sure they may have spotted, I must put my hand up to artistic license in the relocation of Marlow Regatta to its former home on the Thames.

One person, more than any other, turned this book from aspiration to reality. My wife Alison (Dolly) provided boundless support and encouragement from the first chapter, making me feel that I had something to say that was worth saying and even laughing in the right places. If writing a book has anything in common with a chemical reaction, she was surely the catalyst.

About the author

This is the first novel by Simon Murch, a former oarsman who is now a paediatrician and academic. The novel was written while he was enduring one of the lengthiest and most unusual proceedings in British regulatory history — the ongoing GMC hearing into the *Lancet* paper that first recognised bowel abnormalities in autistic children and reported parental concerns of a possible link with MMR immunisation.

Simon Murch admits to having lost one Henley final and three semi-finals, as well as receiving summary ejection from the lightweight national rowing squad just before Henley. He insists that any similarities with his characters stop there, and that any suggestions that he might be grumpy, use bad language, worship unusual gods or enjoy red wine are almost certainly unfounded.

Lightning Source UK Ltd.
Milton Keynes UK
07 June 2010

155234UK00001B/265/P